BRIDGE over HELL

*a novel from Janet Morris' **Heroes in Hell**™ universe*
by MICHAEL A. ARMSTRONG

Perseid Press
P.O. Box 584, Centerville Massachusetts 02632

Bridge Over Hell

A Perseid Press Original
First Perseid Press Kindle Edition, October 2012
First Perseid Press Trade Edition, November 2012
First Perseid Press Electronic Edition, October 2012

Parts of this work have previously been published in similar form as *"God's Eyes"* in Masters in Hell, Baen Books, December 1987 and *"Madly Meeting Logically"* in Rogues in Hell, Perseid Publishing, June 2012)

Book design by Sarah Hulcy; cover design by Sonja Aghabekian
Cover art: Cover image copyright (c) Perseid Press, 2012.
Cover art: Artist: Jonas Lie, circa 1911-12; Detail from oil on canvas

ISBN-10: 0985935154
ISBN-13: 978-0-9859351-5-3

Published in the United States of America

ACKNOWLEDGEMENTS

This novel was originally written under a contract with Baen Books in 1988-89, the second novel I wrote in the grand arc of my career. Due to a misunderstanding having to do with the late Jim Baen's unwillingness to pay the final advance on the accepted final manuscript, *Bridge Over Hell* was never published, although Baen Books graciously reverted all rights back to me. In 2010, Janet and Chris Morris, the creators of the Heroes in Hell shared universe series, resurrected the idea, and invited me to participate in the 21st century incarnation of the project. As a result of renewed interest in the project, Janet and Chris and Perseid Publishing have brought this book into print. I am immensely grateful for them giving my novel a second life, and to all the hellions of the universe for encouraging me and inspiring me.

Several works were helpful to me in writing *Bridge Over Hell*. In particular, David McCullough's *The Great Bridge* provided excellent background information on the building of the Brooklyn Bridge and the lives of Colonel Washington A. Roebling and his first wife, Emily Roebling. Louis Untermeyer's *Voyages: The Life of Hart Crane*, while often packed with irrelevant trivia, contains as much information as the average reader could possibly want to know about Hart Crane, including the fact that he did live at 110 Columbia Heights Road in Brooklyn when he wrote his epic poem, "The Bridge." Readers interested in the poetry of Hart Crane might examine *The Complete Poems and Selected Letters and Prose of Hart Crane*, edited by Brom Weber. An excellent collection of Ezra Pound's poetry (including "Sestina: Altaforte," as well as several other Bertrans de Born poems) is *Selected Poems of Ezra*

Pound. Several editions of Emily Dickinson's poems are also in print.

Carl Gustav Jung's "Answer to Job" influenced much of my thinking on the character of Job; that essay can be found in *The Portable Jung*, edited by Joseph Campbell. Numerous discussions with the poet Thomas F. Sexton of the University of Alaska Anchorage helped me to develop some of my opinions on the modernist poets; I am especially indebted to Tom for introducing me to Hart Crane's poetry and his "logic of metaphor." It should be noted that the late Brian Thomsen, my editor at Warner Books (now Hachette) first told me that most of Emily Dickinson's poetry can be sung to "The Yellow Rose of Texas," a fact later confirmed by Gardner Dozois, Susan Casper, and Tess Kissinger, much to the distress of my ears.

The first three chapters of *Bridge Over Hell* appeared in a slightly different form as "God's Eyes" in *Masters in Hell* (Baen Books, 1987), and the characters of Rabbit and Queequeg also appeared in "Between the Devil and the Deep Blue Sea" in *Crusaders in Hell* (Baen Books, 1987). My novel bounces off several plot lines developed in the *Heroes in Hell* series created by Janet and Chris Morris; in particular, I would like to acknowledge the demented twists and turns of plot developed in earlier anthologies and novels by Janet and Chris Morris, C.J. Cherryh, David Drake, and Robert Silverberg. I'm honored to be allowed to play in their universe.

As always, I am extremely grateful to Janet and Chris for encouraging me in my career and supporting my work.

- Michael Armstrong
Homer, Alaska

ALSO BY MICHAEL A. ARMSTRONG

Heroes in Hell Series:

"Between the Devil in the Deep Blue Sea," in
    Crusaders in Hell
"God's Eyes," in Masters in Hell
"The Man in the Black Cape Turns," in War in
    Hell
"The Rapture Elevator," in Lawyers in Hell
"Madly Meeting Logically," in Rogues in Hell

Novels

After the Zap, Warner Books
Agviq, Warner Books
The Hidden War, TSR Books

TABLE OF CONTENTS

BRIDGE over HELL

Chapter 1

Job stood in the hatchway of the Armored Combat Earthmover, scanning the parking lot of the Oasis Bar for an empty space. Other tanks, troop carriers, jeeps, chariots, and the occasional civilian vehicle cluttered the lot on the edge of the New Hell harbor. Paradise cast its usual ruddy glow through banks of black thunderheads rolling in from the east. Out beyond the mouth of the harbor the *Titanic* rumbled as it slid under for its nightly sinking, its survivors getting their dunking before they hit the streets in drag. Job squinted in the mustard-yellow glare of the parking lot lights, spied a space at the edge of the lot next to the harbor.

A pink VW-style convertible — license plate NORMA — had parked across the line next to a dusky gray hell-made Wagoneer, taking up two spaces. The Wagoneer had to belong to some merc, Job figured — it *looked* armored, with the fat tires and the funny sheen to the windows — but the Bug looked safe: civilian. Job drove up to the Bug, lowered the blade on the ACE, and rammed it, pushing it over the edge of the lot and into New Hell Harbor. The pink convertible splashed into the slimy waters, listed to port, then righted itself and drifted out on the tide. Job popped back down into the dozer, shut the engine off, and yanked the keys out of the control panel. Grabbing his stubby sub-machine gun — the one the Czech hellions called a "Samopal,"or cigarette lighter — he climbed out, dogging the hatch behind him.

The Oasis covered half a block from North Road to the harbor. Just north of the long wharves, and on the main thoroughfare that snaked out of New Hell and into the mountains, the Oasis had become a crossroads for mercenaries moving back to the capital after long campaigns, heading out to sea, or slouching their way to the swamps south of town. Three stories high, the Oasis was a squat concrete cube, windowless except for a few small barred ports on the seaward side. A low wall ran around the roof of the building, with gun slits every ten feet, machine gun nests and mortars at the corners, and barbed wire strung halfway up the sides. Job walked around to the street side of the bar, pushed the heavy oak door inward, and walked into the Oasis entryway.

The bouncer at the door — a brute Neanderthal with teeth the size of walnuts — stopped Job, grunted over to the hat check girl watching a big locked cage containing a small armory. A sign next to the cage read in large capita letters, 'One Weapon, One Magazine, No Shit.' Next to that another sign read 'Rooms To Rent By The Minute, Hour, Day, Week, And Month'; a narrow staircase next to the ammo cage ran upstairs. Job laid his repro Samopal and a magazine of 9 mm parabellum rounds on the counter, slipped off his ammo belt and handed it to the girl, then stepped through the metal detector at the end of the counter.

"He's clean," the hat check girl said to the Neanderthal, signing the words as she spoke them. She handed Job a little disk of metal with the number "7" stamped in it, pushed the Samopal and the magazine back at him. Job slid the magazine into the SMG, checked the safety, and slung it over his shoulder.

"Any action tonight, Shanidar?" he signed to the Neanderthal.

"Quiet, Ombudsman," the bouncer signed back: one fluttering hand rising up was his sign for Job's title. Shanidar lifted a moth-eaten velvet rope and waved Job inside.

Pausing at the top of the stairs to let his eyes adjust to the dim light, Job pulled the hood of his robe down, let it fall back on his shoulders so the Beirut marines standing at the bottom of the stairs could see the blue hem around the hood, a Star of David glinting on a gold chain on his neck. A big black marine grunted at him as Job walked into the bar, and Job smiled. He'd always been a little jumpy around the Americans, worried that they might misread his Semitic features and add him to the body count of their eternal feud against Arabs and Iranians in general and that spook Bill Casey in particular.

Sam nodded at Job from behind the bar, and Job nodded back at the man in the white suit and string tie. A nasty lot of greasy, grimy, mud-smeared faces turned to size up Job as he walked around the edge of the bar, toward a corner table where a man with dreadlocks sat smoking a stinking joint about the size of a panatela. Job glanced up at the newly emplaced machine gun nests in the upper corners of the big warehouse-like room, tried to pay no attention to the little red dot on his chest as the laser sights of the guns tracked him — just for practice, he hoped.

Rubbing a gold diablo between his left forefinger and thumb, Job stopped short when a merc in tiger camo stood up from a table on his right and came at him. The guy reached to grab Job's throat, but Job swung his right hand up, caught the merc's wrist, and brought it down in a slick little *Systema* move he'd learned from an old Spesnatz veteran.

"'Budsman, you owe me," the man growled.

"I do," Job said. He twisted the man's hand around, palm up, then dropped the diablo into it. "We even, Zebediah?"

Zebediah looked down at the gold coin, squeezed it, held it up to the light. "Yeah, sure Job. Sure." He smiled, a gold canine gleaming. "*Yeah*. When'd you get flush, 'Budsman?"

"Oh, you know... got the new budget, Zeb. Things are looking up."

"Sheet," Zeb said, shaking his head.

Job pushed him aside, went over to the corner, and sat down to the Rastafarian's left. He slung the Samopal over the arm of the chair and stared across the heavy walnut table at the man Sam called Rasta Bob but Job knew as Jareem, Son of Zion. The big Jamaican sucked at the joint, breathed in the dope, and blew it back out into Job's face. Job held his breath, felt the dope ooze its way into his eyes, felt the little shiver as the THC snuck into his bloodstream. Reem nodded.

"You're looking well, mon." He jerked his head over at Zeb's table.

Job motioned to a barmaid, pointed at Reem's empty beer bottle, raised two fingers. The barmaid, a black rooted blonde in camo undershirt and tights, nodded, went to the bar, came back and set two bottles of Ping Pao down. "Your beers, Mister Ombudsman," she said.

"Thank you... uh —" Job squinted at the name embroidered in olive stitching on her shirt, "— Norma Jean."

She smiled, ran a hand through the dark roots of her hair. "Marilyn, actually," she said. "Norma Jean's on vacation. This is her outfit. I'm filling in for her while she's gone."

"Well, Marilyn, then," Job said. He reached into his robes, pulled out a lumpy bag, shook two coins out onto the table, and handed her a diablo. "Tell Sam to apply that to my bill." He smiled, picked up one more coin. "And that's for you."

"*Thank you,*" Marilyn said. She blushed, took the empty bottles, and walked back to the bar.

Reem snorted. "You *are* flush. Since when does the Ombudsman go around buying drinks — or tipping barmaids?"

Job took the beer, sipped it, grinned. "Since the Devil increased my budget, that's when."

"*Increased* your budget?" Reem shook his head, his dreadlocks swaying in front of his eyes, then back. "Jah be praised, I find that hard to believe."

"Yeah?" Job reached into a fold of his robe, handed the keys for the ACE to Reem. "Thank Odysseus for the loan of the dozer," he said. Job poked a finger into the bag on the table, took out four diablos, pushed them over to Reem. "For his trouble." Job hefted the bag, smiled, tucked it back in his robe.

"I don't believe it."

"*Believe it,*" Job said. "Don't ask me how or why, but when I finally made it to my desk today - you should have *seen* that ACE cut through the clutter in the warehouse - there was an open safe with about ten thousand diablos in it. A little note from the Attorney General himself said that it represented 'the commitment of the Department of Injustice to the fine work the Office of the Ombudsman is doing.'"

"No shit?"

"No shit."

"Okay, mon, so how come?"

"I got a case — a real case. Devil wants someone out of here, Reem. I've been empowered to do it."

"Soon come? A soul out of Hell?" The Rasta man shook his head.

"Soon come, Jareem. I'm supposed to meet a messenger here tonight to — *shit.*" Job grabbed his Samopal, swung the gun out, clicking the safety off. He heard the snick of rounds being chambered into guns, chairs falling back, mercs standing and cursing. Job glanced to his right, saw Reem reaching behind his back, then looked to the front of the bar.

A tall, emaciated man pushed his way down the stairs of the Oasis, past the marines. Shanidar sprawled at the top of the stairs, clutching his stomach. The thin man's lizard tail whisked behind him, scattering stools as the marines scrambled out of his way.

"Son of a bitch," someone said loudly, "a fucking lawyer."

The lawyer's tail began just below his neck and extended fifteen feet behind him. Boils and pustules oozed from the man's back and dripped down the tail, and he dragged a line of slime behind him. This man walked in sort of a swishing way, turning his body almost all the way to the left, then right. As he turned, Job saw that the base of the tail ran under his buttocks and up through his legs.

Big bottle-bottomed glasses had been shoved into the sockets of the lawyer's face; thin, white hair swept back from his forehead. A little demon hovered next to the man's right ear, buzzing loudly. The lawyer kept swatting at the demon but it would fly away, then dart quickly back. The man wore a tailored pin-stripe suit, blood oozing from its pockets. Across the top of the breast pocket the word ROY burned through the suit, smoke from his smoldering skin wafting through.

"Hold it there, counselor," Sam, the bar owner, shouted from behind the bar. He held up a short-barreled bear shotgun, sliding the receiver back with a loud snick. Someone shone a spotlight on Roy's pasty face, but even in the bright light Job could see a small red dot centered on Roy's forehead: a laser sight.

Roy stopped just inside the bar, his tail twitching back and forth. He held a neat roll of white parchment in his right hand and raised it up, shielding his eyes. "I'm from the Hall of Injustice," Roy said. "I have something for the Ombudsman."

"Kaka," Job muttered. He looked at Reem, shrugged. "My messenger." He put the Samopal down, clicked the safety on, stood up and waved at Roy. "Yo, over here."

"Stay," Sam said to Roy. "Job, go deal with him - I don't want the fucker getting my bar all scummy."

Job went up to Roy, spread back his robes, held out his hand. "You have something for me?" Job felt an itching in his back; the thought occurred to him that he was in the line of fire of about half the weapons in the room, and he didn't doubt that they'd shoot right through him if they had to take out Roy.

"Your case," Roy said. He handed Job the scroll.

Job took it, tensing as he saw Roy's hands drop to his sides, then relaxing a little when he saw that Roy kept his claws in plain sight. Job unrolled the scroll, glanced at the writing, and nodded — the illumination was superb. "Good," Job said. He waved Roy away — the thing exuded a horrible stench that overpowered the rotting smells coming in from the wharves. The lawyer didn't move.

"Sir," Roy said. "Uh, the Attorney General asked me to speak to you about the, uh, importance of this case."

"Yes?" Job scanned the scroll, glanced up, then looked back down.

"It would please the Attorney General if you did your best to process it."

"Sure, sure," Job said.

"It would please the Attorney General — it would please Lord Satan - if you did your *best* to process it."

Job looked up, "Of course." He felt the bag of diablos tugging at his belt. "I mean —" Job rubbed his eyes. "You mean... you mean the Attorney General *really* wants me to do my job?" He'd hoped — hoped — no one had really been serious. Wrong, he thought. *Wrong.*

"Yessir."

"Well." Job smiled. "*Well.* Well, it's not as if I haven't tried. I mean, given my limited resources..."

"Exactly," Roy said. "Which is why they are no longer limited." He reached slowly into his suit pocket, pulled out another lumpy bag. "Your latest appropriation." Tugging open the bag, Roy poured a small handful of diamonds over his rough calluses. The mercs whispered behind Job's back, and he felt more intensely the eyes behind all those guns burning at his back.

"I see," Job said. "Well, would you tell the AG — *and* Lord Satan — that I will do my —best?" His *best.* Usually, in New Hell, doing one's worst was apropos.

"As expected," Roy said. "Lord Satan will be most interested in the results. *Most* interested. Should you fail to deliver satisfaction — should you not give this case your utmost attention — well..." Roy grinned.

"Well what, slimeface?" Job moved toward the lizard man. "What? What can Satan possibly do to me that Y — already hasn't? *What*? Boils? Kill my children? Burn my crops? Come on, Roy. You're talking to *Job*." He thumped his chest with the palm of his hand, looked around the room at the mercs, then waved his hands. "These guys know what I've been through — you don't scare me, shyster. You know that." The crowd of soldiers muttered, laughed.

"If you fail... If you fail, Lord Satan will Reassign you."

"*Pfah*." Job spat.

"The Pearly Gates," Roy said.

"*What?*"

The room fell silent.

"The Gates... the Gates to —" Roy pointed up. "Well, someone has to do it. Someone has to sit outside and shove the damned back down. They do slip through occasionally, you know, just as the blessed sometimes get placed here. Oh, *He* catches them, but they do slip through." Roy swished his tail back and forth. "I understand it's a coveted assignment, so near to the *Lord* and all that. So near to your *Redeemer*."

Somewhere, thunder cracked. Job stumbled back, reached for a bar stool, sat down. The Gates to Heaven? Nearer my God to thee? Just outside, within Divine shooting distance, close to the Being who had caused Job his torment? He winced, recalling the pain. Never. *Never.* He had chosen Hell — chosen it over Paradise, over Purgatory, chosen it because...

...because, he thought, whispering the secret thought in his mind, because Satan and Y - were the same being: two sides of the same entity; an antinomy; good and evil together in one. Hell is being without God, Job thought. And God is in Hell, God is in Satan. And Satan, despite his incredible evil — no, *because* of it — could be trusted to be *not* trusted. *He* — Him, the Other One — could not be trusted *at all*. Job had seen that, had learned that horrible lesson in the most painful way possible. And yet Job loved Him, loved Him with all his heart, and though he loved Him, because he loved Him, Job knew he had to be as far from Him as possible. And so he had come to Hell, the thought occurring to him that perhaps not only did he belong here, he deserved it.

But no, Job thought, The Gates of Heaven? I can never be near the Gates of Heaven. *Never.*

He sighed. "Tell the Attorney General I will not fail. I will do my best to get a soul to Paradise." He held the unfurled scroll up. "I'll do my best to get *this* soul out of here."

Roy nodded. "*Good.* Very good, Ombudsman." He poured the diamonds back in the pouch, held it out to Job.

Job stood, took the pouch, shook his head. He glanced at Sam, glaring at him. "Get the... get out of here, lawyer."

The lawyer turned, swished his tail at Job. Job jumped back as the tail swung around, knocking a table over. The lawyer waddled up the steps and out of the Oasis, his demon fluttering along next to his ear, whispering, whispering, whispering.

"Damn it, Job," Sam said, "Can't you do your business someplace else?"

Job reached into the bag, placed a particularly large diamond on the bar, and shrugged.

Chapter 2

Roebling. Who in the name of Y — was Roebling? Job asked himself. He stared down at the bleached parchment, traced his fingers over the illuminated manuscript, felt the faint grooves of the palimpsest in the lambskin. He rubbed his eyes, leaned back in his desk chair.

While he'd been at the Oasis, a squadron of wraiths had descended on the Auxiliary Records Depository, Office of the Ombudsman, Department of Injustice, and cleaned up the place. The great hemlock doors he'd shattered with the ACE had been replaced. The eighteen titanium panels depicting Job's torments — crumpled by the treads of the dozer — had been hammered back into shape, polished, and re-hung on the doors. Carpet (carpet!) had been laid on the floors of the warehouse, and the millennia of records had been reformatted, stacked, and filed in row upon row of gleaming brown spheres, like shelves of dog's eyes — the new biologic records that Reem the Rasta man had assured Job were all the rage in micro-encoded binary storage. A glassed-in office had been built in one corner of the warehouse, with a heavy oak desk in the middle of the office. Job sat behind the desk in a velvet upholstered chair. On the desk the dead gray eye of a monitor stared back at him, its cable twisting down into the floor, with a little depression for the bioware in its keyboard. Waiting.

Roebling, Job thought. Why Roebling?

He spread the curled parchment out, read the soul's biography: *"Colonel Washington 'Washy' A. Roebling, builder of the Brooklyn Bridge. Born May 26, 1837, died July 21, 1926. Son of John Roebling, designer of the Bridge; husband of Emily Roebling, whom he loved dearly. Civil War hero, kind to dogs and cats. No known major sins. Resisted corruption. Hard worker."*

Why Roebling? Why in Hell?

"Condemned to Hell on order of Y-, Lord of All Creation, for sins committed against Nature and Man," Job read, *"to-wit, responsibility for and causation of the deaths of at least 20 men in the construction of the Brooklyn Bridge, among them: Pat Daugherty, crushed by a granite block fallen from derrick, 10/23/70; John Myers, death from caisson sickness, 4/22/71; Patrick McKay, death from caisson sickness, 4/30/71; John El- liot, killed in fall from New York tower of bridge, 5/15/76; Samuel Cope, killed when leg was caught in cable drum, 6/17/76; 15 others killed in miscellaneous accidents. Also responsible for death of unnamed man, suicided Thanksgiving Day 1856, after he was refused affections of W.A. Roebling."*

He shook his head, stared at the passage. Damned to Hell because men had been killed in construction accidents? Damned because he refused to engage in a homosexual act with a suicide? Job rubbed his eyes. *Those* were sins? That was reason to damn a man to Hell forever? He looked up, stared upon the rows of brown eyes staring back at him, each eye containing the complete known facts of a damned soul's life. If Roebling could be damned, no one was safe. Job looked at the eyes, the dog's eyes — *God's* eyes Reem had called them — and wondered how many souls like Roebling had been un- justly sent to Hell. How many had been sent here by mistake, how many had been processed too quickly? He shuddered again, thinking of his own torment, thinking of the Injustice of Y —

I had thought I was the only one. The only one.

Job picked up the brown eye sitting on the desk, dropped it into the depression on the terminal, flicked the screen on. *Location*, he tapped in, *roebling, washington a*. The scanning laser spun over the eye, transferred its contents into the main banks of the Hell data net, cross-checked the Reassignment files, and came back with *Slab A, central morgue*. Job smiled, amazed that Roebling would be so easy to find. *Latest reassignment*, he typed in.

None, the screen replied.

First assignment, Job typed.

None, the screen replied.

No Reassignment? Job thought. No Assignment? That couldn't be. Roebling had to have been Assigned, at the very least. Had to have been.

Current status? he typed.

Dead, the screen answered.

Job took the eye out, turned the screen off.

"Kaka," he said, reaching for the phone and dialing the number of the morgue.

*

The Undertaker pulled back the sheet from Roebling's body. He lay on a marble slab in the inactive area of the morgue, surrounded by racks of dead in dusty sacks and sarcophagi waiting for the Undertaker or one of Old Shit Mouth's crew to revive them. The sheet covering Roebling's body was clean and white, and though his body had that pasty gray look of the newly dead, it seemed to glow in the dim light. His gray beard had been neatly clipped, like that of General Grant, Job thought, and his blue eyes blazed with a life that made the body seem to be only resting and not dead.

The Undertaker checked the toe tag, nodded at Job. "'Roebling, Washington A.,'" he read, "'5/26/1837 to 7/21/1926.'" This your man?"

Job nodded, sighed. He'd expected trouble finding Roebling; thought he might be off in some hinterland, maybe mind-wiped, maybe-body wiped so he'd never find him. And there he was, newly dead, lying on Slab A, ready for resurrection. "That's him. He just come in?"

Turd Breath turned the tag over, shook his head. "Been here since... since he died."

"This is his first trip back to you?" That was pretty amazing, Job knew. Most of the damned seemed to die regularly, at least every few years — die in the hell sense, anyway — a soul's spiritual body that would be broken, tormented, and resurrected.

"No. His only trip. He's never died here." The Undertaker shrugged.

"Never? Wait a second — hasn't... hasn't he been, um, processed?" Job shuddered, remembering the Awakening, the coming-to that every one of the damned had gone through, even him.

"No. Never." The Undertaker smiled, then shrugged his thin shoulders. "It happens. Not too often, but... well, sometimes we get a soul through here who doesn't wake up. They belong here, of course, else they wouldn't be here. But there's not enough sin — enough evil — for them to come alive here. There's not enough good for them to be elsewhere, either.

These things are very delicate, you see." He coughed, bit at a long fingernail. "We, uh, we don't like to advertise them."

"He'll just lie there?"

Fart Face held up his hands. "Probably. Maybe. Devil knows." He smiled. "And *He's* not telling, eh?"

"But..." Job held up the rolled parchment of Roebling's case. "Roebling's filed appeals. He *has* to have been processed."

The Undertaker pulled the sheet back, looked at his watch. "I'm a very busy man, Sir. He has not been processed. I would know." He grinned. "I would know."

"Thank you," Job said. He turned, let the Undertaker lead him out of the maze of the morgue, back aboveground to the lobby of the Administration Building. Roebling not alive? And yet in Hell? It couldn't be, he thought. *It could not be.*

*

"He's in Hell, Job." Reem held the rubbery eye of Roebling's file between finger and thumb, squeezed it gently, handed it back to Job. Job had loaned it to Reem to run a hack on it, to see if Reem could get some data out of the Reassignments net that Job just wasn't capable of getting.

They sat at the same corner table in the Oasis, ruddy light streaming through a skylight overhead; the bar almost deserted except for one or two Americans at the door, a drunk merc sleeping in the back. A ganja cigar smoldered in an ashtray on the table.

"I didn't think he could be dead," Job said. "He's *got* to be alive. Who filed his appeals?"

"Not alive." Reem held up a skinny finger. "But he's around. Oohh, yeah. He's around." He held out his hand. Job handed him another biochip, some random file, one Reem could use to bust his way into the net again. Reem took the eye, held it up to the light.

Job watched him fondle the rubbery eye. Reem smiled, put it in a little wood case, pocketed it. Reem had a thriving business going in Reassignments. Somehow he'd figured out how to get into the net and put tapeworms — intrusive programs that generated more intrusive programs — into people's files, and get them Reassigned wherever they wanted to be. It didn't last — the Fallen Angels usually noticed the switch and called them back — but it lasted long enough for some damned to rendezvous with a lost loved one, long enough for another round of a feud to be played; long enough for Reem to turn a profit.

Job shook his head. "You're starting to sound like the Undertaker. 'He's not alive.' 'He's around.' What is it? Is Roebling dead or not-dead?"

Reem picked up the joint, inhaled, let the smoke curl out of his nose. "Dead *and* not-dead. Both, mon. You don't understand, do you?" Reem laughed. "Roebling's a *shade.*"

"A shade?"

"Shade, shadow — a wisp, man, a *soul*," Reem explained.

"We're all souls here."

Reem shook his head, dreadlocks whipping around like hunks of molasses pasta. "No, no, a soul of a soul. Part of the soul — the *shadow*. I mean, Roebling came down here *corporeal*, exactly the way he'd died. You know what killed your man? Bends, mon, the caisson disease. Bends and nerves, though he took a long time to go — lived to be eighty-nine, mon, fucking ancient for the early 20th century. Guy was wasted, not even fit to torment. Satan sent him to Reassignments immediately to see if he could be patched up."

Job tapped the table, grabbed his beer, sipped it. He glanced around the room at the Oasis, looked at the hard men by the door, the even harder women along the south wall, the mercs slipping by in ones and twos as the afternoon wore on and the night's arrangements started to be made. He looked at the soldiers — the irregular and regular troops, guerrillas and terrorists, generals and privates, ranked and freelance, all with automatic rifles or sub-machine guns casually slung over their shoulders, probably a round already chambered — enough mercs and soldiers and armament to fight a couple good old fashioned Biblical battles in less than a second. He shuddered.

"Okay: Satan wanted him patched up. And...?"

"The Undertaker couldn't do anything for him — the body wouldn't *dissolve*. The guy just couldn't be touched. Roebling..." — Reem looked around, then whispered — "...Roebling doesn't belong here. That's what I hear. He belongs to... well, he doesn't belong here."

"How do you know this?"

He sat up, stroked his chin. "First thing I tried when you asked me to look at his file was to get him Reassigned. I ought to charge you double. No could do. Fucking net ate my program — might've eaten me, if I hadn't shut down fast enough. Roebling cannot be 'Reassigned 'cause he never was Assigned. Got it?"

"Yeah. Undertaker made that clear. But how could he be — I mean, *Be* — if he doesn't have a hellish body?"

Reem sat back, bit his lip, took another toke. "Like I said: he's a shadow."

"A... a wraith?" Job remembered the wispy, see-through souls that sometimes made deliveries, the ones who had cleaned up his office after he'd broken into it with the combat bulldozer. You saw them sometimes, little outlines of bodies visible only in dust or the right kind of light, pushing a package along the street. They were like half-souls, bodies that had been used up — great for pushing paper.

"Nope — a *shadow*. We're talking the evil, nasty, cruel, demented, tormented side of Roebling. We're talking a part of him that is so little a part of him it can't *move* his body, so it has to cruise on its own. You can't find it because it really doesn't exist. It's like a demon, mon — *that's what filed the appeal.*"

Job sat back, rubbed his chin. "The shadow... the dark side. But it *is* part of him." Reem nodded. "Sophia, Sophia... This *thing* — I'm going to have to find this thing, get it back to" — he shook his head, sighed — "that body on Slab A to get Roebling out?"

Job felt the floor shudder a bit.

"Or at least on his way." Reem put the ganja down. "Soon come, feels like a temblor."

Job grabbed his beer, steadied it. "Or..."

"*Incoming!*" someone yelled.

Reem and Job dove for the floor, covered their heads and crawled under the table. Job stared across the floor, stared as the concrete slab buckled, a crack zigzagging toward him...

The floor cracked open before Job and, like a chick poking its head through an eggshell, a horrid thing rose up out of the slab. It had the head of a goat, the snout of a wolf, the body of a woman, and the legs of a jackal, all covered with oozing boils. The thing stood before Job, spread its arms, revealing leathery wings hanging from its fingers. It pulled the wings around it, then opened them up again. The wolf snout diminished, the goat horns shrunk, and the head transformed itself into a woman's head: her hair, like the horns, curled back from her forehead in a hard carapace, her face covered in fine gray fur. She smiled and little red drops of blood dripped off her long canines.

"Jooobbb," she moaned, pointing a claw at him. "Ombudsman? We must talk."

"Fuck," Sam muttered from the bar across the room. "Damn it, Job, I told you..."

Job got to his feet, dusted himself off. He heard the other patrons of the bar get up, coughing in the acrid smoke, muttering. Extending a hand to Reem, Job helped the Rastafarian to his feet, started to sit back down, thought better of it, and remained standing.

Job smiled at the demon, held out his hands. "Yes?"

"I am Lady... *MacBeth*," she said. "Yes, MacBeth will do, Ombudsman. Your... *assistant*..." — she pointed at Reem — "...has been most helpful to you, and to us. We understand you are looking for *Roebling*, yes?"

"Uh, sure," Job said. "Found him, though. No problem."

The demon scratched a breast with a claw, then ran it up the side of her snout. "Found his *body*, you mean. We know that. No, we do not want his body." She bared her teeth. "We want his *shadow*. You search for his shadow?"

"Yes, yes, his shadow. It seems that is the crucial, uh, element; yes, Lady."

"Gooood. Good. Find his shadow, Job. Find his shadow, reunite him with his body, and bring him whole to me at..." — she rubbed her chin — "...at Ilion, and I will give you something valuable, something that will *enhance* your position, and help you end the Injustice you seek to end."

"What do you mean?"

"I will give you the files — not the God's eyes you think so precious, but genuine files, intact souls, as it is — to three beings damned to Hell that may not belong here. Use them.

Use them to get this *Roebling* creature out of here. Maybe you will get the three souls out, too. Do you understand?"

"Yes," Job said. "But why... why? Who do you work for, Lady?"

She raised a hand, spread her claws, waved it. "It is not... important. But we work for the same interests, the same side. Help me, you help yourself. Do you see?"

"Uh, well —"

"To get Roebling out, you must kill his shadow, send the shadow back to Reassignments. We will then Reassign Roebling to you, to your office, and Roebling and Shadow together, you will come to me. Do you understand?"

"Yeah, but —" he glanced over at Reem; Reem nodded. "Okay. Done."

"Good," Lady MacBeth said. "Good. That man is wise; heed his counsel." She pointed again at Reem. The demon slid her hand into her crotch, pulled out a black silk pouch, handed it to Job. "For your services, and to facilitate your task."

Job took the pouch, hefted it; it had a nice, clunky feel. "Lady." He bowed.

"One more thing," she said. "You will need some assistance. A woman will approach you after I leave. She will offer you her services. Use her, and when you have used her, bring her to us."

Job nodded. "Thank you." He bowed again. "Thank you, Lady."

"At Ilion," Lady MacBeth said. She sank down into the floor, smoke following her down, the concrete healing behind her.

Sam walked around the bar, held out his hand. Job sighed, opened the pouch, spilled out perhaps a pound of cut emeralds into his palm. He selected one, handed it to Sam.

"You're getting to be a real pain, Job," Sam said. He picked up the two empty beer bottles on the table. "Two more Ping Paos?"

"Two more," Job said.

Job put the emeralds back in the pouch, shrugged, sat back down. Reem chuckled, shook his head. "You got any bright ideas?" Job asked him. "Would this shadow show up on the net? Could we find him that way?"

Reem shook his dreadlocks. "Jah be praised, no. Enough static as it is."

Marilyn, the barmaid, came up to their table, set two bottles of Ping Pao beer down. "Your beers, Mister Ombudsman," she said.

"Thank you, Marilyn." He slid a diablo over to her, turned to the Rastafarian. "Okay, Reem, what's your idea?"

"Mister Ombudsman," Marilyn said. "Excuse me, can I ask you a favor?"

Job glared at her, sighed. He could smell it coming: now that he had a little power, every soul in Hell would be hoping that he could do for them what Job was trying to do for Roebling. "Yes?"

"I — I need work," she whispered. Marilyn glanced around the bar, looked at Sam. "This... this just isn't cutting it. I thought, well, I've heard that you might be having some openings, and I... Mister Ombudsman, I can do a lot of things. A lot. I can type. I can, uh, do fun things. I can perform." Job looked up at her, smiled, glanced at her body, the fine hips, the well-shaped breasts, the face... "I can *act*, sir. Do you need an actress?"

Job reached into the sack, handed her a small emerald. "I'll call you if something opens up."

"Thank you, sir." She smiled, knotted the emerald in an end of her shirt. "I'll work hard for you, sir. You'll see. Thank you." She walked away.

Job shook his head. "Women," he mumbled. "Your idea, Reem?"

"Not her," Reem said. "The Devil's, maybe?"

"What? I'm talking about finding shadows."

"Oh," Reem said. He reached for the ganja, took a toke. "No, I thought — Job, that was the Devil's secretary, Marilyn — former secretary, actually. She's on his shit list, I mean, *bad*, Job. Ran off with DaVinci, I hear, then shacked up with Mister Revolution himself, Ché Guevara. Word is that the Devil yanked her back and Reassigned her to this scum pit. She turns a trick now and then, if that's what you like."

"Not really, Reem. Your plan...?"

"Ah: find the shadow. You don't want to put a trace on it, but there's something just as good. Just as good." He grinned, pulled another eye out from a pocket. "Job, you're an aye-ree mon. Funny that the Lady MacBeth would tell you to seek 'my wise counsel.' I was going to give you this — it's on the house." He held up his hands as Job reached into the bag of emeralds. "*No*. On the house, mon. What you want to look for is sha-dows of shadows. You read that file on Roebling again, and you ask yourself, if you were Roebling's shadow, the evil nasty part — the *guilty*, nasty part — what would you do? Shadows of shadows, man." He held out the eye for Job. "This little bit of bioware, let it be your guide, mon. Let it guide you through Hell, eh?"

"Like Virgil to Beatrice," Job muttered, remembering what Lady MacBeth had told him: "a woman will approach you... she will help you... use her and return her to me."

"*Beatrice?*" Reem asked.

"Dante's Beatrice," Job said. "Didn't you ever read that little slime's book? It's in the Welcome Woman's package. Beatrice — the woman who would help Dante get to Paradise. And Roebling." He jerked his head over at Marilyn, taking a tray of beers up to the Marines by the door. "I think I see what you're getting at, Reem. I think I see." He took the bioware from Reem.

Chapter 3

Job ran a hand over his neatly trimmed beard — clipped in the U.S. Grant style — and stared down at the people entering 110 Columbia Heights. He smiled over the brick street, at the facades of the buildings lining it, at the little corner of Brooklyn resurrected on the west coast of Hell, just across the Sea of Sighs from Pompeii. He leaned over the balcony, adjusted the drape of the banner hanging from it. *'Welcome Brooklyn Bridge Builders,'* the banner read. Job waved at a red-haired man entering the door below. The man smiled, waved back.

Roebling, Job thought. They have to think I'm Roebling. He took out a pipe, filled it, played with the tobacco as he'd seen pipe smokers do. Damn cursed stuff. A breeze blew in from Pompeii, and Job sniffed at the faint odor of sulfur coming from the smoldering volcano. In the mountains east of Brooklyn, at the edge of the sham city, he could see lights moving on the hills. A light at the top of a mountain blinked twice at him. Job checked his watch, nodded to himself. Nineteen-hundred, he thought. Right on time.

He'd been amazed at how easy it had all been. Remembering, he thought of the sudden power the Ombudsman's office had acquired when given the Roebling case. Lady Mac-Beth's emeralds had allowed him to commission a replica of mid-Nineteenth Century Brooklyn. Reem's bioware had given him a list of all the Brooklyn Bridge veterans in hell and their addresses. The bag of diamonds had made it possible for him to organize a reunion. And with the crossing of a few palms — rough, callused palms — with diablos, Job had his own free-lance mercenary army. So simple, he thought.

Job turned to go inside, but as he turned, he noticed a thin man in black watching from across the street. A match flickered in the man's hand, and for a moment Job had a better view of the man's face in the dimming light: neat, clipped gray beard, piercing blue eyes, a long nose. The match went out, and the man fell back in the shadows. Job caught the glint of brass, then heard a faint click as the man moved down the street, his cane tapping as he walked away.

"Washy," a woman said from behind him. Job turned, smiled at the brown haired lady in the long skirt. Good, Job thought. She didn't call me by name.

"Emily?" he asked, continuing the charade.

"They're waiting for you, Washy."

"Yes, dear." Job stepped to the woman, let her take his arm. He smiled as he felt her smooth hand, glanced covertly at her figure. Marilyn. As Lady MacBeth had said, a woman had walked up to him after the demon had left, and Marilyn had practically thrown herself at Job. It hadn't taken much — a few more emeralds, a diamond or two — to enlist her services. Marilyn, the Devil's former personal secretary — the great ac-tress herself — was his for the night. *Marilyn.*

Job had thought her a harlot, but her performance as Emily Roebling changed his mind. She was the consummate professional, completely in character, perfect in her disguise. She had become Emily, become Washington Roebling's wife. Job knew he couldn't fool the Bridge veterans, knew he couldn't circulate among them, but none would expect him to: Marilyn-as-Emily would play hostess, Emily would do his duties. But he would make a brief appearance.

Job let Marilyn lead him downstairs, to the head of the staircase leading into the main salon. The Bridge veterans stopped, turned, stared up at him and the strong, handsome woman at his side. Marilyn — Emily — held up her hand and the murmurs of the crowd subsided. The veterans — the Irish, Italian, German, and Scandinavian immigrants who had built the Bridge — looked up at the Roeblings. Marilyn smiled, squeezed Job's elbow.

"Gentlemen," she said. "Gentlemen. Welcome, welcome to the First Reunion of the Brooklyn Bridge Veterans. Colonel Roebling and I are pleased that so many of you could make it tonight — though we do, of course, miss those who, due to circumstances beyond their control, are unable to attend." She smiled, jerking her chin up, and the men laughed slightly. "Colonel Roebling is still recovering from the unfortunate effects of his illness acquired, as you know, from the rigors building the Bridge back in the world. He has asked me to make a brief speech on his behalf." Job nodded, reached into the breast pocket of his coat, and handed her a sheet of crisp white paper.

"'Welcome, Bridge veterans,'" she read. "'It is with great pleasure that I have the privilege of meeting with you tonight. Aware as we are of the unique events that bring us together here'" — Marilyn spread her arms — "'we must also be aware of our great accomplishments in other worlds and in other times. We gather here tonight to celebrate those accomplishments, and the heroism of those who so nobly gave their lives in the building of the earthly Brooklyn Bridge.'" The men began to clap, but Marilyn held up her hand. "'But I have asked you to gather here tonight for another purpose. We cannot rest on our laurels,'" Job smiled, "'even in the situation we find ourselves in. I have gathered you together tonight to ask your aid in another great undertaking, an undertaking more arduous, more ambitious, and, indeed, more dangerous than that which unites us here tonight. What is this Great Undertaking, Gentlemen?

"'You may have noticed the great chasm separating our Fair City from the great island of the Old Dead on the opposite shore. Gentlemen, you may have heard of the great danger there is in crossing to that shore, even in sturdy warships. You may have heard of the Great Monsters that lurk in the depths of the Sea of Sighs. But you may also have heard of the great riches that await us on that distant shore. Gentlemen, there is one way, and one way only, to safely get to that shore. I have sent emissaries to the Island of Vesuvius and the cities of Pompeii and Herculaneum, and the Old Dead have agreed to join us in this Great Undertaking, if you are willing. Gentlemen, are you willing? Are you ready to join with me and build — rebuild, here in this Hell — the Greatest Bridge of All Time? Gentlemen, will you join with me to build the Brooklyn Bridge'?"

The men stared up at the Roeblings, looked at each other, whispered to each other. One man said, "You've got to be out of your fucking —" but was punched into silence. A tall, beefy man raised his arm, glared around at the crowd, then nodded. "Colonel Roebling, I'm with you." He stared at the crowd. "John Myers is my name, and you know who that is. I died in the caissons, Sir, the first man to do so, but I don't care. I'll die again — hah, I've died ten times already! What the hell! We'll build your damn Bridge!" The veterans roared their approval and others chimed in with Myers.

"Daugherty, Sir! I'm with you!"

"McKay, Sir! I'll do it again!"

"Cope, Sir! Count me in!"

Men began shouting their names, and Job smiled at their willingness to torture themselves again. Did they really think they could build a bridge, he thought. In hell? He was amazed at the perseverance of the human spirit. Even in hell they struggled. Even in hell they would attempt the impossible. He smiled at the idiocy of such souls, smiled at the idiocy of his own soul.

"Let the fireworks begin, then!" Marilyn shouted.

Job started, glanced at her, then nodded. That would be the signal. The men turned, went to the great open windows looking west, to Pompeii. Out on a raft just off the coast a cannon shot shells high over Brooklyn. Streaming fountains of flames roared forth from the waters. The darkness overhead vanished in the stroboscopic glare of exploding shells. Rosettes of sparks flowered in the sky. Then Job heard another sound, a faint sound, a thumping that grew louder and louder until the window panes rattled with the noise.

Choppers.

Job nodded at Marilyn and she ran down to the main floor, past the men, out to the front doors. Job heard shouting, some sort of commotion, then saw Marilyn being shoved back inside by a man in desert fatigues, a black and white kaffiyeh covering his face.

"PLO!" a man shouted — Mullen, Job saw. Mullen ran toward the fireplace, grabbed a poker, and rushed the man holding Marilyn by the throat. One of the guerrillas turned toward Mullen, raised his Hellishnikov rifle, and fired a quick burst at him.

"Damn fool," Job muttered. Job moved to the far end of the landing, out of the line of fire, and watched as a squad of IRA regulars burst through the French doors on the sea side of the main room.

Plaster flew as the IRA troops fired bursts across the room. The bridge veterans ran from side to side, first to the exit, then back to the French doors, then from one end of the room to the other. More PLO guerrillas poured into the room, and the two armies slowly squeezed the veterans into a huddled mass in the middle. The armies circled them, automatic rifles pointed down, occasionally jabbing someone trying to escape.

Two PLO fighters dragged Marilyn toward the French doors. She looked up at Job, ducked down on the railing. Her mouth opened. "What?" she seemed to be saying.

Job shook his head. That hadn't been in the plan. That hadn't been in the plan at all. Job waved at them, and the taller of the two nodded, then shoved Marilyn outside. In the light of the still exploding fireworks he saw them drag her across the lawn to the sea, and then she was gone.

The bridge veterans sat in a heap in the middle of the salon, hands locked behind their heads. The PLO and IRA mercs stepped back, rifles pointing at them. One guerrilla looked up at Job, motioned with his rifle at the men on the floor. "Now?" he seemed to say. Job stood up, shook his head. The bridge builders looked up at Job. One of the guerrillas raised his rifle at Roebling.

"No!" Myers shouted.

"Yes," a man said from a small balcony opposite Job, looking down at the room. Job smiled, eased his cane forward, slowly raised it up.

The man looked down at the guerrillas. He stepped into the light, tall, erect, his steel blue eyes appearing to glow, even in the bright light of the chandelier. The man stared across at Job, down at the men, then back at Job. Job looked at him and he looked at Job, and for a moment Job felt like he was looking at himself, then remembered who he was and who the man across was and what he had to do.

"Colonel Roebling?" Myers asked, looking up at the man on the balcony. "Colonel?" he said, looking over at Job.

"No," Job said.

The man on the balcony smiled. "Yes," he said. "I am Roebling." He glared down at the guerrillas. "Put your weapons away. I presume you are paid. Whoever paid you, consider your price doubled if you spare these men."

The guerrillas looked up at Job; Job nodded. Their rifles snicked as safeties were clicked on. They slung their rifles over their shoulders, nodded at each other, relaxing, and moving out of the room and onto the lawn, like football players after a long game.

Roebling looked over at Job, the end of his cane between his feet. Job raised his own cane up and over the top of the railing, let it rest gently on the top of the rail. He pressed a stud in the head of the cane, listened as the cane began to hum faintly and waited for the hum to cease.

"You wanted me to come here, didn't you?" Roebling asked.

"Yes," Job said.

"Emily," Roebling said. "Was that Emily?" Job nodded. "Where have they taken her?"

Job motioned toward the sea. "Pompeii, probably. I don't know."

"It was really Emily?" Roebling asked.

Job shrugged. "That's who she said she was," he said, lying.

"Emily... Why have you called me here? Why these men?"

The veterans looked up at the two Roeblings, from one to the other. They brushed off their jackets, some moving toward the bar near the fireplace.

"To build a bridge," Job said.

"Really?" Roebling asked.

"Really," Job said, lying again. The hum ceased on the cane, and he moved it slowly toward Roebling, until its end pointed at him.

"Who are you?" Roebling asked.

"Job," he said.

Roebling raised his eyebrows. "The Ombudsman?"

Job nodded. "The Ombudsman."

Roebling closed his eyes, let the cane drop to his feet, and gripped the rail. "Why are you really here?"

"To take you," Job whispered. "To kill you, Sir."

Job felt for the little stud on the cane and touched it. A light shot out from the end of the cane, and a flash of silver flew across the room, hitting Roebling in the chest. Blue sparks shot across Roebling's chest, flashing into sparkling webs, shimmering around his body, enveloping it in a plasma cloud. Roebling raised his hand, pointed; his mouth opened, shut, and he shook his head. The blue web wrapped around and around Roebling's body, covering him until he was a mummy of blue light. The light spun faster and faster, a water-spout of energy, whirling around and around, shrinking into a sphere the size of a beach ball, then a globe, then a baseball, then a marble, and then a dot that vanished into a faint pop. Roebling's cane wobbled on its tip, and gently fell to the floor.

*

Job walked across the glass plain of Ilion. His bare feet left faint footprints in the fine ash covering the plain. A rim of rubble ringed the crater, and beyond the ring Job saw wisps of smoke curling into the ruddy sky. Which battle was it? he wondered. What armaments had they used this time? Clouds of ash rose up behind him, soiling his coarse woven robe. Roebling walked beside him, still stiff from his resurrection. He walked like an automaton, his movements clunky. The Undertaker had told Job he would be like that until his shadow got adjusted to his body. Job stopped, and Roebling came to a clumsy halt next to him. The Colonel leaned on his cane, glanced at Job.

"Soon come," Job said, repeating the words Reem used to say to him. *Soon come: be patient, you know that your Redeemer lives. Soon come.*

The glass before them cracked open, and Lady MacBeth rose up out of the glazed dirt. She stood before Job, spread her arms, flapped her wings, wrapped them around her, and emerged, wearing a women's face this time, with golden ringlets curling back from her forehead, hardening into gold metal on her shoulders, flowing over her body in spun cloth. Two hoofed feet poked out from under the gown. She let her wings fall back, held out a clawed hand to Job.

"You brought the shadow," Lady MacBeth hissed. Job nodded. "Good. Good. And where is... the woman?"

"Marilyn?" Job asked.

"Yessss. Satan is quite displeased at her absence."

Job shrugged. "The mercs took her. Pompeii, I think."

"Pompeii? That was not in the plans." Job shrugged again.

Lady MacBeth sighed. "Well, Satan has ways of dealing with the Old Dead."

"Did you bring the... material?" Job asked.

"Yesss," she said. She looked at Roebling. "He is intact? Body and soul together? There are no little Roebling shadows running loose?"

"Intact," Job said. He smiled at Roebling, looked down. "The plasma gun Satan acquired for me did its trick, thank you." And, Job thought, Reem's bioware did its trick, helped him get the Bridge veterans together, helped him set the trap that would bring the Shadow Roebling to defend his men when they were endangered by the PLO and IRA troops.

"Goood," Lady MacBeth said. "He looks whole enough." She poked Roebling's arm with a tip of her finger, and his flesh hissed at the touch of the claw. "But some things aren't quite working right yet, eh? Ah, well, perhaps it is good not to feel pain. Is that so, Colonel?"

Roebling grimaced, said nothing.

"Well," she continued. "Yes, I have the material."

"Good," said Job. "Very good. How did you get it anyway?" He thought of Reem, Reem the hacker and his ganja-inspired forays into the hell data net.

"New programmer," Lady MacBeth said, "Ada Lovelace, know her?" Job shook his head. "Crackerjack computer jock. She plucked 'em out of one of those new biochip arrays. Damn shame, though — she had to reference them through a data block search, by vocation, as it were. Still, they're files." She waved her hand, and three bioware spheres, the God's eyes, appeared in her palm. Job reached for them.

"Uh-uh-uh... not yet," she said. She pulled her hand back. "Do you understand how to use these souls? Do you have any sort of idea for getting them out? I must know before I trust them to you. What are you going to do with them?"

"Going to do?" Job asked.

"How will you use them? How will you get Roebling out of Hell?"

Job sighed. "The souls you have brought me — whoever they are — may get out, may not get out; that will have to be seen. Roebling" — he glanced at him — "Roebling will, Y-willing. Roebling will lead them out, or they'll lead him out..." He shook his head, grinned sheepishly. "Well, I don't know exactly. I just sort of thought I'd wing it. My resources, you know, are limited."

Lady MacBeth rattled her teeth. "Ombudsman, Ombudsman... You're not very good at this, are you?" Job shrugged. "Well. Well. May I make a suggestion?"

"Please."

"At least one soul — so I understand, my source seemed a bit confused — has made it out of Hell: Aziru the Amurrite. The rumor goes that the Seven Judges of the Ananaki yanked Aziru from a chamber deep below and up into heaven. Who knows? If Roebling" — she pointed a steel tipped claw at him — "can be purified, a chance exists that he may be able to get out, like Aziru. Aziru, see, redeemed himself..." Job frowned. "Yes, I know this sounds like Sunday school prattle. Aziru proved contrite in the eyes of the Ananaki: his Judges. So if Roebling can find and meet the Judge of his time, like Aziru... perhaps? Perhaps."

"So to get out he'll have to find his Judge?" Job glanced at Roebling. "And these poets will help him — help us?"

"Perhaps," Lady MacBeth said. "Perhaps not. In any case, you must try."

Job shivered, remembering the lawyer, Roy's, threat. "I must try."

"Excellent. Excellent. One more thing. You claim your resources are limited? There is, well, another soul that can help. Not a soul, exactly..." The demon held out her paw, claws uncurled, and a tiny model of a bridge appeared in it. She handed it to Job. "The Bridge. The Brooklyn Bridge. You know of its demise? Sometime in the Twenty-First Century a barge slammed into the New York tower and brought the thing down."

"Never!" Roebling said. "I built the bridge to last forever."

"The only forever is here," Lady MacBeth said. "My apologies, Colonel; I did not make myself clear. The barge was loaded with CD-73, a rather nasty explosive developed in that era. Terrorists."

Job took the brass model from her, and felt it tingling in his palm. "So this... this bridge, too is here?"

"Why not?" she asked. "Troy is here, Alexandria, Memphis, Thebes, Pompeii... why not the Brooklyn Bridge? Or even Brooklyn, eh? Damned, damned like all of us — well, why not? It assisted in numerous deaths, the cursed structure. The Bridge... the Bridge must atone for its sins, too. It will assist you, like a ship, like a ferry, like those things that rumble under the ground, those things that fly above the clouds. The Bridge shall be your passage to... who knows, eh?" She pointed a long claw at the Bridge. "Some say the Bridge may be a manifestation of Satan Himself, that it has the power to create other hells, to, well, bridge the gaps between the hell of New Hell and the hells beyond. Again: who knows, other than Satan?"

Job nodded. "Who knows?" He brushed his fingers over the detailing of the model, touched its towers and cables and the little white lights blinking on it. The brass felt warm to his skin. "How does it work?"

"Ask it," she said. Job nodded, stuck the model inside a large pocket of his robe. Lady MacBeth gestured at Roebling.

"You will give us his shadow now?" Job waved his hand in assent. "Goood." She pinched Roebling's shoulder. "The Shadow Roebling will be of great use."

"His shadow must stay here in hell," Job said. He smiled. "It is only a little evil, and so weak, as it is."

"Powerful enough," Lady MacBeth said. "Powerful enough." She smiled, her canines oozing blood, her long tongue licking around her mouth. "Very well, Job, very well. If you think you can get someone out of here, we will entrust you with these other souls." She held out the eyeballs of data. "These are not like your... dog's eyes, yes? These are true God's eyes, every nuance of the soul. Just add blood, stir — bubble, bubble, toil and trouble, eh? — and the souls will come to you."

"Uh, could I have them in hard copy?" Job asked.

"Hard copy?"

"Please."

Lady MacBeth sighed. "One moment." She popped the eyeballs in her mouth, chewed and swallowed them, rubbed her stomach, then puked up a stream of putrid white stuff. She rolled the stuff around in her claws, patted it, and squeezed her hands together until the white stuff began to smoke. She opened her hands, and handed three small leatherette-bound books to Job.

Job took them, glanced at the names still smoking on the covers; he did not recognize them. "Who are they?" he asked.

"Poets," the demon said. "That was the category Ada managed to call up. Poets. I don't really know them myself."

"Poets," Job murmured.

"Poets." Lady MacBeth sneered. She reached with a claw toward Roebling, touched his throat, and drew it across his neck. A cut opened up, and a line of blue blood oozed from the wound. Lady MacBeth grabbed Roebling's beard, yanked his head down, so the blood dripped to his feet. The pool of blue blood whirled, grew, and shaped itself into a replica of the engineer. She released his beard.

The hairs from Roebling's face drifted away in a shower of gray, and he fell back — clean shaven — into Job's arms. The wound at his neck knit itself together.

Lady MacBeth reached for the shadow's hand. The shadow grasped the claw, let himself be led to her. He shimmered, slowly coalescing into real form. The shadow looked back at Roebling, smirked, then turned away. Roebling shuddered, looked to Job.

"Come," Job said. "Come. We will find these poets." He held the three booklets in his hand, then stuck them in the pocket with the bridge model. "Poets," he said. "Poets in hell." He took Roebling's elbow, and walked away from the demon, across the plain of Ilion, toward the cone of a volcano glowing blue on the horizon.

The demon wrapped her wings around the shadow, gathered him up into her, and sank down into the depths of Hell.

*

Job waited until Lady MacBeth had vanished down into the ground with the shadow, then stopped. Roebling walked clumsily, with a palsied twitch to his body. Poor soul, Job thought, He's been through too much this day: awakening in hell, reunited with his evil part, and now separated once again. He laid a hand on Roebling's shoulder.

"Rest," he said.

"I... I do not feel well," Roebling said. He sat down, rubbing his smooth chin. Job squatted next to him.

"None of us do, not here." The Ombudsman stretched, pulled the sling of his Samopal over his head, and laid the submachine gun on the glazed ground, barrel pointed away from him. The bridge model jabbed him in his side, and he took it out of his pocket and set it on the stock of the gun. Something clicked inside the gun, the trigger cocked back, and the Samopal began firing. Roebling and Job jumped up and away from the firing gun, but the bridge model held it steady. Within seconds the magazine emptied, and the ejected cartridges landed on the roadway of the bridge model. The brass melted into the Bridge and it shimmered and doubled in size.

"Ahhh," the Bridge said, burping. "Thank you. That tasted very nice. Could I have some more?" As it spoke, the pedestrian walkway between the two roadways wriggled around. The Bridge skittered over to Job on the legs of the two towers and held up the end of one roadway, like begging arms.

"Um... um, sure," Job said. He took two more magazines from his ammo belt, held them out to the Bridge. "Do you want them in the gun, or...?"

"Just give them to me," it said.

Job set a magazine down on one roadway, then about the width of a man's hand. The magazine sputtered in a series of brief explosions, and again melted into the Bridge. Job laid another magazine down, the Bridge ate it, and it grew once again, to about the height of a goat and the length of a large alligator. "More? More?"

"I, uh, might need these," Job said, patting the remaining magazines on his belt.

"Well," it said. "Well. All right. All right." Two lamps at the end of its "arms" — the roadways — swiveled, looked up at Job and Roebling. "My... my Lord, it's him." It waved one roadway at Roebling. "HIM. My maker. Colonel, colonel." The Bridge kneeled on its forward legs — the three columns of the tower facing them — and bowed the top of its head — the top of the tower. "How..." — the Bridge straightened out — "...how may I serve you, Maker?"

"Well..." Roebling said. He turned to Job.

"Can you bring to us these poets, uh..." Job reached into his pocket, pulled out the three books, read the names stamped on the cover, "...Hart Crane, Ezra Pound, and Emily Dickinson?"

The edges of the Bridge roadways warped upwards in a smile. "My pleasure." It waved one arm at Job. "Could I have... could I have more bullets?"

Job sighed and handed the Bridge another magazine.

Chapter 4

The hot blood courses through me. Hot, hot, yes, I feel the hot blood, the damning blood, I am all blood and wisp and not body, pure soul, pure id, evil — that is what I am, evil. The shadow, he calls me, he who would damn me here, he the Ombudsman, he who is Job. I belong in hell, he says, not in Roebling, not in — yes, W.A.R. — not in Colonel Washington A. Roebling. But I do belong in W.A.R., yes, I *am* W.A.R., as much a part of him as pancreas and kidney and Isles of Langerhans. I am W.A.R., Job be damned, and I will get out of this hell or no one — do you understand me, Job? — no one gets out.

At least in one piece. At least whole. And I — I, the pure evil in the Colonel — am what makes him whole. Surely you will see that, Mr. Ombudsman, surely?

The Lady escorts me, she wraps her fine goat legs around my thighs; she takes me to new heights of pleasure, and then she escorts me through the very rock of this underworld, here and there: we do our duties. This hell is like cheese! It is riddled with holes, riddled with tunnels, a whole new world underneath and through. The Lady warns me, though, tells me to beware the blue spots, the cold, ice blue spots, the holes and gaps and tunnels where *He* has asserted his presence. *He* is here too, *spiritus mundi,* in the body of that pure spot of goodness, that *Angel*, Altos, and (worse, worse), in His Grace. Satan says it is *He* that holds this hell together, but I say it is *He* who tears it apart. Well, like that philosopher builder Fuller said, tensegrity, eh? Things in tension: *His* grace against Our Evil, the tension between the two making a structure. His Grace is here, here in the pot of boiling essence that all must dip their flesh into when they receive their first torment; and it is here, too, in the pitiful good deeds some overwhelm evil sense to do. It is here — damn her — in Hope, that dreadful urge toward Redemption that keeps this hell from being a true hell, the hell we shades and shadows so desperately seek.

Damn this Grace! Damn it to heaven! Damn the holes in our hell! Damn *Him*, He who could not keep worse enough alone! Damn Him! Well, I will show Him, pitiful Creator. I will come to *His* world, come show Him what it is like to have Things That Should Not Be Here *there*.

I will be everywhere, my essence, my nastiness, my horror. I will spread my filth to all who Roebling encounters, spread it to those he might encounter. The Lady MacBeth has endowed me with certain powers. I will be there. Oh, malfeasance, I go now already. As the good Lady commands, I pour my blood into *her*.

Into Marilyn.

Chapter 5

Leviathan spat him onto the beach opposite Pompeii, and Hart Crane gathered himself up. As his footsteps left pink question marks in the ruddy, fine sand, Hart picked up the ground white lumps of his bones and poked them back into his body. He watched, fascinated, as the naviculars and astragali of his ankles grew back to their original shape and muscles wound around them, tendons stretching to calcanei, from metatarsals to phalanges.

What was that line about bones in "Melville's Tomb?" he thought. Something to do with "bones like dice?" Hart shook his skull, clicked his jaw. The poetry — he could never remember his poetry. He grasped at the image; ah: the bones of drowned men washed up on the beach, and they were the only messages of doomed sailors. Yes, that was it, the tortured metaphor he created — an embassy, an emissary, bones and bones tossed on the sand, random chance; here he was put back together, his message delivered. Metaphor, he thought, all metaphor: souls, bones, everything. The logic of metaphor, that had been his theory. He cocked his skull out to sea. *Metaphor*.

Hart glanced out to sea and saw Leviathan raise his great head, shaking it, bits of blood and flesh flying to shore. Dipping his hand into the Sea of Sighs, Hart let the fingers of his left hand crawl back onto his palm, let his flesh ripple over his body and snug itself around him.

Sure beats Fart Breath, he thought, remembering his first forty-seven resurrections on Slab A, the table of His Satanic Majesty's Undertaker. Poor sucker, Hart thought, so many bodies, so little time... Still, he knew that if he had *really* hated being reborn, Satan would have fit him into the Undertaker's schedule. Only Hart's pleasure on the Undertaker's table kept him from it. The first rule in hell, Hart remembered the Welcome Woman telling him on his arrival long ago, was "If it feels good, it's denied." There was a corollary to that rule: "If it's denied, it will feel good."

Satan couldn't deny him death, Hart thought. Got him there. He rubbed the plastic tag on a chain around his neck, felt the familiar bumps and grooves of the letters etched into it. Hart stopped, let go of the tag. *The ripcord*, he thought. *It is there, too.* Holding the tag out from his chest, he read his name in the hard black material, felt the silver links of the chain running up and into — he felt it — the back of his neck. The ripcord: Satan had given it to him again, that local version of cyanide that could whip his body back to the Undertaker — or back to a walking Resurrection — before anyone could stop him; that toy that wiped knowledge of any action he had undertaken on behalf of Satan and that gave him perfect deniability.

As he had attempted before and before, with each new awakening, Hart tried to remember what he had gone through in his lives in hell. Dim memories came up to him, blurred faces, a maelstrom of moments of déjà vu, but nothing substantial, nothing real: only memories of his life, and vivid memories of his deaths, starting with the death that sent him to hell, that night of April 27, 1932, on the *Orizaba* when he had climbed over the rail of the steamship and jumped into the sea. Forty-seven deaths had followed since, and although he couldn't remember the time before those deaths, he remembered whom he had killed, and how he had died: the deaths had burned themselves in his memory, each one vividly recalled, each one easily savored.

His pink toe, already tanning to dark brown in the light of Paradise, stubbed a bottle. Hart looked down, smiled at it: he knew it would be there. Always the bottle, always the note, always the faint whiff of whiskey oozing out to tempt him, to tease him. He uncorked the bottle, raised it to his lips, and sucked out the stale air, letting the faint taste of the Devil's own brew tickle his taste buds, the only taste of booze he could ever get. Satan always sent him to the dry districts. "I'm no fool," Satan had told him once. "If I send a lush like you to a wet county, you'd fuck up every assignment."

As he sucked on the bottle, a rolled-up piece of paper hit his lips. He bit down, pulled the note out, and unrolled it. "Watch the Bridge," burning, branded letters spelled out in the yellow paper. The upper case letters licked at the edges of the note and it flamed into black ash. Hart Crane let the ashes fall away onto the sand, and looked toward Pompeii, toward the strait separating it from the mainland.

The Bridge rose from the sea.

*

Harold Hart Crane stood on the shore and watched the great granite towers of the Brooklyn Bridge build themselves up from the muck of the sea. He heard the sighs of the damned, digging deep in the caissons, excavating the foundation. From the bottom of the sea the bricks rose in quick rows, three columns for each tower, the portals between the columns cathedral windows without glass. Great cables strung themselves between shore and tower and tower and shore, thinner cables dropping from the suspension cables to the bridge deck one hundred feet below. It had taken fourteen years to construct the original in the world of the living, Hart knew, but in hell the bridge resurrected itself in minutes.

The Bridge spread its roadway into Pompeii, then extended the road east, into the rocky shore of hell's west coast. A small city had sprung up on the mainland side of the bridge, a city of red-brick row houses, shops and warehouses, cafes, wharves and docks. Hart walked inland, over a rise, and toward Brooklyn Heights. He came upon a cobbled street that became asphalt, and wandered down the deserted streets, his streets. He smiled, and wondered for what and why the Devil had given him such pleasure.

Down the streets of Brooklyn, up Columbia Heights, Hart felt himself drawn — he knew exactly where — to 110 Columbia Heights Avenue, his old apartment, the one he had written his great poem in. Of course, he thought. Of course. He had a glimmering of what Satan was up to — was it not the greatest suffering to give the damned that which they had loved the most, let them taste it, remember it, and then yank it away?

Emil. The Devil was going to give him Emil Opffer, his beloved. Would the Devil let them be reunited? Hart could hope; even in hell, he could hope.

Hart opened the door to the building, walked toward the brass cage of the elevator. He walked by it — even in 1924 it hadn't worked — heading toward the stairs, but as he passed the elevator, its door slid open. Hart shrugged, stepped inside, and the elevator rose up to the fifth floor apartment. He walked out of the brass cage and to the apartment.

The door creaked open as he approached it, and he went in. The rooms were the same, exactly as they had been when he and Emil had lived there in 1924: the same water stained walls, the same chipping paint on the radiators, the same glorious view west of the Brooklyn Bridge, and now, of Pompeii, the new Sodom where Manhattan had once glimmered. Hart walked to the window, flung back the dusty drapes, and let the dank air flood into the room.

"Hell!" he shouted, "Glorious Hell, wondrous Pompeii!"

The steaming city sprawled across the new island of Vesuvius — Adam's Isle, some called it — Pompeii on the east flank, Herculaneum on the south, the volcano rising up between the two ancient towns. Sulla ruled there, Hart had heard — now where had he heard that? — Lucius Cornelius Sulla, Sulla the Dictator.

Vesuvius belched out thin wisps of steam and occasional ash, spreading a purple haze over the island. Lights and torches flicked on as Paradise set behind the mountain, and Hart could hear screams biting through the dark. Pompeii, the city of the Old Dead: he did not feel an urge to visit there.

"Harold?" a voice boomed from behind him.

Hart spun, turned to see Satan flickering in the center of the apartment, the bat-thing Michael digging into his shoulders. Satan wore his usual human garb: pointed beard, hair greased back, pin-striped suit immaculately tailored.

"Lord?" Hart said. "Lord Satan, are you in the flesh?"

"In the flesh?" he chuckled. "Oh, *never* in the flesh, not a spiritual being like me." He shook his head. "I know what you mean... No, I regret that I cannot grace your fine living quarters" — he spread his arms at the dingy walls — "with my physical presence. I am here in *spirit*, so to speak."

"You present an awesome presence, Lord," Hart said.

"As do you, Harold." The Devil snickered at Hart's baggy wool jacket, yellowed shirt, and greasy tie. "Harold, you are probably wondering why you are here — I mean, here at One Ten Columbia Heights, Number Five?"

"I got your note, Lord. 'Watch the Bridge.'" Hart turned, waved a hand at the Bridge. "It's still there, Lord."

"Very good, Harold. You are doing an admirable job. Yes, the Bridge is still there. But there is more to your task, much more."

"I suspected as such, Lord."

"You are to watch this Bridge, Harold."

"Yes sir. All the time?"

"No need to. You may use... that." Satan waved his arm, and a small video camera appeared, mounted on a tripod by the window. A video console about the size of a refrigerator appeared next to the window, six flaming apparitions of Satan reflected in the blank screens of the console. "That will make your life easier. Video cameras watch all of Brooklyn — every alley, every street, every doorway — and that computer digitizes every image at ten-second intervals and records it on a hard disk. You can program the console to play back a sequence from one camera, or 'follow' an object through space."

"Ah, Lord," said Hart, "like the device I used on the Marti kill?"

"Not as crude, Harold — better." Satan smiled. "We do a *few* things right in hell, when necessary. You are to watch for a blonde woman, a very sleazy-looking blonde woman — Marilyn, my secretary, the only joy in my dismal existence" — the familiar on his shoulder dug its claws into his skin — "excuse me, Michael — the only *human* joy. She has left me, that bitch, gone off to that sick island of Old Dead — a whore, I understand — and left me with... with Alice B. Toklas. *Miz* Toklas, excuse me."

Hart smiled. "Gertrude Stein's friend?"

"Her *friend*, yes, Harold." Satan's image flickered out for a second, then came back. "Get Marilyn, Harold. I *want* her back."

"You want me to go into Pompeii, sir?" Hart shuddered at the thought.

"No, Harold. There is no need. Now that the Bridge has been built, the Pompeiians will come over it soon enough. Brooklyn should tempt them — the stores, the shops, the warehouses, the intrigue... Marilyn will come, sooner or later. There's a dossier on her in the console. Figure out how to get her to come to Brooklyn. When she does, the cameras will catch her. The console computer is programmed to cross check every person who comes over the Bridge. If you miss her as she comes over, the computer will let you know. You are then to track her down in Brooklyn. But when she comes, when you find her, I want you to bring her back... the *hard* way." Satan smiled.

Hart smiled, rubbed his chin. "A straight trip to Slab A, Lord?"

"Very good, my faggot poet. Yes, straight to Slab A. With this." The image of Satan reached out of the field of view, came back holding a gleaming blued-steel gun, the barrel, action, and stock all one smooth unit except for a slight bulge on the left side just in front of the trigger. A scope was mated to the top. Satan held the gun toward Hart and pushed it through the image field. It shimmered as it passed through and materialized in midair, floating in front of him. Hart stepped forward, took the gun, caressed it.

"It's beautiful, Lord."

"A plasma gun, Harold. After your time. It has an accurate range of a thousand yards, the scope a magnification of three hundred times. You know about plasma guns?"

"I've seen them, Lord." He remembered that rather tricky assassination attempt on LBJ, when the squad of Texas Rangers had whipped out plasma guns and fried his head off — resurrection number 42, hadn't it been? "They are very, uh, effective, sir."

"*Very*. It has a flat trajectory. Aim and shoot. You'll love it. Kill the bitch, Harold. Kill her and send her back to me. Kill whomever she's with and... "

"Lord?" Hart did not want to say it. His heart raced, and though he smelled treachery, he had to believe that this time Satan would not deny him, not after 32 successful assassinations, not after all the good work he had done for His Satanic Majesty.

"Kill Marilyn, and you will be reunited with your beloved Emil."

"Lord... Oh, Lord." Hart kneeled, held the plasma gun over his head. "Thy will be done, Lord," he said.

"Cut the crap, Harold," Satan said. He shimmered into nothing.

Chapter 6

When morning came, the Pompeiians had already begun coming over the Bridge. Hart heard crowds milling about in the streets below. Factories hummed, street vendors hawked their wares, and all sorts of vehicles rumbled through the low city canyons. Hart quickly got out of bed, threw on his robe, and went to the video console. He played back the tape, back to early morning when the first Pompeiian — a Roman soldier on horseback — came across the Bridge. Lights whirred and flashed as the computer cross-checked each image, video cameras spaced along the Bridge adding additional perspectives. No Marilyn. She had not come. Hart sighed, walked over to this bedside table, and got a cigarette.

He paced the room, tapping the bottom of the cigarette pack, opening the fresh cellophane, pulling a cig out. Death's little luxuries, he thought. The Devil's Children got some perks. An assassin who had to wait long hours for his kill, Hart got fine cigarettes, not the sulfurous herbal shit most of the dead smoked, but real tobacco: Balkan Purgatories made by heretic monks in the northern mountains. He lit up, sucked in the cool smoke, looked around the room.

Hart's gaze fell on the two dimples in the queen-sized mattress of his bed. He squinted, went to the left side — not his side — and buried his nose in the pillow.

"Emil," he said.

Emil, he thought. The pillow held the rough, sweat smell of Emil, the smell of the wharves, the smell of the hold, the smell of the sea that the sailor always had about him. The briny, salt smell clung to Emil's hair, clung to everything he touched and wore. Emil had been there, there in his bed, there with him. Hart shook his head, dimly remembering a body next to him, a nervous embrace, and someone — him? — murmuring "Emil, Emily, Emily." Emily? Emil? He shook his head at the confusion.

He brewed a pot of fresh coffee on the small hot plate in the kitchen — another perk: Antiqua Guatemalan seized from a small band of Ché's dissidents — and dressed. Hart put on what he liked to call his Ninja poet outfit: loose black pants, his rumpled black coat, a black turtleneck, and black umpire shoes with black socks. He hadn't had shoes like that in his time, but on his tenth assassination he had offed someone from the 1980s who wore a pair, and grabbed them before the body went back to the Undertaker.

Setting the coffee down on the windowsill, just out of spill range from the video console, Hart sat down and called up Marilyn's dossier. He paged through the file, reading about her habits, her husbands, her films. Hart smiled, ideas forming in his head. Marilyn. Miss Marilyn, a/k/a Norma Jean. Vanity: that was the rub, her — he chuckled at the thought — *Achilles* heel.

What was that line in his poem? he thought. Something about touching "those hands of yours that count the nights," — hands, what, smeared?, streaked?, no — ah, yes, he recalled — "*stippled* with pink and green advertisements." She'd come to Brooklyn, all right. She would come.

Hart filed the dossier, began running the surveillance system through its paces. As the images flicked by, screen after screen, Hart saw that Brooklyn was slowly filling with dead, the New Dead from the East, the Old Dead from Pompeii, soldiers from Mao's Celestial Kingdom, caravans from the interior, dead newly Assigned. Camels and horses and oxen clomped down the streets, dodging more modern vehicles: motorcycles, trucks, cars, or ground-effect tanks. More dead would flock here, he knew, as soon as word got out about a new, open city. No restrictions, so anyone could come. And it was *new*, which meant that Brooklyn would work for a while, that hell's bureaucracy hadn't begun to foul things up.

He chuckled at the facade of it all. A ruse. Brooklyn was a ruse, a city resurrected to appease Hart, a city designed to lure Marilyn over from Pompeii. The Devil did things the hard way, Hart thought. Why couldn't he just send one of his hot shot commandos, Nichols or that crew, plunk them down in a Huey in Pompeii and just waste the whorehouse Marilyn was supposed to be at? Why the ruse?

Hart knew: how else do you pass the time in Hell? Quick and efficient was for God Almighty; arduous and dirty was for Satan. The Bridge, Brooklyn, this apartment — himself, Hart thought — all of it was done for the Devil's amusement. Well, fuck it, he thought. Hell was the Devil's game, and he'd play along, as he'd always played along.

Yeah, he'd play along. And as long as he could play, he'd up the stakes and make the game more interesting. Hart finished his coffee, set the video cameras on record, slung his plasma gun over his shoulder, and went out.

*

When Brooklyn had been born the day before, the streets had been clean, the walls of the row houses freshly sandblasted, and the paint fresh. That morning, as Hart Crane walked into what he thought would be the shopping district, the city already was turning dirty. Horse dung steamed in the middle of the streets. Soot blackened the chimneys and roofs of the brownstone warehouses along the wharves. Even the shining steel cables of the Bridge had tarnished to a dusky gray. Some of the Romans had set up a purgatorium next to a new restaurant, and vomit flowed out of oak barrels into the gutters. On the corner where Columbia Heights Avenue came into the main throughway of the bridge, the dead body of a headless woman, slowly dissolving into the asphalt on its way to another hell, shimmered as its soul went back to Reassignments. Hart glanced at her clothes, looking out of habit for jewelry, but saw that she'd already been looted, if she'd had anything worth looting. He adjusted the strap on his plasma gun, walked on.

The filmy dress of the corpse had reminded him of his idea, his plan to lure Marilyn over to Brooklyn. From what he'd read in the file on Pompeii, Sulla ran an archaic city. He didn't allow much modern in there, only some weapons, a few ground-effect vehicles, nothing from what Sulla considered the corrupting influences of the 20th century. Hart didn't know exactly why Sulla disdained what the Old Dead called "middle technology," but he thought it had to do with Che and the Dissidents — don't appear to align with Che's time, Sulla probably figured, and the wrath of Satan would be less likely to come down on him.

Suited Hart fine. If Sulla didn't allow middle-tech in Pompeii, Hart would make damn sure it would show up in Brooklyn. The 1950s was Marilyn's peak, if he knew his history right, and after the stifling antiquity of Pompeii, Hart could almost bet Marilyn would come over to grab what she could of *her* time.

Color television. Transistor radios. Rhinestone earrings. Gold lamé. Fuck-me pumps. Mascara. Eye shadow. Platinum-blonde hair dye. Yeah, if Hart had read the computer dossier on Marilyn right, she'd be ready to kill for a taste of '50s paraphernalia. Damn bitch must be pulling at her black roots by now, he thought. Norma Jean. She wasn't going to let Norma Jean surface, Hart knew.

On the northeast corner, opposite the corpse, Hart saw the thing that would reel Marilyn in like a fly-starved trout: a Woolworth's Five and Dime. The gold letters on a red background spanned across the facade. In the front window a tasteful display of modest woman's suits had been set up. The store was drab and boring, but the location was perfect. Hart opened the door and walked inside.

A prim, brown-haired young lady stood behind the cosmetics counter, helping a gray-haired, Victorian-era gentleman. As Hart stepped up next to the man, he heard him say, "for my wife, Emily."

"A present, then?" the clerk asked.

"Oh, yes," the man said. "She's in Pompeii, and I dare say they don't quite have this sort of thing there, eh?"

The woman blushed. "I think not."

Hart caught the woman's eye; she nodded. "I'll be with you in a moment, sir," she said. She held up a pair of crotchless panties, folded them, then put them in a little box and packaged them for the man.

"For my wife, Emily," the man said to Hart. "She's working as an entertainer in Pompeii."

"An entertainer?" Hart asked.

"Yes," said the man, beaming. He reached in his breast pocket, pulled out a gold pocket watch, opened it, and showed Hart a picture. "My wife, Emily."

Hart stared at the photo, a sepia tinted shot of a stern looking woman with a chubby face and a smile that looked like she was suppressing a laugh. "She's... quite lovely," Hart said.

"Yes," the man said. He clicked the case shut. Hart caught a glimpse of the initials etched into the case just before the man put the watch away: W.A.R.

"Do you live around here?" Hart asked, just to make conversation.

"Columbia Heights," W.A.R. said.

"That's quite a coincidence," Hart said. "So do I."

"Really?" he said, taking the package from the clerk and signing a slip of paper. "Well, perhaps we'll run into each other some time."

"Perhaps," Hart said. The man left the store.

"Can I help you?" the woman asked Hart.

"Yes," said Hart, leaning the plasma gun against the counter. "May I speak with the manager?"

The clerk blushed again. "I *am* the manager," she said, holding out her hand, "Miss Wood. Call me Natalie."

"Ah," Hart said, taking her hand. "Then allow me to introduce myself. I am a, well, sort of an entrepreneur, Miss Wood, and... well, has anyone told you how *glamorous* your store could be with a slight alteration in its appearance?"

Miss Wood smiled, raised her eyebrows, and shook her head. "This place? Why, no, Mister Crane. No. But *do* tell." She adjusted a pin in her Gibson Girl coiffure, and leaned forward, hand under chin. "Do tell."

Hart laid his pitch on her. With the location of her store — right there at the base of the bridge — Miss Wood could draw in the Pompeiians, seduce them with the wonders of the Twentieth Century. All it would take would be a little advertising, a slight change in the store's stock, a different window display...

Miss Wood was a pushover, Hart knew. As he talked to her about how she could increase her sales and attract a more classy kind of clientele, he saw the mousy facade of the clerk tumble away. Good girls didn't go to hell, Hart thought, even if they *had* been Woolworth's clerks. She probably had been repressed in life, never allowed to live her fantasy. Now he was giving it to her, letting her be what she wanted to be: glamorous, influential, romantic. Miss Wood was in hell now, and he could make her dreams come true.

"We'll name it after a great king," Hart said, "to give it a little class: Frederick's." Hart chuckled, imagining the transformation of the five-and-dime. "Frederick's of Hell.

*

Walking back to his apartment that night, Hart passed W.A.R. on the street a few doors down from his building. W.A.R. tipped his hat at Hart, puffed on his pipe, and continued down the street. Hart squinted at the face: W.A.R. reminded him of somebody — the beard, the receding gray hair, the cold blue eyes; he had seen him somewhere before. He shrugged, forgot about it. So many different people from so many eras were in Hell, a lot of them infamous in their own time, it was always hard to remember exactly who had been who. Some were transformed when they got to hell — younger, missing parts replaced — while others were transformed from Reassignment. Many disguised themselves, for fear of retribution from old feuds or new.

At his apartment door, Hart started to put the ancient brass key in the lock, then stopped. Someone had been in his room. He smelled the faint odor of pipe smoke — real tobacco smoke — and sensed, somehow, the recent presence of an intruder. Unslinging his gun, tapping the "arm" button, powering it up, Hart crouched down. He slipped the key in the door, slowly opened it. When the bolt slid back with an almost silent click, he kicked the door open, swinging the gun down, hunched, a low target, fanning the gun across the room.

Nothing.

He stood up, skittered over to the closet, flung it open, poked the gun through the empty space, then sidestepped to the small kitchen, peering around the corner of the little alcove behind the refrigerator.

Nothing.

Hart relaxed, glanced under the bed, nodded. He looked toward the open window, noticed a waft of pale-blue smoke curling out. He ran to the window, pointed the video camera so it looked down, clicked on the monitors, and slowly panned around the outside of the building.

Nothing.

Okay. He laid his gun against the console, wound the tapes back, tapped in the code for the apartment's video camera. The images clicked along at ten second intervals, showing him the progression of shadows across the floor. One frame flickered black, and the next frame showed the apartment door closing, only the sight of a man's leg moving through the doorway. The frame after that showed the empty room again, except for a cloud of fine smoke — pipe smoke? Hart thought — curling up to the ceiling. A few frames later showed Hart kicking the door open, crouching around and looking very foolish.

Spooling the tape back to the blank spot, Hart watched the sequence again: empty room, blank spot, shot of man leaving room, empty room. Someone *had* been in there — someone with a key.

Someone who had erased the evidence of his passing —
or whose presence could not be recorded.

*

A week later, Hart dropped by the old Woolworth's for its
reopening as Frederick's. Miss Wood had asked him to write a
poem for the occasion, and he had revised a stanza he'd
thrown out from his own "The Marriage of Faustus and Helen"
— a stanza obscure enough to fit the event, he thought cynic-
ally. Pompeiian ladies, almost identical in their diadem hair-
dos and sloppy, muddy make-up, clustered around on the
sidewalk before the store. Early Twentieth Century New Dead
gawked at the garishness of the display: azure green mannequins in gold lame crotchless panties, coupled mannequins in
erotic poses, arrays of love toys, and perfume in chintzy crystal-
line bottles. Miss Wood had altered her own appearance to
match the store, abandoning the high-necked long dress for a
black leather mini-skirt with bolero jacket, her hair teased off
her face and hanging down her back. She clapped her hands
to quiet the crowd and introduced Hart.

"From our very own Brooklyn, the famous poet, Hart
Crane!"

Hart nodded at the scattering of applause — who in hell
knew him, the most obscure of the Modernists? — and cleared
his throat. "A brief poem on the occasion of the opening of
Frederick's of Hell," he said. "Ahem:

Refractive rainbows, spectra spread
Infinite indigos and violets of Vesuvius
Limbs and belly untethered, the jewel
Winking from your natal pit; azure eyes,

*Lids in penumbra: your cheeks blush at the
Sigh of thighs gone liquid. Come, Helens,
Come to Frederick's and cast off your cocoons,
Butterflies bathing in the new dawn."*

"Wonderful!" said Miss Wood, clapping her hands like a schoolmarm. "Wonderful, Mister Crane. Would you do the honors?" She handed him a pair of pinking shears. Bowing slightly, Hart took the shears, spread the blades wide over the silver ribbon in front of the door, and cut it, opening Frederick's. He stood back, waved Miss Wood forward, and quickly stepped aside as the torrent of consumer-goods starved Pompeiians stormed into the store.

Hart stood by the door, his gun slung loosely on his back, looking into the faces of each person as he or she came in. No sign of Marilyn. She might have altered her appearance dramatically, he thought — she was, after all, an actress. But he'd seen the tapes of her movies, read Mailer's rambling essay in the photo book, and he knew he could spot her, knew that walk, knew that famous pout. She might not come to Frederick's on its opening. But the bait was set, and she'd come.

Leaving the spectacle of the opening behind, Hart followed the stream of Pompeiians backward, toward the Bridge. He walked up its long ramp, up the walkway going down its center, over the horses and carts passing by below. Hart thought of Emil, of the glorious time he had spent with his beloved, of walking across the Bridge with him, "the cables enclosing us and pulling us upward in such a dance as I have never walked and never can walk with another," he remembered writing in that silly letter to Waldo Frank. Emil, dear Emil, he thought. Will we be reunited?

At the center of the bridge, where it was suspended a hundred feet above the Sea of Sighs, Hart sat on a bench, watching, watching. He unslung his gun, laid it across his lap, then raised it, sighting on pedestrians below, testing the scope.

"Doing a little hunting, young man?" a voice said next to him.

Hart stood up, swung the gun around, pointed it at a bearded man. He relaxed, lowered the weapon: it was W.A.R. "Just testing the scope."

"A fine weapon," W.A.R. said. "May I?"

Hart handed him the plasma gun, carefully pressing his thumb to the security switch above the arming button, turning the gun off.

W.A.R. grasped his walking stick between his knees, held the gun up, sighted down it. "A most remarkable specimen. I believe this is one of those plasma guns?"

"Yes," Hart said. "Yes, it is."

"The last person I saw with one of these," W.A.R. said, "was a close associate of His Satanic Majesty."

Hart said nothing.

"Well." W.A.R. handed the gun back to Hart.

"A wonderful view, isn't it?" Hart said.

"Indeed. I stroll here often. This is a glorious bridge." W.A.R. took out pipe and pouch, tamped the tobacco in, lit up. Real tobacco, Hart smelled.

Hart pulled out his own cigarettes, lit up. "I've seen you often in the neighborhood," he said. "Shall we walk back together?"

"Certainly," said W.A.R.

Hart and W.A.R. strolled back to Brooklyn. Paradise dipped down behind Vesuvius in its quick, equatorial plunge.

The lights along the cables flickered on, casting gleaming reflections on the sea below.

"Again the traffic lights that skim thy swift

"Unfractioned idiom, immaculate sigh of stars —" W.A.R. said.

"Beading thy path —" Hart continued, *"condense eternity:"*

"And we have seen night lifted in thine arms."

"You know Hart Crane?" W.A.R. said.

"Very well," Hart said. "The Bridge, right?"

"Yes," said W.A.R. "He was after my time, but my dear Emily sent me his book on my arrival in hell. He wrote on a subject special to me."

"The Bridge?" Hart felt his pulse quicken.

"The Bridge," he said. *My bridge.* My dear wife and I built this bridge. My father designed it, I started it, and crippled from the bends, guided my wife in finishing it, me watching the construction from my apartment — there" — he pointed toward Columbia Heights — "and dear Emily shouting the orders to the men. Twenty men died to build this bridge," W.A.R. said, "four of them buried alive in the concrete of the foundation. And for that sacrifice Emily and I were damned to hell — to here." W.A.R. stopped in the middle of the Bridge, looked out to sea. "Ah, but it was worth it. It was worth it."

"Roebling," Hart said, "You are Roebling."

"Colonel Washington A. Roebling," he said. "Yes. You know me?"

"Oh, I read an article on you once." Hart smiled to himself. Of course he knew Roebling.

"And you, young man, who are you? What is your sin?"

"Belushi," Hart said, hoping Roebling hadn't seen him at

the Frederick's opening, or ever known the fat comedian. "John Belushi. Gluttony." It was sort of true, Hart thought.

"Ah, well, there are worse sins." They walked on, Roebling tapping his cane on the wood planking.

"You said your wife is here?" Hart asked.

"In Hell, but not with me. In... *Pompeii.*" He pointed with his stick at the city. "Sulla has stolen her. I aim to get her back." He smiled. "Didn't I see you at that old Woolworth's?"

"Frederick's, now," Hart said. "I think we met."

"Yes, Frederick's," Roebling said. "A stroke of genius, Miss Wood had. I hope it works in my favor. That store should draw the Pompeii ladies like flies to sugar. I do hope my Emily decides to visit."

"Does she know you're here?"

Roebling shook his head. "Satan has parted us. But if she comes here, I will seize her until she comes to her senses. And if she doesn't come to her senses, then I'll" — he held his walking stick up, and sighted down it like a gun — "well, she'll come to her senses."

"I'm sure."

Hart and Roebling had come back to Columbia Heights, to Frederick's. Roebling stopped, turned to Hart, took his hand. "A pleasure chatting with you, Mister Belushi. I'd walk with you further, but I have some business on the wharves to attend to. Let us have dinner at my club sometime, yes?" He reached into a pocket of his vest and pulled out a small, yellow card, handed it to Hart. "Ring me."

"A pleasure, sir," Hart said, taking the card. He watched Roebling walk north on Columbia Heights, tapping his cane as he went. Hart looked at the card. "Colonel Washington A. Roebling," it said, "110 Columbia Heights, No. 5. CHAos-6574."

*

The door clicked shut. Hart opened his eyes at the sound, reached for the gun slung over the bedpost, grabbed it, armed it, and rolled out of bed, crouched on the floor. He stood, ran to the door, flung it open and glanced down the stairwell. Someone walked through the front alcove; Hart heard the tap of a cane, then the loud clunk of the outside door shutting. Hart went back inside, to the console, punched in the codes for the street video cameras. The cameras went blank for a moment, then flickered back on as they caught the back views of a man carrying a cane just rounding a corner, or a man with a cane ducking between two carriages as he crossed the street. Hart gave up.

He played back the tape of his apartment camera. The camera showed — in infra red — Hart sleeping on his bed. Dawn broke. For a brief moment, the camera showed Hart lying on the bed next to someone else — a man, Emil? — and then the next frame showed Hart sleeping alone. Several frames after that were blank, and then showed the door closing shut, Hart rolling out of bed, and Hart running to the door.

Too many blank spots, Hart thought. Yet someone had been in bed with him. Who? He lit a cigarette, paced the room, watching the smoke rise in lazy curls. Smoke, Hart thought. It's like a spirit in my apartment. Smoke... *Roebling*. Roebling smoked.

Roebling's calling card... Roebling lived in his apartment. Not then, not in his time — now, in hell. We share the same apartment in this place, Hart thought. My Lord — am I *sleeping* with Roebling? But how is it that we pass each other? How is it that he doesn't see me when he wakes? How is it that we could live here simultaneously and yet not simultaneously?

Madly meeting logically, Hart thought, thinking of the lines in his "Voyages IV":

All fragrance irrefragably, and claim
Madly meeting logically in this hour.

Hart smiled, stubbed his cigarette out. Of course: he and Roebling had lived in the same apartment in life, but at different times. And here in hell, the pattern continued. One of them — Roebling, probably — was moving from a time before to a time later. Shells within shells, times within times. Could the rumors be true? Could there be more than one hell?

Chapter 7

Hart swung by Frederick's later that day. While he trusted the video system, he didn't trust it entirely — things broke in Hell far too frequently. He had made a deal with Miss Wood: she was to let him know if any blondes came into her shop from Pompeii, particularly if they had dark roots.

One had.

"When?" Hart asked Miss Wood. He held out his tin of Balkan Purgatories to her.

"Thanks," she said. Hart lit her cigarette. "This is wonderful, Mr. Crane. Ahhh." She waved her hand. "This morning. Oh, I don't know, a few hours ago. She came in with a bunch of Pompeii ladies — a chauffeur in a pale-blue ground effect Nixon dropped them off. They were looking for jewelry. The blonde woman wanted to buy a cameo ring. She didn't look blonde at first, because she had pulled her hair back so only the roots showed — maybe two inches of dark roots — and twirled the blonde ends in a bun. When she turned around I noticed the blonde bun. She had on a Pompeii gown like the rest of the ladies, but with her hair and make-up she looked different from them. I recognized her as New Dead right away."

"You recognize her from your time?" Shit, Hart thought, I hadn't ever thought to ask Miss Wood what time she was from.

She looked down. "I don't remember my time," she said. "Satan wiped me completely when I got here."

"Here? In Brooklyn?"

"Here," she said, "in hell."

Damn, he thought. He'd offed someone like that — a New Dead who couldn't even remember why they were in hell. That was serious shit.

"I'm sorry."

"Don't be," she said. "Whatever I did to be here, it must have been real bad. Sometimes I'd rather not know."

"Yeah." He tapped his fingers on the glass counter, stared at a display of dildos. "Which way did the Pompeiians go?"

"North," she said. "They said something about checking out some boutiques and then going to the hairdresser's. They had an escort — couple of soldiers."

"Thanks, Miss Wood."

"Thanks for the cigarette, Mister Crane."

*

Back at his apartment, Hart played back the Bridge cameras. Quiet and still until Paradise-rise, trickles of Pompeiians — and a few others going back to Pompeii — came over the Bridge. The portal cameras caught each face as it came into Brooklyn. He clicked through the progression of dead: New Dead, Old Dead, most dressed in First Century robes, some in more modern attire. The console computer automatically cross matched each face with that of Marilyn's, and each time came up negative.

He switched on the Frederick's camera, followed the tapes back to mid-morning, when a ground-effect Nixon Continental limousine stopped in front of the store, two Roman soldiers jumping off running boards and raising the darkened bubble of the passenger compartment. Four Pompeii ladies stepped out, walked into the store. The camera froze on each face; Hart could hear the computer whir as it cross-checked each woman. A fifth woman stepped out, and the camera across the street from Frederick's caught the back of her head: a blonde bun on top of brown hair. As the sequence clicked to the Frederic's camera, the frame went blank, then came on again, catching the back of the woman's head as she walked inside.

Hart tapped in the codes for the Bridge cameras, watched a quick progression of images until he saw the Nioxn limo floating over the center span. About mid-morning the pale blue limousine, its passenger bubble darkened, whizzed under the western tower. Two Roman centurions stood on the running boards, looking tough and mean-ass. Another soldier drove the limo from an open cockpit at the nose. Hart played the tapes that followed the limo over the Bridge and into Brooklyn. Once its bubble was backlit by the rising Paradise, and he counted five heads inside the passenger compartment. Again the cameras followed the Nixon as it pulled up in front of Frederick's. And again four women stepped out and the screen went blank for a moment.

"Shit," Hart said. He played the sequence back, banged the console as it came to the blank frame. The screen jumped, and for a moment showed clearly the face of Marilyn, just like Miss Wood had said: brown hair pulled back into a blonde bun. Hart smiled.

"Got you, bitch," he said.

Switching over to the Bridge cameras, he watched the Pompeii-bound lanes to make sure Marilyn or the limo hadn't slipped back over. She hadn't. Just to be sure, he checked the wharves, watched the nearly empty ferries as they sailed to Pompeii. He noticed Roebling hanging around below the great tower, staring at it, sighting along his walking stick. Odd, Hart thought. But he didn't notice Marilyn. Good, he thought. She's still in Brooklyn. Hart turned the console off, got his gun, checked the charge on it — full — and went out.

Hart walked along the edge of the Pompeii-bound lane until he came to where the suspension cables met the bridge deck. Ox carts clomped by, but most of the pedestrians took the promenade deck suspended between the two lanes. Waiting until no traffic came by, Hart climbed up the railing and to the northern cable. He slid under the guard lines along the side of the foot-thick main cable, and began walking up the Bridge.

Back in the world he'd done this once before. It had been 1925, and he had been very drunk, and Emil had left him. He remembered vaguely thinking he might suicide, but about halfway up the cable he'd become so scared of the height that it was all he could do to hold on. When he let the fear go, Hart had sat down on the cable and remembered feeling the Bridge hum through his crotch.

Now he climbed, and now he felt no fear. The rubber soles of his umpire shoes stuck to the rusty tarnish of the steel. Plasma gun slapping his back, hands gripping the guard wires, Hart climbed. Paradise hovered dead overhead, its dusky glow fighting to get through thick red clouds. Vesuvius spat out thin contrails of steam, steam whipped west and to Purgatory. Under the Bridge the dark shape of Leviathan cruised, swimming the Sea of Sighs, ready to feast on any who dared swim the channel between Pompeii and Brooklyn.

Up. Hart stopped every ten yards to look down at the deck, watching for Marilyn, watching for a pale-blue ground-effect Nixon Continental limousine. He went on, up and up and up, until he came to the flat top of the towers, nearly three hundred feet above the sea. The main cables snaked through an opening at the top of the tower, across supports holding their weight, and back down. Hart ducked through the opening and came to a short ladder that led to the top of the tower.

He poked his head out, glanced around. No one was up there. Of course no one was up there, he thought. Paranoid. Who would be up there? Hart pulled himself up, walked to the edge, sat down, knees in front of him, and watched.

The old assassin routine, he thought. Watch. Smoke a cigarette, watch again. With the high-power scope on the gun, Hart had the luxury of being able to scan a long distance, waiting, then scanning again. He tracked the approach of any new vehicle, anyone walking onto the Bridge. At the base of the tower he looked down, checking the boats and ferries. Hart knew that he might miss Marilyn, that if she wanted to she could slip onto a boat, slip across the Bridge, but he figured that she wouldn't, that she didn't know — or didn't suspect — someone was looking to take her out. Hell, Hart thought, if she was stupid enough to walk around Brooklyn, guards or not, why would she expect an assassin on top of the Bridge?

Late afternoon came. Hart had heard there was a curfew for Pompeii of Paradise-set. Marilyn would have to come across the Bridge before nightfall. Hart scanned the Bridge, then grinned.

Ah, he thought. Bingo.

The pale-blue limo had turned onto the Pompeii-bound ramp of the Bridge. Hart tracked it, zoomed in the scope: the same two soldiers, looking a little tired, the driver in the cockpit up front. The passenger bubble was raised and opaqued. Shit, he thought — could it be armored against plasma loads?

It was possible. Only some tanks were supposed to have the proper armor, but he didn't think a civilian vehicle would. The bubble might stop lasers, but not plasma charges.

A ground-effect tank pulled onto the ramp behind the Nixon. "Fuck," Hart said. The tank paced the limo. The soldier sticking up out of the turret, hands grasping the handles of a 20mm three-barreled Gatling gun, didn't look mean-ass, just deadly efficient.

Hart clicked the tracking sight of his gun on, armed the gun. He heard the reassuring whine of the plasma gun's batteries cycling up, firing the barrel with the negative charge that would shoot the bullets out. Four shots, then thirty seconds before another round. He sighted on the tank gunner, fired.

One: the gunner pitched back, head and upper torso atomized. The 20mm gun swung around, and the body pitched against it. The tank roared ahead, passing the limo on the right.

Two: the driver of the Nixon dusted the bubble with the ash of his existence. The limo swerved, slammed into the guardrail, whirled around, and stopped. Smoke poured out from under the skirts of the air cushion.

Three: the guard on the left running board of the limousine raised his laser gun, swung it out horizontal in front of him, then looked down, as his lower body disappeared from below him and the seared ends of his intestines whipped out from his abdomen.

Four: the guard on the right jumped off the limo, rolled, ducking behind the side of the car. His body peeled apart, like a knife slitting a shrimp, and crumpled into little bits of charred flesh.

Hart counted, waited for the gun to recharge. The tank pulled in front of the Nixon, shielding it from anyone firing from straight on, but doing nothing for death from above. The turret swiveled, then the 200mm main cannon slowly raised up, searching for a target.

"Shit, here comes Slab A," Hart said.

His gun whined, clicked, and a red dot blinked in the scope. Hart aimed, shot at the base of the limo's bubble. The bullet hit the bubble right at the seam, the plasma charge was released, and a line of blue sparks circled the bubble, climbed up the sides, met at the top, then shimmered away, revealing the passenger compartment.

All the women inside were blonde. All wore gold lamé dresses. Each woman's hair had been styled in the same shoulder-length, upswept hairdo. Their make-up was exactly the same, and they each had the same little mole on the right cheek.

"Damn you, Satan," Hart cursed. He powered up the scope, went from woman to woman, looking, squinting, staring. Kill 'em all, he thought, and let the Devil sort them out.

He fired, four quick shots to the chest, four heads bursting into ash, four bodies flopping out of the limousine, seared necks smoking. The fifth woman didn't scream, didn't puke, just jumped from the car and ran down the Bridge. She kicked off her spiked heels, and ran. Hart focused on her left hand, noticed a cameo ring on one finger. The ground-effect tank sped up to catch her.

Hart smiled. Marilyn. No one had a walk — a run — like that. And the ring... Miss Wood had said Marilyn was looking for a cameo ring, and now this woman wore one. He tracked Marilyn, waiting for the gun to recycle, waiting for the little red light to come on. He was in the flow, the trance his mind went in when he was making a hit. Only the world in the sight existed for him, only he and the target, everything else exterior, non-existent.

"No," a voice said from behind him.

Hart didn't turn, kept watching Marilyn. "Roebling," he said.

"I won't allow you to kill Emily," Roebling said.

Hart felt something cool press against the small of his spine, just above his coccyx. "No," Roebling said. "She's mine. I won't allow you to take her from me."

"Damn it, Roebling, that's not your Emily." The red light clicked on. His arm twitched. Hart felt the cool thing press harder into his back, wondered what it was — ah, the cane.

"It's my Emily. I should know my Emily."

"That's fucking Marilyn, damn you," Hart said. "She's the Devil's damn secretary and I'm going to take her out, even if you do kill me."

"*No*," Roebling said.

"Emily's not in Hell, Roebling," Hart said, guessing. "She never came to Hell. Only you. *She's not here, damn you.* Let me take Marilyn out."

"I'll kill you, Crane."

He knew, Hart thought. "Go ahead," Hart said. "Kill me with your little stick."

"Cane-derringer," Roebling said. "I'll kill you. I swear."

Yeah, Hart thought. The tank sped up beside Marilyn. Someone on top of the tank shouted at her, arms dangling over the turret's edge, ready to pull Marilyn up. She ran, getting closer and closer to the tower. Have to take her out now, Hart thought, before she gets under me, or in the tank.

"Emily's dead!" Hart screamed. "Dead to you!" He didn't know how he knew, he just knew. "Emily's in Heaven!"

"No!" Roebling screamed.

Hart fired.

The soldier on the tank reached down, arms hanging over the side of the turret. Marilyn grabbed his arm, and he yanked her up. The plasma bullet hit her just below the shoulders. The soldier pulled Marilyn up and over the top, headless. He held her up, her legs kicking against the side of the tank, still running. He glanced up at the tower, let Marilyn's corpse fall to the side, and shook his fist.

A rod of hot iron pierced through Hart's waist, ran through the fat of his skin, and came out harmlessly to the right of his belly button. He felt the hot bullet flatten against the tower below him. Hart rolled over, felt a trickle of blood ooze out below him. He swung his gun around, aimed at Roebling, and fired. The shot hit his stomach; the plasma released, shimmered around him, and ate Roebling up. His cane clattered to the ground. Hart felt his eyelashes burn away, smelled the sickly smell of burning hair as his head flamed. He rolled again, pulling his coat up, damping out the fire.

The cable exploded behind him. Drops of molten steel splashed up onto the deck, one glob just missing his foot. Hart scampered away, to the north side of the tower, looked down at the tank. The 200mm gun pointed up at him, fired another round.

Hart got to his feet, ran to the edge as the other cable exploded. He reached down, fingered his ripcord. Time to go? he thought. *No. I can get out of this one.* Wires sang out of the tower, and he heard a screech as the smaller cables scratched down the side of the tower. Lowering his gun, Hart aimed at the inside suspension cable — the middle north cable — fired, watched fascinated as it split in two. He looked down.

The south lane — inbound, to Brooklyn — fell to the sea, spilling carts and cars and horses and people into the waiting mouth of Leviathan. The north lane — outbound, to

Pompeii — warped, one side tipping down to the south. The tank slid into the guardrail, flipped over it, and tumbled to the water. Cables whipped the air, some tumbling away, others wrapping around the tower.

"Oh, fuck," Hart said. He slung his gun over his shoulder and ran to the remaining cable, the north one. Hart dropped down the hatch on the north side of the tower, climbed down, then ran down the main cable, down to the deck, down to earth.

Cables snapped behind him, but the main cable held. He heard asphalt tumble away, heard screams and cries of people trapped on the Bridge, or drowning in the Sea of Sighs. Hart ran, gun slapping against his back. He ran until he came to the bridge deck, jumped down on it, ran along its crazily slanted surface. He stopped, caught his breath, and looked back.

The east tower — on the Brooklyn side, the one Hart had just come down from — shuddered, bricks tumbling off its side. The lights on the main cables came on, still working, as Paradise set. Cables were outlined not as smooth lines, but chaotic jumbles, maelstroms of stars against the night. The Brooklyn-bound lane fell from the east tower, deck slapping against the water.

Hart turned, ran across the north span toward Pompeii. Only when he was on solid deck, only when the lane didn't tilt, did he slow. He half-walked, half-jogged under the west tower. The cables sang and creaked, but they held. He slowed to a walk, panting; safe.

Satan appeared before him, his familiar, Michael, perched on his shoulder. "You did well, Harold," he said.

"Thank you, Lord." Hart leaned forward, hugged his knees. "Roebling... Roebling thought Marilyn was his Emily."

"To him, she was," Satan said.

Hart looked up at the flickering image. "But Emily's in" — he pointed up — "the other place, right?" Satan nodded. "Will he know, Lord?"

"Never," Satan said. "It's a common problem. People, and souls, sometimes don't see things as they really are."

Hart stood up. A man shimmered next to Satan, took on solid form. The image held up a cane, pointed it at Hart. "Roebling?" Hart asked. He had the grey beard, the coat...

"Yes and no," Satan said.

The image wavered. His shoulders became wider, he became taller, and his face hardened, the beard disappearing, the top hat becoming replaced by a wool sailor's cap...

"Emil," Hart whispered.

The image of Emil Opffer opened his eyes, stared at Hart, then raised the cane. The end of the cane sparked, Emil was bathed in a blue light, and he disappeared.

"*Emil!*" Hart screamed.

"Emil, yes," Satan said. "Emil was here, sort of — in Roebling, in you." Michael dug his claws into Satan's neck, and Satan smiled.

"Damn you, Satan," Hart said. "Damn you —"

"— to hell, Harold?" Satan chuckled. "To hell?" He laughed again and shook his head; his image flickered away.

Hart fell to the deck of the bridge, convulsions of anger and grief tearing his body. He pounded his fists on the bridge until the heels of his hands were raw and bloody. Rubbing at the bullet wound in his right side, he felt the blood drying and winced at the slight pain. When the tears had stopped, and the grief begun to subside, Harold Hart Crane stood up and looked back at the Brooklyn Bridge. He raised his plasma gun, and cut away the remaining wires.   As the bridge slowly collapsed behind him, he slung his gun over his shoulder and walked into Pompeii.

Chapter 8

Ezra Pound stared down at the peninsula thrust out into the northern sea like a crooked finger. Pink pack ice surrounded the peninsula: a bay along the peninsula's southern edge that extended perfectly flat and smooth to the far horizon. Hovering above the foothills ten miles to the south, the airship *Italia II* waited for the brief dawn to break. Campfires flickered in the lowlands and valleys of the foothills — the fires of the Dissidents. Halfway up the crook of the peninsula searchlights blazed, barrage balloons blackening the sky. Occasionally a mortar burst from the area of the searchlights, and another mortar would be returned from the foothills.

Flying over the Great Range west of New Hell — they'd become the Smokies, and then turned to the Alps to the north — the blimp had wound its way through shifting mountain passes, across the great desert controlled by Mao, and up the coast, along ranges that changed not into new mountains, but new nations. Finn Malmgren, the navigator, had charted a new course daily, one map at a time, as Ez saw fit. The poet hadn't even let Umberto Nobile, the blimp's captain and builder, know where they were going — he had only said, "Fly the ship."

Ez stared through binoculars at the blazing lights to the northwest. He let them rest from the cord around his neck, turned to Nobile and Malmgren. "Good work, signors. We have reached our destination." He waved a hand at the search-lights. "Free Hell — home of the Democratic Resistance."

Nobile nodded. "Ah: I'd thought we were carrying cargo for them."

"Cargo?" Ez snorted. "Of a sort. What do you think our mission is?"

Nobile waved back at the hold. "Guns, ammunition, medical supplies, food... Are we not running supplies to the Resistance? You'd said in your broadcasts that the DEVO Pact counterrevolutionaries had taken back part of hell from Che and the Dissidents." He smiled at Ez. "You never *did* say where."

"There," said Ez. "Purgatory, General. The Purgatory Peninsula." He unrolled a map of the area, tapped an "X" pen-ciled in two-thirds of the way up the peninsula. "This entire coast is controlled by the Dissidents, but the Resistance has liberated the peninsula. The peninsula is all that keeps the Dissidents from sweeping north across the ice and into Purga-tory — all that keeps them from seeking the justice they *think* they deserve."

Nobile nodded. "And we will go resupply them?"

Ez smiled. "Hah! Resupply them? Hardly." Ez reached behind him, and pulled out his Teller plasma gun. "No, sig-nors. We go to Free Hell not to save them, but to destroy them. We go... to wipe them out. And when we have destroyed them, and nothing stands in our way" — Ez looked forward, at the horizon beginning to glow dull red — "then *we* will escape — escape, signors, to Purgatory!"

"*Escape...?*" Nobile whispered.

"Escape," said Ez. "Are you with me?"

"Escape." Nobile smiled. "I had thought you... a slimy, conniving bastard, Pound. I misjudged you. How do we know that you won't betray us? How do we know that Satan won't stop us?"

Ez shrugged. "I have come this far. It is God Almighty who is all-powerful, not Satan. Well?"

Nobile turned to the rest of the crew. "Finn, Giuseppe? Francis? Ettore? Vincenzo? What do you say? Is this madness? Or should we join Pound?"

"It is madness," said Malmgren. "But we should join the poet."

"Si," said Giuseppe. He turned to the other men. "We will fight with you, with the poet."

"I do not like this, Pound," Nobile said. "It stinks of treachery." He stared out at the mountains below, then smiled. "*You* — Amundsen knew. You had him killed because he would not go along with you?"

Ez smiled, thinking of Roald Amundsen's corpse back at the New Hell airport before they'd left. "He was... reluctant."

"But won't he betray you on the Undertaker's table?"

"No — well, perhaps, but not for a while. The Undertaker is so, so *busy*. And he babbles so much: he hardly cares what the resurrected think." Ez grimaced, recalling his last Reassignment. He stared at Nobile. "Are you with me, General? Shall we make a go for it?"

"It still stinks, Pound." He looked at the other men, at Ez's plasma gun — his Teller — slung at this side. "Still, I really don't have any choice, do I? We'll do it, then, Pound. We'll wipe out this counterrevolutionary camp, and then make the run for Purgatory."

"Benissimo," said Ez. "Benissimo." He slipped a piece of paper to Giuseppe. "Broadcast a message on this channel to the Resistance: Papiols, come! Let's to music!" Ez turned to Nobile, held up his right hand like a claw. "When the day breaks, and Paradise is at our back, we will attack. The Dissidents will fire at us, but we will be too high for their rockets to have any effect. The Resistance will lower the barrage balloons and let us into their encampment. When we are in..." Ez smiled, closed his hand into a fist, and shook it.

"Si," said Nobile. "Stations, men. Malmgren, take the ball turret. Vincenzo, Francis, Ettore, your stations. Signor Pound, I give you the honor of the bow turret."

"Grazie," said Ez. He climbed forward in the *Italia II*'s command nacelle — the fuselage of a B-25C bomber mounted upside down on the belly of the blimp — and to the General Diabolic Minigun mounted in the bow.

Paradise rose behind the mountains east of the blimp, lighting the plain of the frozen Sea of Purgatory into a flaming mirror. The steel roofs of the Resistance camp glowed in the dawn, the windows of the fort blazing back the Holy Planet's glare. Nobile steered the *Italia II* into a gentle wind from the west, and kept a level altitude over the Dissidents' camps. Flak burst a hundred feet below them, the bursts of smoke silver puffs against the white plain.

Giuseppe broadcast Ez's message, and the reply came back from the Resistance: "Bertrans, to the music."

"To the music," Ez whispered, and then, to Nobile. "Descend, General. Let's take them out."

The blimp roared down, a cloud of vengeance, its engines screaming, a low, shrill screech rising from a loose fold of rubber flapping in the descent. Someone in the Resistance compound began winding the barrage balloons down. The *Italia II* came over the edge of the compound, high walls like a crater's rim. Nobile yanked the wheel hard, to the right, swinging the blimp around so that the nose swiveled on a point five-hundred yards dead center over the compound.

"I'll keep her in a low circle, nose down, Pound!" Nobile yelled to the poet. "Fire at will!"

Ez sighted down the barrels of the Minigun at the fort below. Low buildings circled the parade ground in the center, the searchlights mounted on the roofs. The barrage balloons were winding down on giant spools mounted in the esplanade running the length of the compound wall. Ez expected to see men coming out of the bunkers, men ready to bring the blimp down. His eyes flicked right to left, searching for a watchman, a lookout, anyone. A lone figure suddenly appeared at the center of the fort. Ez smiled, flicked the Minigun's trigger forward, and fired.

The bullets fell in long, lazy loops, a narrow funnel of fire descending to the figure, surrounding it, enveloping it. The blimp came down, lower, the Minigun's rounds tightening into a column of lead. The lone figure raised its arms at the blimp, spread its wings, and caught the bullets.

Dust swirled around the creature below, dust and fire and smoke and eviscerated bullets, sweeping the Minigun's force into it, pulling the bullets down, yanking the bullets, the charge, the powder, the cartridges, the very gun itself down into it. Ez pushed back from the gun, let go, pulled his cape before him as the GE Minigun was ripped from its supports and out of the blimp.

More, Ez, the voice said inside his head. *Give me more.*

Ez pulled his Teller forward, squeezed ten quick plasma bursts through the broken turret, waited for the gun to recharge, then fired ten more. The plasma charges fell down on the thing, its blue light flickering, enveloping the cloud around it, joining the dust, the smoke, the lead, the steel. The thing opened its great mouth, swallowed, and sucked the tornado into its maw. Ez heard his Teller cycle and fire, cycle and fire, until its batteries were exhausted. Behind him, Nobile fought for control, fought to take the blimp out of the spiral, to no avail.

Dust cleared. The thing at the center of the Resistance camp rose up, larger and larger, its wings spreading to cover the sky. It reached up with a hand the size of the blimp, and with a gentle finger, touched the blimp's nose. The *Italia II* swirled around on the tip of the finger, slowing and slowing like a top, until it rested level in the sky.

"Lord Satan," someone behind Ez whispered.

Ezra, Lord Satan said, *You have done well.*

Ez gulped. "I came to please you, Lord Satan."

You came to destroy my resistance, Lord Satan said, *but I am the Resistance.*

"I... I see that, Lord."

Why? Have I not been good to you?

"Very good," Ez said. "But..."

The truth, the voice said inside him. *The truth, Ez.*

"I... It is not enough. I wish to escape."

Oh, said Satan. *Well. I am disappointed, but not surprised. All wish to escape my dominion. Even I wish to escape my dominion.* Satan lowered a finger, and drew a charred gash across the peninsula, across the Resistance compound. *There. My powers diminish there. I am too close to purgatory, do you see? Escape then. Cross the line and see.*

"Props full reverse," Nobile whispered back to Ettore.

Nobile knows, Satan said. *Yes, props full reverse. Run for it. I give you a chance.*

Satan touched the nose of the blimp again, and pushed it. Ez glanced down, saw the *Italia II*'s shadow pass over the black gash in the peninsula. Satan smiled, pursed his lips together, and blew. The blimp slipped backward, her props screeching as they gasped for purchase, and then Satan raised his wings.

"Props forward!" Nobile yelled. "Finn, Pound, get out of the turrets. All hands — brace for impact!" Nobile swung the wheel around again, turning the blimp's stern behind them, their back to Satan.

Ez came up out of the nose turret, pushed by Nobile, and took a jump seat against the port wall, across from Francis at the elevator controls. Finn rose up from the belly turret, strapped himself in next to Ez.

Satan's gale hit the blimp from behind, tossed it forward on a wave of hot air, like a cork in a raging surf. Nobile gripped the wheel, twisting and turning with the buffets of Satan's wrath. Struts creaked and groaned from the spine of the blimp, the engines sputtered and gasped as the carburetors adjusted to new qualities of air. A chill spread over the blimp, frost forming on the walls of the nacelle. Ez pulled his cape around him, then smiled.

This is how it should be, he thought. *It will work.*

He stood up, spread the cape back, and went up to a wall of the nacelle. A dark cloud spread across the peninsula, and a horrid flapping whipped the air into hundreds of small tornadoes. Snow swept by the ports of the nacelle in streamers of broken white. Ez rubbed frost from a port, looked up at the blimp bag above. A thin sheen of red ice slowly built up on the flat-black rubber. He turned to Nobile.

"General?" Ez asked.

Nobile glanced over at Ez, nodded, looked away. "Now what, Pound? Do we still escape? Or incur Satan's wrath even more?"

"Escape, Signor. Escape in the only way we know."

He nodded. "Die again?"

"Another spin of the wheel."

"Another torment?"

"Perhaps it will be better." Ez shrugged.

"Perhaps."

"I only meant to say, General, that... that you showed great nerve." He jerked his head back, toward the sound of Satan flapping his wings. "I mean, thinking ahead of Satan."

"I'll probably pay for that, Pound." Nobile shrugged. "What now? What next?"

"There is a village ahead, near Purgatory. If you can make it?"

Nobile smiled at Ez. "If." He tightened his grip on the wheel. "Where?"

Ez took the chart that had been spread on the table, held it in front of Nobile. He pointed at the tip of the Purgatory Peninsula. "'Middle finger,'" he said. "Qitiqliq. There is a small camp there — mostly whalers and such. It's something. If we live...?"

"Bene," Nobile said. He looked at the map, then stared forward into the gloom.

Ez went back to the port, opened it, and leaned out. His black cape flying behind him in Satan's gale, he watched the pink ice spin off the props and strike the underside of the blimp bag. The ice built up on the cracked wood blades, flew off in fist-sized chunks, and tore into the bag of the blimp. In the scream of the gale, he thought he heard the gentle hiss of the hydrogen leaking out of the bag. The Purgatory Peninsula seemed to rise to meet them, seemed to grab at the *Italia II* and yank it down to hell.

Ez ducked back inside the command nacelle. "The ice is building up," he said.

"What?" Nobile yelled back.

"The ice. It's building up on the propellers, breaking off in little chunks, and shredding the blimp bag."

Nobile turned back, smiled. "No problem. Amundsen installed shields. He checked them himself, assured me they would work properly. We had that problem on the *Norge*."

Ez stuck a hand out the window, reached up, pulled a piece of tattered rubber inside, handed it to Nobile. "Amundsen's a son-of-a-bitch."

"Fock," said Nobile.

Ez stepped forward, to Nobile's right, leaned against the console and looked at Nobile. "Odd, isn't it," he whispered, "how only Malmgren saw Amundsen die?" Ez pointed with his chin back at Malmgren, hunched in his jump seat. "And now Amundsen isn't here to see us crash?"

Nobile jerked his head toward Ez, bit his lip, then looked over at Ettore. "Ettore, take the wheel, please."

He strode up to Malmgren, Ez following, and, grabbing the lapels of the navigator's jacket, yanked his head up. Malmgren reached for the catches of the safety belt holding him into the jump seat, but Nobile slapped his hands away.

"Finn! Did Roald die?"

Finn Malmgren looked up. "Die? Of course — that's why he's not here."

Nobile reached down into Malmgren's shirt, pulled the gold chain looped around his neck, the ebony tag at the end of the chain with Malmgren's vitals engraved in it — a ripcord. "Ah, Signor Important?" Nobile asked. "What is so special about *you* that you need a ripcord? What information could you possibly possess that would make you want to suicide instantly?" Nobile looped the chain around his hand, twisted it tight. "What *is* this little toy, and what happens if I pull it now?"

"Umberto," Malmgren croaked, "no, no...." Malmgren bit down on his tongue, but it moved around in his mouth, a viper aborning, bloody froth dripping out his lips. "I... I must speak." His voice changed its timbre. "You have asked for the truth. The ripcord is not a suicide device, not a gadget for spies and saboteurs, though that is what those who wear it would like you to believe. It is a *torment* — my torment. The coward's curse, we who wear it call it. I am forced to tell you this. Lord Satan tests us, sends us into battle, gives us special missions. The ripcord is our way out, a clean death, a painless end. It wipes the slate clean, takes us back to what we were when we came into hell."

"That is so bad?"

"No, no — yes, it is bad, for the one thing we remember is that we pulled the ripcord to escape dying, escape pain, escape suffering — escape *truth*, do you see?" Malmgren looked down. "I have pulled it seven times already. Each time I come close to enduring, to going beyond my fear. If you pull it... The Devil does not make such fine distinctions. I will wear the cord again, forever and forever, until I die an honorable death."

Nobile twisted the chain in his hand. "Then.... Then, answer me: Did Roald die?" He turned the chain tighter, until its links cut into Malmgren's pale throat.

"No..."he croaked. "No, I lied. *He* told me to lie."

"Kill him," Ez said. He reached for Nobile's hand.

"*He?* Who?" Nobile asked. "Roald?"

"*Pound*," Malmgren said.

Nobile turned, let the man drop. Ez reached forward, snatched the chain, and pulled. Malmgren's mouth opened, gasped, then his eyes dilated into black pools, and the body fell into itself and disapeared. The air popped around the space where Malmgren had been.

"*You,*" Nobile said, staring at Ez.

Ez smiled. "Me," he said. "Well, who else? Who helped you build this blimp? Who had Amundsen and Malmgren assigned to you? Who thought up this mission?"

"You," Nobile whispered. "But why?"

"Think, Umberto. *Think.* Think why Amundsen died in the World."

"But..." He shook his head. "But we settled that."

"Oh?" Ez snorted. "Oh? Is anything *ever* settled in hell? Ever?"

Nobile looked down. "Never," he said quietly. "*Amundsen* thought up this whole operation?"

"Amundsen? No, hardly — but close. Close."

"Satan," Nobile said.

"Ah, yes — our friend, Lord Satan." Ez stepped away, held his black cape out like wings. "Satan, Lord and Master." He flapped the cape back and forth, then wrapped it around him and sat back down. "Did you really think the Big Guy would actually let you *fly* to Purgatory?"

"*You* said that. You said he is not All-Powerful." Nobile glanced aft, at the bulkheads of the blimp. "As you pointed out, Satan *did* let us build the *Italia II.*"

"Yes, He did," Ez said. "Oh, He certainly did. And why did Satan let us build this blimp? Why did He let you get this far?" Nobile has to know, Ez thought.

"To torment me," Nobile said. "To punish me." He looked out the window, at the raging storm.

"Yes. *Yes.* And why else?"

Nobile stared at Ez, looked into his dark brown eyes. Ez smiled, tobacco stained teeth glinting out from black lips. Nobile turned away, shook his head. "*You*," he said. "To deliver you — to *this*?"

"*Bene*, Signore Nobile. Bene." He fluttered his hand, making a mock bow.

"Fock," Nobile said. He straightened up, smoothed the lapels of his wool jacket. "Fock *you*. You will get where you will. And I, I will do then what I am to do: I will land this ship safely and protect my crew."

Nobile walked forward, took the wheel from Ettore. The clouds had parted briefly, and the tip of the peninsula stretched before them. "OK," he said. "Then we go down there." He waved at the crew. "Landing stations — crash stations. Spread the word. I want everyone ready to jump if we have to. Dress warmly, too." He glared at Ez. "*You* just stay out of my way."

"As you wish, Captain." Ez bowed at him, swept his cape across the deck, and sat down again.

The *Italia II* spun around in the gale, turned into the wind. Footsteps rang on the steel deck of the catwalk as Giuseppe, Ettore, and Vincenzo ran to the landing stations fore and aft. Francis remained at the elevator controls, with Ez and Nobile in the main nacelle. Ez reached into the chest pocket of his black jacket, pulled out a tin case of cigarettes. "Captain?" he asked Nobile.

"Fool!" Nobile said. He reached over and, with the back of his hand, knocked the tin out of Ez's hand.

"Signore, those are *Purgatories*," he said. "Do you realize how hard they are to get?" He went down on hands and knees, began picking up the cigarettes.

Nobile ignored Ez, gripped the oak wheel, fighting to keep the blimp into the wind. Francis struggled next to him, turning the elevators, the two men trying to fly the blimp down. She barely responded. Ez gathered up his cigarettes, stuffed them in his vest, and stood. He looked out at a frozen lagoon looming before them, watched it recede below. Nobile turned the blimp about, let the wind take the airship into the coast, trying for another approach.

"Release ten-percent gas, all balloonets," he shouted in the ship's intercom. The needles on the gas gauges jerked, then began to fall down. They lost more altitude.

"You want to come down fast?" Ez asked.

"Shut up," Nobile said.

"I just had an idea," he said.

Nobile sighed. "All right. Let's hear it."

"Send all the men forward. Pump the water ballast forward, too. The nose will drop." He held his hand out straight, then pointed the fingers down. "See?"

"*Bene*," Nobile said.

Ez shrugged. "You learn a few things in poetics," he said.

"All hands forward," Nobile shouted. "Pump ballast forward."

The *Italia II*'s nose dropped, the deck slanting at forty-five degrees, pencils rolling off the console. A cigarette rolled by Ez's foot. He stomped on it, reached down, pulled the flattened cylinder up, stuck it in his mouth. The ice rose up to the blimp, faster and faster. Francis turned the elevator wheel level, but the blimp stayed nose first, at forty-five degrees. Nobile locked the rudder wheel, stepped over to Francis, and heaved with Francis at the elevator controls to pull the ship out of the dive. Something screeched overhead, and Ez looked up. He heard a loud snap, then something whipping around above them. The elevator wheel spun back, tossing Nobile and Francis to the floor. The *Italia II* fell into a steep dive. The lagoon came at them.

"Damnazione!" Nobile shouted. He got up, yelled into the intercom. "All hands aft! Quick, quick." He looked at the intercom light; it didn't come on. He hit the switch, then pounded the console. "Francis! Run! Tell them to go aft!"

Francis nodded, climbed up into the catwalk above. They heard his footsteps thunder forward.

Nobile grabbed the main wheel, looked over his shoulder at Pound. "Ez! Prepare to crash!"

"Right," Ez said. He went back to the jump seat, strapped himself in, pulled the cape around him.

"Shit," Nobile said.

He fought with the helm, not daring to leave it, alone with Ez, all his men forward. Qitiqliq rose up to greet them, a little cluster of huts on a small mound between the great sea of ice and the Purgatory Peninsula. As they came down, Satan's gale seemed to stay above them, and they descended into calm, the light of Paradise gentle on the ice. The ice rose up, and Nobile gripped the helm as the blimp hit.

The nose of the blimp hit first. Like the nipple on a great baby bottle, it collapsed, pushing in. The forward section of the catwalk hit next, the edge of the keel cutting a long groove in the ice before the force crumpled the steel, pinning the men in the forward section between the base of the catwalk and the top of the spine, crushing them as the crash bent the steel. The command nacelle hit next, the B-25C fuselage ridiculous looking upside down, the nose bouncing on the ice, then wedging into an ice crack. The nacelle cracked at the top, ripping loose from the spine, separating from the blimp. The four engine nacelles broke apart, one propeller spinning into the ice, the others spinning up into the blimp bag, cutting it to shreds. The bag split open, and the balloonets inside burst, hydrogen spilling into the air.

Nobile slammed into the console, was thrown against the starboard bulkhead, then yanked from his feet and slammed shoulder-first into a seat post. A bone cracked in his back. He turned his head, looked up at Ez. The poet remained strapped in the jump seat, head down between his knees, arms crossed over his head. Ez looked up, saw light pouring in as the remains of the blimp rose up and away, freed from the weight of the main nacelle. Ettore waved from part of the spine still attached to the stern.

The main nacelle slid across the ice, then came to a stop. Ez sat up, unstrapped himself, walked over to Nobile. He stood over the General, a limp cigarette in his lips, then kneeled down.

"You OK?" Ez asked.

"Fock no," Nobile said. "I think my back's broken."

"Yeah?" Ez reached down, pressed against Nobile's spine. Nobile's face contorted as a searing pain roared through him; he winced, closed his eyes, cursed. "You're right, General," Ez said.

"Leave me," Nobile said. "Let me go back... back to Reassignments."

"To Fart Breath? No, you'll be fine," Ez said. "Let me move you."

"No!" he screamed. "Let me —"

"Ah." Ez reached underneath Nobile, rolled him over. Something cracked at the base of Nobile's neck. "How's that?"

"I..." Blood bubbled from his lips. "I... thank you, Pound. That's better." Nobile stared up at the caped poet. "Lord Satan, I have failed."

"No," Ez said. "You have done well, Umberto. You have fulfilled your mission. You're a... *heck* of a pilot. Thank you for delivering me to Qitiqliq."

Nobile grimaced. "Ebbene, Signor."

"An admirable job." Ez waved at the wrecked nacelle, shrugged. "A bit rough on the landings, but otherwise... fine. I'll go get help."

"Not... necessary, Pound." Nobile spat. "Ah. Ah. Back I go."

"Hold on, chum."

"No... no, I go."

Ez shrugged. "As you like." He stood, looked down at Nobile.

"See you, Pound," Nobile hissed.

"Not bloody likely," Ez said. He watched as Nobile heaved one, two, three last ragged breaths, and then went back to Reassignments. He reached down, closed Nobile's eyelids, and got up.

"Hell of a way to fly," he said. He took the unlit cigarette out of his mouth, smoothed it, stuck it back in. From his vest pocket the man in the black cape pulled out a book of matches, lit the cigarette, turned, and tossed the flaming match back at the remains of the *Italia II*. Ez pulled the cape over his shoulders, pulled the Teller forward, and began walking to Qitiqliq. A cloud of hydrogen burst aflame behind him, the flames licking at Ezra Pound's cape, and then receding. He sucked at the Purgatory, and smiled.

Chapter 9

Three men stood on the ice on the lagoon side of Qitiq-liq. Ez walked toward them, waved. A half dozen men and women moved out on the ice toward the poet, dragging small sleds. One woman, her face caked with grease so thick Ez could hardly tell she was a woman until she spoke, stopped him.

"Any survivors?"

He shrugged. "Maybe. I don't think so."

"Yeah?" The woman smiled. "Lots of corpses?"

"You can be sure of that."

The woman nodded, began running toward the burning remains of the blimp. Ez looked back, saw smoke rising from the wrecked fuselage and the engine nacelles, thought he saw the blimp bag floating over the flat coast. He turned back toward the three men waiting for him.

One looked tall, at least a foot taller than the other two, maybe six and a half feet, Ez guessed. He had odd designs tattooed on his face, a jet-black top knot on his head. The tall man leaned on a long staff, a harpoon, Ez saw, with a rusty barbed point about a foot long on the end; he wore a long parka made of some animal, with large ugly spots on the hide. The other two men were shorter, and bundled in similar parkas, with breeches and knee-high boots below the parka. They had hoods drawn up over their faces, so Ez couldn't see who they were or what they looked like. The two shorter men both held rifles, the business end of the barrels pointed politely down.

Satan's wrath had died down almost as soon as the *Italia II* had crashed, and only a light wind blew at his back. Ez pushed his cape back, freeing his arms, and held his hands in plain sight. He walked up to the three men, stopped, took a last drag on his cigarette, then handed the butt to them. The man in the middle, the shorter man, took it, sucked on it, and handed it to the other shorter man. He inhaled the last of the cigarette, then tossed it into the snow.

"You our man?" the guy in the middle asked.

"What do you think?" Ez asked.

"I don't think, I just do," the man said. "Devil said 'a whale that flew' would come to us, and we were to kill it if it didn't die, but not to kill the man in the black cape. That you?"

Ez smiled, whipped the cape around, then let it fall back over his shoulders. "Yes."

"Devil said we'd know you in other ways, know you by your weapon — and your smoke. Good smoke." He reached down, picked up the cigarette butt, turned it over in his hand. "Purgatories?" Ez nodded. "Yeah, I know your type. Let's see your piece."

"Piece?"

"Your gun," the other shorter man said.

"Ah." Ez reached behind him, under the cape, and swung his gun out on a leather sling. He unclipped the sling from the barrel, handed it to the man in the middle.

"Just an Ezekiel?"

Ez shook his head. "Not an Ezi. More than an Ezi."

The man in the middle ran his hand over the short barrel, unfolded the stock, and examined the grip. The barrel was smooth, with no action, and the grip was slightly larger, without the grip safety Ezis had. "A *Teller?*" The man raised an eyebrow.

"Ezi body," Ez said, "just to fool the citizens, but you're right: it's a Teller automatic, with a ten plasma-round cycle. You can set it for single fire, burst, or full auto."

"Sheet," the man said. He handed the Teller back to Ez, and Ez folded the stock, slung it back over his shoulder. "Okay, you're our man. I'm Barker. This is Ukalliq — 'Rabbit,' we call him, if you can't pronounce it right — and this tall dude here is Queequeg." Nobody shook hands.

"Pound," Ez said. "Ezra Pound. Call me Ez." He laughed. "'Call me Ishmael.' You *that* Queequeg? Melville's Queequeg?"

Queequeg spat. "Everyone tells me of this Herman Melville. Melville this, Melville that. I do not know this Melville. But if you mean, am I the Queequeg of the *Pequod*, yes, I am that one."

"Okay," Barker said. He was all business, Ez noted. "Devil comes to us in one of his forms, a hooker, as it was, all big tits and lubed legs ready to pump anything that moves, and tells us that one of his 'children' — that's what he said — would be coming to our friendly little village. We're to render any assistance you require."

Barker pulled back his hood, and Ez saw that he had bright blue hair, cut short in a fuzz, pale orange skin, and brilliant violet eyes, like a color photo developed wrong. A Mistranslation, Ez thought — someone who had gone through the Undertaker's hands, but had been changed in the process.

He scratched his blue hair. "You the poet, that Pound? Um, heard you added a few stanzas to the Bloody Sestina. How's it go...?

Satan swear the heavens' thunder will clash!
Loud screech dread demons in battle rejoicing
Horn to horn, claw to claw, knives opposing!

Rebels, tyrants, and kings — none shall have peace
With mortars and rifles, powders' music
Their souls will run blood seared into crimson!

"You *that* Pound?" Barker asked.

Ez grimaced. "Yes, I'm *that* Pound."

"Glad to have you here, man." Barker smiled. "Come, out of the cold. Rabbit, go see to the rescue." He shook his head. "Come, Ez, come taste our simple hospitality. You bring us great riches. Meat! Fresh meat! We'll feast tonight."

"Feast?"

"On the survivors." Barker cocked his head at the wrecked blimp. The people with the sleds were dragging back odd lumps of something. "The best meat, the only kind you can digest up here."

Ez turned, looked at the woman with the greasy face as she pulled what looked like Nobile's upper torso on a sled. She laughed, showing him a mouth of more gaps than teeth. "Demons rejoicing," Ez mumbled, and followed Barker to the village.

*

The whalers sat around the oil lamp in Barker's sod house, gnawing on Italian fingers, licking the little bits of flesh from the bones. Every now and then a whaler would rush from the main room and to the back of the house, where Barker kept a honey bucket. They'd come back with a satisfied grin on their face, and dig once more into the pot of human meat stewing in the corner. Ez politely nibbled on a bone — he hoped it wasn't Nobile — but he had no taste for dead people. He'd rather be constipated.

"What you up here for?" Barker asked.

"Why am I in hell?" It was a common question, Ez thought, like "Where do you live?" or "What do you do?" had been on Earth.

"No, in Qitiqliq?"

Ez shook his head. "I'm afraid I am not at liberty to speak of that." He hated the formalism, but it had become like a mantra to him, to others in Satan's service.

"Not even a little background?" Barker grinned. "I mean, yeah, an important guy like you has his own agenda, sure, but you want our help, you have to give us something."

Ez nodded. "Fair enough. Sure, a little background: I've come for your Gap."

"Gap?"

"Well, that's what some physicists call them. Hell-time's little fuckups. The theory is that hell's riddled with them, particularly near hot spots, volcanoes, fumaroles, that sort of thing. I'm not sure I buy that theory, though — but then, I'm just a poet. Personally, I think these Gaps are just weird volcanoes that don't act like the volcanoes you and I know."

"The Devil knows hell's got enough volcanoes," Barker said.

"Too many," Rabbit said. "Not like on home, where the land was flat and did not steam."

"Spare us," Barker said. "We've got a fumarole or two, if that's what you mean — volcano complete with a little hot spring, inland about twelve klicks. That's where we do our laundry." He laughed. "Hah! No, nothing so fancy. It's more an oozing creek that flows out of a small cave. I've never been in the cave. Queequeg has, though."

"What'd you see?" Ez asked the harpoonist.

Queequeg set down a forearm, leaned back, farted. "Darkness," he said. "The hot river glowing orange, and a blast of cold air blowing along the walls. I did not go far." He smiled. "I thought I had heard the voice of a woman, but I was wrong."

"You will take me there," Ez said.

"Yeah, sure, he will, if the Big Guy wants it. But why?" Barker asked. "I mean, other than that it's His wish. What's so special about this 'Gap,' if it exists?"

Ez sighed. "This sounds peculiar, I know, but... Well, some of the folks in Authority — particularly the Old Dead types — think that these 'Gaps' are manifestations of almighty god's Grace — or gods' grace, pick your deity. They don't like the idea of hunks of Grace polluting the precious evil of hell. Satan wants us to find it, try to bring it back, or get it out."

"Grace?" Rabbit asked. Ez saw the look on his face, and could guess what he remembered: the horrid pot many had stuck their hands in when they had first come to hell, the misty presence that had judged them and given them their torment. "How can you remove it?"

"Never mind that. We won't touch it." Ez grinned. "Think, comrades, think: if it *is* almighty god's Grace, why would it be here?" He waved his hand. "No, no, not in the Hall of Injustice, but here, near a hot spring?"

Barker squinted. "A tunnel? A leak between hell and... and Paradise?"

Ez nodded. "Yes, but not a leak. Say the physicists are right, that it *is* a 'Gap,' a warping of space and time — really, a bridge, if you will, between hell and... Well, it could be a bridge to some other place that *may* be Paradise — certainly not hell. Not hell at all."

"The Grace marks the spot?" Rabbit asked.

"The Grace *makes* the Gap." Ez rubbed his beard. "Oh, I don't really know. I may have screwed up the physics — some guy named Newton explained it to me once, but I still didn't get it. Anyway, Satan thinks the Gap's there. And if it is, and we can go into the Gap..." He let them imagine it.

"Escape from hell?" Rabbit asked. "Get out?"

"Yes. A bridge over hell — a way out!" Ez smiled.

"Escape?" Barker asked. He stood up, walked away from the fire, gnawing on a finger. "I don't think so — we are not like those Dissidents. Like you, we work for the Devil, not against him. Even if you *could* get out..." Barker shook his head. "Man, I don't get you dudes always talking about escape. What makes you think heaven'd be better? This hell isn't so bad. It's a lot like life, in a way." He held up the chewed finger. "Food's crummy, it's hard to take a shit, and you can't trust hardly any-one." Barker laughed. "It's the struggle, Pound, that makes it worth living. The adventure. The new stuff you learn. New sights In that respect, hell's *better* than earth, than living. You can take more chances, 'cause you cannot die. Heaven — why should I want heaven? Heaven would probably be *boring*: harps and clouds and a bunch of pansy-asses." He spat. "Rabbit, tell him about Qavvik."

Rabbit nodded, swallowed a piece of meat. "A... a great man, a shaman, came to us a while back. I had heard of him in my world. This man, this hunter, taught us an important les-son. Satan had sent him here as a torment. Satan made him hunt whales, but his torment was that Qavvik would never *catch* a whale. Satan thought that would drive a man like Qavvik crazy, but Qavvik didn't mind. It was the hunt that mattered to Qavvik, not whether or not he caught a whale. The hunt, see? We learned that from him, that it didn't matter if you had meat, it didn't matter what your reward was, but how you *struggled*. Qavvik taught us that, and though we have had our share of misery, our struggle" — Rabbit smiled — "our struggle has been pure. Of course" — Rabbit grinned even more — "such an attitude drives Satan crazy. Fortunately for Him, we are weak and sometimes forget ourselves, and believe there should be rewards." He reached for another piece of meat simmering over the fire. "And sometimes there are."

"And what happened to this Qavvik?" Ez asked.

"He became the whale," Rabbit said.

"Ah — you see! So there is escape, yes?"

"Escape *in* hell," Barker said. "Escape into other things, a bettering of one's condition, a change in attitude, redemption, sure. But escape from hell? There is no escape from hell."

"But there is," Ez said. "I have heard of it. There *must* be — why else petition the Ombudsman? Why else would the Devil give us hope?"

Rabbit grinned. "Easy. To torment us." He dangled a piece of meat in front of Barker, and Barker snapped at it as Rabbit snatched it away.

"But if there were not some chance, who could believe the torment?" Ez asked. "Think."

"Maybe," said Barker. "But the Man sent you here to us, told us to help you. I don't buy this shit about almighty god's Grace. You here to help Satan? Or what?" He spat out a bone, wiped his lips with the back of his orange arm.

Ez held up his hands. "Help him? Yes. Help myself? Yes, too. Satan has told me to remove almighty god's Grace, or the Gap, or whatever. I will do his bidding, loyally and willingly. But I will remove that Grace *behind* me. I will take it with me to the other side." He grinned. "So? You with me? Can you lead me to this fumarole?"

Barker grunted. "You want to try to pull a con on Satan, that's your business. Satan told us to help you, so our ass is covered. I don't like pulling shit on Satan. But if there's adventure..." His lips broke into a smile, showing golden teeth. "Then you can count us in. We could use a little action. This place gets too damn cold anyway." He turned to the harpoonist. "Rabbit? Queequeg?"

Rabbit nodded. "Sure. Qavvik would approve."

"A woman's voice," Queequeg said. "*She* was real." He stood, held his right hand out. "I will lead you."

*

East of Qitiqliq, in from the Sea of Purgatory, the land sloped up to miles of low foothills. A broad river braided its way across the slope from the lagoon toward the hills. Lakes periodically dotted the expanse — ice-free lakes, lakes of liquid nitrogen and other such gases that froze at very low temperatures. Slightly acidic clouds hung over the hills, pale red like anemic lips, rolling down on the coast in the evening, searing the stunted trees that struggled to grow. Snow sometimes fell, a pink snow, covering the sod houses of the village, whirling into gullies, etching the lagoon ice clear.

The whalers — Barker, Rabbit, and Queequeg — set out with Ez early the next morning. Paradise hadn't graced the village with its light yet, but its glow was refracted over the horizon, making the sky glow dark red under the low clouds moving in from the Sea of Purgatory. Paradise continually baffled Ez: he'd seen it from a hundred places, and each time it rose and set in a different pattern, even at two places at the same latitude. Sometimes it set in the east, sometimes in the west, once in the north, and once it did not set at all. He'd seen Paradise in all colors imaginable, all patterns, once even in stripes like Jupiter. Once he had seen it mirrored, reflecting back at hell hell's own light — Paradise's true color, he'd heard.

Queequeg led the way, followed by Ez, with Barker and Rabbit taking up the rear. A light snow had fallen the night before, and Ez gladly let the harpoonist break trail. Rabbit had loaned him a pair of fur boots — mukluks, he called them — and a parka, but he still wore his great black cape.

Seven miles into the foothills, up a narrow valley and out of sight of the coast, they came to a low volcano, its cone blasted down into a wide crater, red steaming hissing along its sides. The volcano blocked the valley, closing off the narrow pass.

Queequeg pointed up at the volcano, at a stream of lava oozing from its base. "There," he said, "that's where I heard the woman's voice."

The four men picked their way over tuff and pumice, through basalt canyons and along the edge of a thin stream of lava. Flowing back into the mountain, the lava came from a large opening, steam rising around the cave's edge as water dripped down the face. A rock tumbled down the volcano, bounced off the lip of the cave, and splashed into the stream.

Barker pulled his M-666 rifle forward, an assault rifle he had chosen not because it did anything wonderful, but because he was used to the feel of it. He clicked a magazine in, turned back to the others.

"Lock and load, gentlemen. I have a bad feeling."

Ez swung his Teller out, checked that the plasma gun was charged, held it in front of him. Rabbit chambered a thirty-ought-six round in his Sturm und Drang rifle, and Queequeg dropped a harpoon bomb down into the barrel of his Pierce & Anger whaling gun.

"Hey, no sweat," Ez said. "It's just a damn cave."

"A damn *dark* cave," Barker said. "I don't like dark places." Barker reached back into his rucksack, wrapped a flashlight to the barrel of his rifle with a velcro strap, and flicked the light on. They walked in.

The lava flow lit the cava a deep red, hell's blood beating through hell's veins. Barker's light stabbed against the far wall. A piece of rock broke loose from the top of the cave, crunching into fragments as it hit the floor. A dull rumbling came from within the mountain.

"How far in did you hear the lady's voice, Queequeg?" Barker asked.

Queequeg turned back, looked forward where Barker's beam fell. "Around the bend ahead," he said, "at the head of that passage. I did not go further."

The passage narrowed, a short ledge of successive old courses of the flow built up on the edge of the current stream. Barker took the point, leading them through.

"Shit," he whispered as he rounded the bend.

Ez followed Barker, held an arm up to his eyes as he followed him into the chamber. The stream of lava stopped in the middle of a bubbling lake about fifty yards wide covering the floor of a spherical chamber. A beach circled the lake, and steps had been cut from the beach up the sides of the chamber to a series of ledges rimming the room. In the center of the chamber's dome a column a yard in diameter blazed down into the molten lake. The shaft crackled and hissed as the golden light hit the air of the chamber; where the light fell on the lake, it pushed a vortex of lava back.

"Almighty god," Rabbit said.

"Almighty god's Grace," Ez said. "Or, a Gap." He picked up a hunk of pumice, tossed the spongy rock through the beam. The pumice lit the edge of the shaft where it entered, briefly flared green, and disintegrated into red motes.

"Try a round," Barker said to Rabbit.

Rabbit raised the Ruger to his shoulder, aimed and fired level at the shaft. The crack of the rifle firing reverberated around the chamber; the shaft flashed green and hummed briefly, something shot up the center of the beam, but they did not hear the bullet strike the opposite wall. Rabbit slid the receiver back, ejected the shell.

"I'll try the Teller," Ez said. He held the gun braced against his hip, the barrel level and pointed straight forward.

"Uh..." Barker reached out, tilted the tip of the barrel to the left, so that the gun was at an angle to Ez's waist. "Try that." He waved Queequeg and Rabbit over next to him, to Ez's right.

Ez fired, and the plasma shell fired straight and flat, bounced against the surface of the shaft, and ricocheted back to the chamber wall left of Ez. The charge flickered against the wall, snapping and cracking, then fizzed away, leaving a blister on the edge of the chamber.

"The shaft repels the plasma charge," Ez said, glancing back at the smoldering hole, "like a magnet. Good thinking, Barker."

"Just a hunch," he said. "I'm no physicist, but I'd say the shaft and the plasma charge are the same thing." He stepped up to the shaft, held his hand out to it. "Cold — like the pot of Grace at the Ministry of Injustice." He turned to Ez. "That your 'Gap?' Your Grace?"

Ez shrugged. "Satan knows, but it has to be." He stepped up next to Barker, held a hand up to the shaft, slowly pushed the palm toward its circumference. Ez glanced at Barker, pulled his right hand back, raised his left hand up. "Just in case — I'm partial to my right hand," he said, and pushed his hand in.

A woman's voice sang through his mind, familiar, nagging. The words jumbled around, running into each other. He cocked an ear, listened, pushed his hand in deeper. Words became clearer to him, his words sung by the woman, her voice a voice... a voice of an angel, Beatrice, he wanted to say, but why Beatrice he did not know. The words became shapes in his mind, images like the sounds that his poems became before he set pen to paper — a couplet, the ending lines to "Paradise," another sestina he had been composing:

Rising, opposing, cries to Paradise clash,
Seize our sins, purge our peace, redeem our souls...

Ezra Pound pushed his hand in further, but the next line, the line he knew he would compose, did not come, only a shudder that pushed his arm out, and the woman's voice whispering in the spot in the center of his head where stereo went to hide. *Finish it, Ezra. Finish it and you will be redeemed.* And then the three men were clutching him, rubbing the frost off his forearm, and Rabbit was muttering, "He glowed. Ez, you *glowed.*"

"She..." Ez started to say, turning his face to the three men, a peaceful smile on his face, his black cape fluttering behind him. "She was beautiful," he managed to add, as the volcano erupted beneath their feet, the floor melted, and the boiling lake of lava exploded up, coating the shaft of light; and they were consumed.

Chapter 10

Emily Dickinson sat opposite a waterfall pouring out of a gap in the mountainside, her back to the foothills rolling down to the caravan camp and the Sea of Sighs west of her. Her notebook spread before her, she nibbled the end of her pen as she groped for the next word in the third line: *Death screamed for me, horribly / A long melodious sigh / That sent shivers up my spine...* She scratched the last line out, looked up at Paradise poking through the clouds to the east. A rock clattered down from the stream above the waterfall, and six Chinese soldiers scrambled out from behind the misty spray. Emily stood, waved her straw hat at the black uniformed little men. They waved back, nodded, returned to the cave, down the passage that nice Dissident Mr. Cienfuegos had told her led back to one of Mao's supply dumps — or a tunnel. She glanced over at the opposite side of the gorge, thought she saw brush move. Deer, she thought, or a dog — maybe a *bear*.

Sighing, she looked down at the page, shook her head, and shut the notebook. The words just would not come today. Emily laid the book inside her carpet bag, on top of the neatly folded black jumpsuit and her broken-down Swedish Mouser rifle and bandolier of 6.5 cartridges. Her fingers brushed against the soft fabric of the jumpsuit, the gentle nap of the black wool. She thought of changing into the jumpsuit, but decided against it: the men in the trade caravan had their notions of what a woman should and should not wear, and tight jumpsuits, Mouser rifles, and bandoliers were not part of that dress code. She clicked the carpet bag shut and walked down through the head-high brush and low trees to the clearing a couple of hundred feet below.

Five minutes away from the waterfall, about halfway to the camp, the woods behind her rattled and the ground quaked. Emily jerked around, grabbed a short tree, and held onto the swaying trunk. A small cloud of dust rose from above the waterfall, and a tumble of rocks roared down the slope, sealing the cave. The tops of the trees rippled in the wake of something big moving through the sky; she squinted, thought she saw a blurred shape against the low clouds, thought she saw steel glint, and then the thing was gone.

Emily brushed a loose strand of hair back from her face, ran a fingernail down the arrow-straight part in the center of her head, tucked the stray hair into the tight bun at the nape of her head. Her long white dress felt clammy against her back. Gathering up her skirts, she tied them in a knot at her waist, ready to run. To the west the campfires from the caravan threw sooty clots of smoke over the low trees. At the edge of the camp clearing, above the caravan, she stopped, set her bag down, and rested.

A great black bird, one of those helicopters that the Dissidents spoke of in fear, settled down into the caravan camp, next to a red and gold wagon — the wagon of that blonde woman, Tamara, Emily had found herself despising. Tamara and a big hairy man — the Babylonian, Enkidu — came out of the wagon, and some strange men jumped out of the helicopter. Moving around the helicopter, but not firing their weapons and keeping well away from the slowly turning blades, the traders of the caravan watched Tamara and the strange men talk. Tamara and the strange men boarded the helicopter, turned and said something to the hairy man, Enkidu, and then he ran after her and into the belly of the bird. Its wings whirling around and around into a blur; the bird rose up, hovered, and began to spit fire from its nose.

Screaming, the great black bird swung back and forth in a long arc over the caravan, its nose shooting cannon shells and bullets at the traders, sundering arms and legs from the men's bodies, flaying their skin, putting holes in bodies where holes did not belong. The cannon of the great black bird cut the wagons into kindling and then into sawdust, made fires out of the fine cloth tents, made death and carnage and chaos of the orderly camp.

Emily ducked down behind rocks, pulling brush over her, hand clasped to her mouth to keep from screaming, tears roaring down her face and sweat coursing over her back. She'd wanted adventure, yes — that was why she had left the security of the brick house in New Hell, that was why she had hiked with her dog Carlo to Che's camp in the foothills north of New Hell, that was why she had joined the caravan west, through Mao's Celestial Kingdom, all the way to the Sea of Sighs. Adventure — but not death. Not this.

Carlo. She looked over her rock, her hiding place. She had left Carlo in camp, left him chained to her wagon, because Carlo had been bad and she could not trust him to stay with her. "Carlo!" she screamed, and started to run down into the camp, into the maelstrom, into the death and carnage the helicopter created, but sense told her to stay, told her that Carlo either had been killed or had crawled, whimpering, to someplace safe. Either way, she could do nothing.

In a minute the massacre ended and the helicopter flew away, back to wherever it had come from, back to the place where people like that could go and live with themselves, however people like that lived. Smoke cleared. Moans rose from still living bodies. Dead bodies glowed the way bodies sometimes did in hell, and melted into the rocky soil. Emily rose up, clutching her bag tightly, her chest heaving and sobbing, muttering, "Carlo, Carlo, Carlo."

She found him, still chained to her wagon, his collar halfway up over his neck, a long gash down his side, his chest rising and falling slowly, froth bubbling from his lips. Emily unsnapped the chain, loosened his collar and slipped it off, then held the big hound's head in her lap.

"Carlo, Carlo," she whispered.

Carlo looked up at her, brown eyes narrowed and focused. He tracked her hand as she stroked his forehead. He breathed a raspy breath, sighed, and his eyes dilated. A thin line of blood ran from his mouth. Carlo shuddered once, legs kicking out, and then he relaxed. Emily closed his eyelids, and stood.

Walking by the smoldering wreck of her wagon, she wandered among the bodies, searching for anyone living, anyone who could still live. But the few living ceased moaning, and their corpses flamed away, one by one. A man groaned near what remained of her wagon. She knelt next to him, rolled him over, face up.

"Miss Dickinson," he said.

"Senor Cienfuegos," she said.

"I... I will not survive. You must" — the Dissident grimaced — "help. Our intelligence tells us a city will rise on the coast. The city... the city will arise to trap a woman named Marilyn for the Devil's own purposes. You" — he gasped, panted for breath — "must help this woman. A man named Mister Frank will help you."

"Mister Frank?"

"Si. Tell him 'Gomez' sent you to work for him. This Marilyn woman may come to Mister Frank — to you. Do whatever" — he shuddered — "whatever she tells you. *Anything, no matter how silly it may seem.* Understand?"

"Yes — si. Marilyn. Whatever she tells me."

"Good. And go with her. If she asks you, go with her. Go with her. She is with the Revolution. You must give her this." Cienfuegos opened his left hand, showed Emily a cameo ring, the profile of a proud looking woman set against sardonyx. "Swear it. Swear that you will do this."

"I swear it."

"Good. Good... "He closed his eyes. Emily held his left hand, and when he died, took the ring from him.

She stood, slipped the ring on her finger, and looked around at the havoc. Emily Dickinson raised her fist.

"For the Revolution," she said.

In the morning, she saw that Brooklyn had been born on the broad plain below the hills of the destroyed caravan, on the West Coast of Hell, on the Sea of Sighs, just opposite the Island of Vesuvius and the City of Pompeii.

*

Where all the citizens of Brooklyn came from, Emily did not know. As she walked down the streets, people seemed to arise from subway stations, from alleys, out of manholes. Some had the dazed look the newly Reassigned had; others looked dirty and tired, like her, and had probably come out of the mountains. Most of them seemed to be of her era, the late

Nineteenth Century, though some seemed more modern. None had yet come from the West, from Pompeii or Herculaneum, over the gleaming new Brooklyn Bridge, *The* Bridge, arisen from the Sea of Sighs.

Down a tree-lined boulevard running along the coast, Emily felt herself drawn to a two story brick house with a short porch, four Ionic columns holding up the roof. She entered, walked up the stairs to a room, found an oak writing desk by the window, fresh quill pens in a holder, unlined parchment laid out. Of course. In the closet hung six identical, starched white dresses with high collars. Of course, of course.

Changed into a new white dress, bathed and scrubbed of the caravan dirt and sweat, the carnage blood, Emily strolled down the boulevard — Columbia Heights, she idly noticed it was named — and toward a major street that fed into the bridge. A man on a horse dressed in some sort of tunic came off the bridge, a banner fluttering from his spear.

Shopkeepers, barbers, shoe repairmen, clerks and doctors raised blinds from their windows along the main street. Old ladies swept the sidewalks, and gentlemen with canes tipped their hats to her as Emily walked by. She stopped in front of a leaded glass window, the words *'Mr. Frank's of Brooklyn'* etched into the panes. A hand lettered sign in the doorway said *'Help Wanted.'* The door rattled a brass bell as Emily walked in.

To her right, two couches faced perpendicular to each other; a large glass coffee table was in front of them, with glossy oversize magazines arranged on top. A tall, thin woman, her red hair arranged in tight braids wrapped around her head, sat on the couch and leafed through a magazine. Two rows of five leather upholstered swivel chairs lined both sides of the long walls of the room, facing wide mirrors. Porcelain sinks had been set in front of each chair, chromed hoods on swivel arms next to each sink. Bleeding snake heads littered the floor around the chair of a masked woman; a hood covered her scalp and the dull thrum of a hair dryer reverberated through the room. On a wall above one couch hung 11 x 16 glossy , hand-tinted photos of women with upswept hairstyles that looked like frozen surf. Behind a white topped desk a man sat, scribbling something in a ledger.

"Excuse me," Emily said.

The man jerked his head up, his mouth open. He quickly smiled, half rose, then sat down. His jet black hair swept back from his forehead in little waves, and he had a pointy goatee and a thin mustache. "Miss?" he asked.

"Mister, uh, Gomez sent me here about a position." She pointed with her chin at the sign. "Are you Mister Frank?"

"Ah, yes," he said. "Mister Gomez sent you? Good, good." He rose again, bowed. "Miss —?"

"Miss Dickinson," she said, peeling off her white kid gloves and extending a hand to him. "Miss Emily Dickinson."

Mr. Frank took her hand, pressed it lightly, and glanced at the cameo ring. He smiled, let go of her hand. "You are a stylist?"

Emily laid a hand to her chest. "Of sorts, though my poems cover many subjects."

"Poetry?" Mr. Frank waved at the empty salon chairs. "No, no — of *hair*."

"Of hair?" She patted her neat bun. "Well, I do my own, of course —"

"I see... "Mr. Frank said. "I really need hair stylists." He shook his head. "Mister Gomez sent you?"

"Yes."

"Well, perhaps there's something you can do to help..."
He looked around the room. "You write poetry?" Emily nodded. "Then I assume you can write? Do figures? Answer
phones? Be civil?"

"Yes, yes, of course."

"Good." A timer dinged on the counter next to the woman sitting in the swivel chair. Mr. Frank moved from behind
the desk, waved at the vacated chair. "I need a receptionist.
Can you start now while I go comb out Miz Medusa's lovely
tresses?"

*

'Death screamed for me, horribly / A long melodious
sigh,' Emily wrote, as the bell on the door tinkled, 'Scratching,
scratching at my breast / And oozing down my thigh.' She set
the pen down, looked up.

Five women walked into Mr. Frank's. They all wore the
gold trimmed tunic that Emily had learned was common dress
for Pompeiian ladies. Four of the women had their hair arranged in the fashionable First Century A.D. diadem style of
rows of ringlets along the crown. The fifth woman wore her
hair in a blonde bun, though the hair at her scalp was dark
brown. The half-blonde woman stepped forward, the four
Pompeiians behind her.

"We'd like to get our hair done," she said. "Is an appointment necessary?"

Emily glanced over at the empty chairs, the empty
couches, Mr. Frank's three assistants lounging in their swivel
chairs, reading magazines and smoking cigarettes. "Usually,
yes," said Emily. She opened an appointment book, held her

pen above the lined paper. "But I think today we could fit in a few walk-ins. Your names?"

"*Marilyn*," the blonde woman said. She leaned forward, touched Emily's pen. "No last name, dear. Just 'Marilyn.' And the other girls... we'll just call them Ginger, Susan, Terry, and Beth, if you know what I mean. No sense getting the Pompeiians riled up, you know?"

"Of course," Emily said. *Marilyn*, she thought. A ripple like cold ice squirmed up her spine. "And what services shall you require?"

"The works, honey." Marilyn reached down, picked up a placard on Emily's desk showing a woman with blonde hair styled in a chin length, upswept style. "Shampoo, set, cut" — she undid the bun, touched the dark roots of her hair — "*and* color." She ran a long fingernail over the photo. "God, I've been *dying* for a platinum blonde, teased and sprayed, to-die-for bouffant 'do.'" Mr. Frank had gotten up from his chair, was walking up to her. "Think you can handle it, toots?" she asked him, setting the placard down.

"Miss M — ," he started.

She held up her hand. "First names only: *Marilyn*."

"It would be an honor Miss — Marilyn. An honor." He bowed. "The other ladies, too?"

"Same thing," she said. "Exactly the same. Do me first, then the Pompeii honeys." Marilyn tapped the placard. "It's kind of a campaign of mine: make Pompeii blonde, see?"

"Uh, yes, yes, of course," Mr. Frank said. "Well?" He waved at an empty chair, and Marilyn moved toward it, running fingers through her blonde-brown hair.

Emily rubbed the cameo ring that Mr. Cienfuegos had given her, looked up at Marilyn, back at the ring. "Excuse me, Miss Marilyn," she said. "Did you know a Mister Cienfuegos?"

Marilyn whirled, her lips parted slightly in a little *O*. "See-en-FWAY-goes... Cienfuegos? Uh, no. Why?"

"He was a friend of mine. He seemed to know you. Shortly before he died, he said that I might meet you, and that if I did, I should give you this." She slipped the cameo ring off her finger, handed it to Marilyn.

"It's... it's lovely. How — how did you know? I've been looking for a ring exactly like this. Thanks. Thank you." She put it on her finger, stared at Emily. "Do I know you?" Emily shook her head. "Maybe...?" Marilyn leaned forward on the desk. "You're out of the Nineteenth Century, aren't you?" She pulled a hair pin loose, and a long strand fell down over Emily's face. "I knew someone like you, I think, but they didn't have this stuffy high collar, this tight little bun."

"Miss Dickinson is a bit, ahem, old-fashioned," Mr. Frank said, avoiding the eyes of the Old Dead ladies. "You know, I've tried to persuade her to update her look, like *all* the ladies of Brooklyn are doing.... Just a *little* trim, Emily." He snicked his scissors at the loose strand of hair.

Emily pushed back from Mr. Frank. "Father says it is not proper for a woman to shear her crowning glory." She tucked the stray hair back behind her ear. *Marilyn*, she thought. She bit her lip, remembering Mr. Cienfuegos's words: *Listen to Marilyn.*

"Crowning glory?" Marilyn reached out, began yanking pins from Emily's bun. Waist-length hair fell forward like a curtain over her face. Emily bowed her chin, kept the hair in front of her. Marilyn pushed the hair away from her face, grabbed in from the back and held it up off Emily's shoulders. "You call that 'glory?' Girl, Mister Frank's right — you should get a *little* trim." Marilyn took Mr. Frank's scissors, pulled a section of Emily's hair up from her forehead, and held the scissors up to it about six inches from her scalp. "Yeah. Cut this shit off."

"Cut it?" Emily looked up at the scissors poised at her head. "Cut it... now?"

Marilyn opened the scissors. "Now? Why not? *Yeah.*" She motioned with her chin at the placard on the desk, the photo of the woman with the silver blonde hair. "Yeah, *now.* Cut it like that. You can join my campaign, Emily. What say, Mister Frank? A little trial run on Miss Dickinson before you do us?"

"Well..." Mr. Frank rubbed his goatee, smiled. "Of course, Miss Marilyn, if Miss Dickinson doesn't mind...." He grinned, waved at the waiting salon chair, daring her. "*Do* you...?" He chuckled.

Emily thought of what Senor Cienfuegos had said: 'Do whatever she tells you, no matter how silly it may seem.' She bit her lip, reached for the ends of the hair Marilyn held on to. "Why, of course I don't mind," she said. "I really *had* been thinking of 'updating my look,' as you say. Go ahead, Miss Marilyn: cut it. *Cut it,* damn it." She bit her lip harder, shut her eyes.

"All right," Marilyn said. She closed the scissors, and a lock of hair fell away. She handed the scissors back to Mr. Frank. "Finish it up, toots."

Emily rose, opening her eyes, tugging at the shorter piece of hair. She swept the remaining hair back over her shoulders, the shorn hair drifting to the floor. "Yes, let's finish it up, toots," she said, holding her head high.

Do as she says, Mr. Cienfuegos had told her. *Follow Marilyn.*

The poet strode bravely to the chair, her hair whisking at her waist, the cut hank curling up at her chin. Emily touched the soft ends of her long hair, then let her hands fall to her hips. For the Revolution, she thought.

For the Revolution

Chapter 11

Emily Dickinson sucked in her breath as two-foot-long strands of her brown hair fell down her shoulders and onto her lap. Marilyn stood next to her, supervising Mr. Frank of Brooklyn as he cut. His scissors flashed, shearing away the Amherst dowdiness, cutting back the dull brown of her reclusiveness. The chin-length locks left on her head seemed to bounce up as the years of growth fell away.

"Great, great," said Marilyn. "That's the look, Frank." She pointed at the placard with the photo of the blonde woman. "See, like this: slightly longer in the front, shorter in the back, and clipped at the nape."

Emily winced as Mr. Frank pulled a hank of hair down in front of her face, opened her eyes as he trimmed bangs across her forehead. He pushed her face down, buzzing the hairs of her nape with an electric clipper. "What's he doing?" Emily nervously asked.

"Hey, don't worry, honey," said Marilyn. "It's going to look fantastic. Frank's the best. Trust him."

Mr. Frank set the clippers down, pulled her head back over the sink, and started working something wet through her hair. The stuff smelled acrid, harsh, and stung her scalp slightly. Mr. Frank wrapped her head in a towel and left her alone. She closed her eyes, drifted off to sleep, then woke up as he unwrapped the towel and laid her head back over the sink. He rinsed the stuff out, worked something else in, and then wound her hair on rollers. He lowered a hood over her head, and she let the warmth of the hair dryer wash over her neck as she watched the scissors of Mr. Frank and his assistants flash over the heads of Marilyn and the four Pompeiian ladies. A small carpet of brown and black hair grew on the floor of Mr. Frank's salon.

As the blast of the dryer whirled around her, Emily wondered if Mr. Cienfuegos knew what he was doing. "Go to a man named Mister Frank," he had said before he died. "Tell him 'Gomez' sent you to work for him." But the last part of the message hadn't been immediately obvious: "Do whatever Marilyn tells you, and go with her. Go with her." Emily had no idea what Cienfuegos meant, or how it fit in with the Dissidents's plans, but she had sworn to fight for the Revolution, and she knew that the Cuban's words would someday make sense.

As she looked down at the long strands of her hair still clinging to the apron, Emily wondered what Father would think. She knew he would probably not approve, just like he would not have approved of her leaving New Hell, just like he would not approve of her taking up the company of Rebels, just like he had not approved of George, of Leonard, or of Benjamin, or any of the young men who had wooed her. Emily smiled. But Marilyn — *Marilyn* — had been so convincing, her words so strong. "Cut that shit off," she had said, and Emily had, by Satan, she *had*. Father was dead, Emily was dead, and if he was in hell she hadn't seen him, and as long as she was in hell, she was going to live her life — her afterlife — her way.

Marilyn. Emily watched Mr. Frank combing out Marilyn's hair, and smiled as he teased her dyed hair into the flipped bob of the placard. Marilyn. She had followed Marilyn's advice, like Mr. Cienfuegos had told her, and there she was under the dryer, even if Father would not approve; she smiled wickedly — *especially* because Father would not approve.

Mr. Frank finished with Marilyn, then came to Emily and raised the hood of the dryer. The rollers clattered to the tray next to her, and Emily shut her eyes as Mr. Frank combed her hair out, spraying some perfumed aerosol on her hair, spraying and teasing, spraying and teasing. His comb made *scrick, scrick* sounds as he pulled it through the gummy strands. She opened her eyes, keeping them away from the mirror, daring not to look until the combing and the patting and the whispered comments from Marilyn stopped. As Mr. Frank turned her around to face the mirror, she closed her eyes.

"Finished," Mr. Frank said.

"Oh, do I dare?" Emily asked, thinking of that nice Mr. Eliot's poems she had read on the caravan.

"Nothing to dare do but look," Marilyn said. "It's *done*, honey."

Emily opened her eyes and stared, fascinated, at the blonde woman in the mirror. The blonde woman patted the upswept hair flipping at her chin; Emily patted the upswept hair flipping at her chin. The blonde woman touched the waves swept back from her forehead, the wispy bangs above her eyes; Emily touched the waves swept back from her forehead, the wispy bangs above her eyes. The blonde woman smiled, and Emily smiled back at the blonde woman in the mirror: a glamorous, stunning blonde woman that Emily realized with a cold shiver was her reflection.

"We could be sisters, Emily," Marilyn said, stooping next to her and looking with her into the mirror.

"Twins," Mr. Frank said. He turned, waved at his assistants, finishing up on the Pompeiian women. "Sextuplets."

Emily grinned, shook her head, watched, thrilled, as the hair gently bobbed back and forth. Father definitely would not approve. Father definitely would be *furious*.

*

Crouched down behind the back seat of the ground effect limo, Emily huddled, her long white dress tangled around her hips. A stiletto heel of one of the Pompeiian lady's pumps jabbed her in the thigh. The smell of burnt hair filled the cab. *Follow Marilyn*, Cienfuegos had said. If she had known it would come to this, Emily might not have taken the dying man's advice. It did not bode well when Marilyn had invited her to Pompeii, and the only space had been the little jump seat in the back of the pale blue limousine. *Follow Marilyn*. She had thought it inauspicious that the limo was being escorted by a tank. *Follow Marilyn*. She sighed. Well, she *had* followed Marilyn, and maybe it had been a dumb idea, but there she was.

Two more blue bolts flashed overhead, the same kind of blue bolt that had vaporized the bubble of the limo. Someone screamed, a shrill screech. Emily ducked lower, gripping her carpet bag tightly, the hard feel of the Mouser inside reassuring. She waited for the screaming outside to stop, for the crackle of the blue light to fade away. Acrid smoke drifted into the cab of the limo, then washed away on the breeze. Emily poked her head over the edge of the back seat, looked out.

The person who had been firing at them from the top of the bridge tower had either run away or fallen. She looked down, drew in her breath at the sight of the four Pompeiian women in their new silver lamé dresses, their neatly coiffed heads blown away. Emily felt a heaving in her stomach, closed her eyes, and fought the nausea. Let disgust become anger, and let anger become action, Mr. Cienfuegos had said to her once, and she followed his advice. Grabbing her carpet bag, she jumped out of the car and past the tank that had been escorting the limo.

The Brooklyn Bridge shuddered; looking up, Emily saw several of the suspender cables break loose from a main cable and whip down to the deck of the bridge. She gathered up her dress and ran toward Pompeii, away from the wreck of the limousine and the tank. Her foot caught on something and Emily fell, sliding along the asphalt, her white dress ripping.

A blonde head stared back at her, a head like her head, with the same upswept hairdo, the same mole on her right cheek — a mirror, Emily first thought. Emily rose, the head stayed where it was, and as she got up she realized that the head was only a head, that it had no body.

Marilyn, she whispered.

She looked back, saw Marilyn's body lying by the side of the tank, the lamé fabric of her dress melting into little brown globs. The turret on the tank whirred, the cannon barrel rising, and fired up at the tower. Emily ducked as a shower of melted steel cable rained down beyond her. She got up, still clutching her carpet bag, and ran from the tank and its destructive orgies.

Emily stopped, looked back at Marilyn's head, then ran toward it, grabbing it by the hair, and dashed back the direction she had come. The head wriggled in her grasp; she clutched it tighter, running, running to the other side.

A shot from above answered the tank, making that same crackling sound again. Emily ran on. One of the main cables screeched as the wound cables inside came undone, swirling in a maelstrom of steel. The deck of the bridge tilted. Emily fell, slid down into the guardrail. With the crook of her arm, she grabbed a cable, still clutching the carpet bag and Marilyn's head. She kicked, her feet found purchase, and she knelt, leaning against the cable. Marilyn's eyes opened, and she looked up at her.

"*Emily*," Marilyn's head whispered.

"No..."

"Emily, kiss me."

"What?"

"Kiss me, please. Kiss me."

"*No.*"

"Do it. Do it for me." Marilyn turned her lips up at Emily.

"No...." Emily closed her eyes, felt the head rise toward her, felt her hands bringing it up to her face. She pressed her lips against Marilyn's, against her warm lips, against her cool teeth. Something passed from Marilyn into her, an electric breath, a shudder of sensuality. Emily sucked in Marilyn's last breath, held it in her lungs, pushed the head from her, and breathed out.

"Thank you," Marilyn said. "Thank you. Release me."

Emily relaxed her hand, let the blonde hair slide over her fingers, let Marilyn's head fall into the Sea of Sighs. She saw the tank slide over the edge of the bridge and tumble in after Marilyn. Emily pulled herself up the tilting deck and stood. Steadying herself along the guardrail, she ran on the twisting deck, up to the other side of the lane where it leveled off, and onto the approach into Pompeii.

More cables exploded behind her, more cars and trucks fell into the water. Emily glared at the twisting roadway before her, dodging hurtling bridges, running from vehicles tumbling and crashing around her. Sweat ran down her back, down her body, the exertion somehow making the dress seem tighter. She wiped a forearm across her brow, the skin seeming to ripple beneath her touch. Her cheeks grew tighter, her lips seemed to swell. Gasping for breath, Emily watched her chest rising and falling, her breasts heaving and seeming to expand.

A piercing pain ripped up her spine, down every nerve of her body. Emily fell to the ground, rolling off the bridge and onto the smooth grass of Pompeii. A shrill screech ripped from her lips, and her vision blurred. She turned, looked back, and through misty eyes saw the Brooklyn Bridge twist apart and destroy itself. A lone man dressed in black walked toward her.

She rolled, ducked behind a bush in a pocket park at the base of the bridge. Panting, lying in the cool grass, Emily relaxed, caught her breath and waited for the man to walk by. Her body quieted its shudders. She stood up, her filmy white dress hanging in strips from her body. Emily pulled the torn cloth from her body and stood naked in the dawn of Paradise. She ran long-nailed hands over her smooth skin, over the gentle curves, the firm flesh. Turning around and around, Emily held out her arms to Paradise. Warm blood, hot blood, blood she had never felt before, rippled through her veins. Emily walked to a pond in the Pompeiian park and stared down at her reflection.

"Marilyn," she said.

Emily, a voice said inside her. *Emily*.

She smiled, reached inside her carpet bag, and slipped on the black jumpsuit folded up inside — the tight jumpsuit Che himself had given her, but that she had been too embarrassed to wear. She retied her black leather boots. She fastened the bandolier around her shoulder, and then she assembled the Mouser 6.5 mm rifle and slung it over her shoulder.

Marilyn, she thought. *Marilyn lives within me.*

Stuffing the remnants of her white dress into the carpet bag, she kicked it into the brush at the edge of the pond. Then, like the man in black who had walked past her earlier, Emily Dickinson walked into Pompeii.

Just as she rounded the street to the public baths, Vesuvius erupted.

Chapter 12

Oh, the light, the blue light, the light of Grace. What is this man doing? Why does Satan endow them with such weapons? Her body seemed so safe, so soft: the cool curves, the feel of her skin, the touch of her teeth. It cannot end. Roebling. I had thought to meet Roebling this way, in her body — in Marilyn's body. She fooled him once, fooled me once. I came to her, then; came to Marilyn (disguised so cleverly as Washington A. Roebling), came to their silly little party. Job tricked me, the bastard. I had thought to trick him, to use Marilyn on Job, on W.A.R..

It almost worked. I could feel Roebling's body longing to come to this Brooklyn, longing for his Emily who he thought resided at 110 Columbia Heights. But Job held his grip on Goody Two Shoes Roebling, and the trap I had set for him trapped me. Satan sent that damn poet Crane to get Marilyn, and he let that poet believe his lover, Emil, was in Brooklyn. And the love of my Emily pulled me from Pompeii, yanked me from Marilyn's body, and I came back to Brooklyn yet again. Damn Satan! Damn me! You would think I would learn. Never. Never. Satan had to send that poet here — that assassin.

Satan! He gives his children these little toys, these little weapons, these guns that spit the blue light, the light of God Almighty's Grace. What power! What cruelty! He knows what it does to us, to all in hell who have even a bit of evil in them. He knows that the evil cannot abide the invasion of the good, and so our bodies — or our souls, or our shadows! — must resist the intrusion, and in so doing, explode. Malfeasance!

Bullets I could resist. Arrows I could devour. Cudgels I could deflect. Shrapnel I could expel. But not this, not this plasma, not this essence of divinity. No. It comes to me and seeks me and if it finds me — no.

This man hunts me. He knows some of me remained in Marilyn, knows that despite my temptations I left enough of me in her to move her body, to plant thoughts in her mind. It was I who told her to make her thighs liquid for Sulla. It was I who told her to become the perfect Pompeiian lady. It was I who told her to go to Brooklyn, to cross that bridge and enter the New Dead city. It was I who led her to her pitiful Twentieth Century dreams, her disgusting lust for 1950s decadence. And it was I who saw her, saw the other Emily, that dowdy poetess. It was I who transformed her, I who made her another Marilyn! Marilyn moves at my impetus, and she creates new Marilyns, new coy traps to capture Roebling, to even capture Satan himself! I, the shadow, move her to my wishes.

Oh, visions of my own Emily tempted me, and yes, I strayed. But I recovered! I tried to prevent Crane from killing my Marilyn. I failed. All right, he destroyed that shell of me. Big deal. Zap, that Roebling fizzled away again. So I went back to Marilyn, back to that little teeny part of me I'd left in her to do my doing. Reunion! Oh, all of us were together again, every last evil bit of me, Washington A. Roebling, and Marilyn. How clever! When he fired that plasma blast at me I escaped down to Marilyn. What shrewdness.

What stupidity.

And now he, that assassin, that faggot poet, seeks me again, seeks us. He aims. He fires. He kills the other Marilyns. But he won't kill me, not this Shadow. I have one more ace up my sleeve. He will not destroy me.

Ah, I see him aim. I turn my head as the Roman soldier reaches down to pull Marilyn up to the tank. I see the lights focus. I see Hart Crane aim, a shot at my upper torso — a good shot, a heart-lung shot. This assassin knows his business. But I, the shadow of Roebling, know my business. I slide up Marilyn's spine, into her cerebrum, into her brain, up the very sheathes of her nerves, into a corner dark and safe from the dread charges of God Almighty's grace. The blue bolts sear into her back, through the heart, the lungs, severing the head from the body, cauterizing the spine and the arteries and the veins. I am loosed! I am sundered! Marilyn and I roll around inside this head. She bleeds. She fades away. So long, Marilyn! Back to Reassignments! Back to Lord Satan! Only I remain.

Emily Dickinson comes to me. I whisper her name. I kiss her, enter her body, and we become one, Emily and little ol' me, the Shadow. Wa-hah! She thinks I am Marilyn. Those thighs! Those breasts! I look at her through her eyes, and I think she is Marilyn.

But what is this searing flash, this roaring blast? What rough angel comes slouching to Pompeii to be born? What volcano erupts in our face?

Vesuvius! Lord Satan, it is Vesuvius!

Chapter 13

As Hart Crane walked into Pompeii, a light rain of grey ash dusted his head. He pulled his collar up and brushed the ash from his hair. Small lumps of pumice fell from the sky, striking the cobbled street and breaking into tinier pieces. Hart turned back around. The last granite blocks from the Brooklyn Bridge tumbled into the Sea of Sighs, only the base of the towers remaining. In a small park near the anchorage of the bridge a naked blonde woman ducked behind a bush. Hart blushed, quickly looked away.

A soldier led a horse down the street toward Hart, toward the ruins of the bridge. Horse and man seemed to hold still, an organic statue, but as Hart stared closely at the man, his hand seemed to close tighter on the horse's reins. Hart noticed other Pompeiians moving down the street, all in postures of flight, all seemingly frozen still like the man and the horse.

Vesuvius rumbled.

Through the darkening clouds lightning bolts flashed and sprays of sparks shot up. Hart reached into a coat pocket and wrapped a scarf around his mouth. The air grew thick with ash and sulfur. Larger flakes of ash mixed with glowing embers showered the streets. Hart readjusted the sling of his plasma rifle forward, and bumped the charging button. The batteries of the rifle hummed as the charge cycled on. He reached down to turn the rifle off, but noticed that ash whirled around him, pushing away from his feet. The fine gray powder settled in a yard wide circle radiating from the poet. He kept the plasma rifle on for the moment.

The right hoof of the horse moving toward him touched the ground. Thickening layers of ash built up on the soldier's head, on his short cape, on the rump and neck of the horse. Sidewalks disappeared under the thickening rain, limbs of trees cracked silently under the strain of the fallen ash. Quick flashes of red thunderbolts lit the volcanic night. Hart Crane walked down the street, a static sphere around him pushing the ash aside.

Vesuvius rumbled and roared.

Hart glanced up. A red wall moved down the flank of the mountain, boulders tumbling at the face. Like a froth of viscous surf, the nu'ee ardente — the glowing cloud — swept down Vesuvius. Pushing ash and smoke before it, the avalanche of lava burst out of a lateral fissure, its intense heat consuming oxygen, its intense force shearing off anything above the ash line. The wind devoured the heads of the soldier and the horse, blasting them into little bits of charred bone and flash. Hart held up his hand to ward off the blast, quickly jerked his ripcord out, ready to yank it and go back to Satan.

He let go of the ripcord. The fire storm streamed around him, rushing by and meeting in the wake of his body, as if he were a boulder in the torrent of rapids. Hart felt the plasma rifle hum against his waist. He reached down, patted it. A sphere of buzzing static shimmered around him. Somehow, he thought, the rifle keeps the ash and heat from incinerating me.

Dark clouds obscured Brooklyn across the strait from Pompeii, the surface of the Sea of Sighs revealed only by glowing rafts of pumice. Hart moved toward the bridge abutments, beginning to regret destroying his only path of escape. A figure moved from a clump of boulders in the park near the remnants of the bridge approach. His plasma shield a teardrop bubble, Hart approached the clump of rocks, letting the shield sweep toward the rocks, sweeping away the ash protecting whoever had hidden behind them.

A woman in a black jumpsuit rose from the rocks and into his aura. Hart held out a hand to her; she grabbed it, and he pulled her to him. Her blonde hair stood out straight from her head, a ten-inch translucent penumbra, and her rifle glowed with a blue light. He stared down at her brown eyes, her thick lips, her fine white teeth. The firestorm whirled around them.

"Who?" he asked.

"Em," she said. "Em - i..." She shook her head. "I don't know. Em." The blonde woman hugged Hart to her, clutching him, burying her head in his chest.

"Em," he said softly, thinking, Marilyn; and then thinking, no, Marilyn: he had killed Marilyn. Hart Crane held onto the woman, holding her, holding her, the charging light on his plasma rifle glowing softly, the crackling static shield around them humming.

*

A steel tongue flickered out of the shaft of blue light and pulled Ez and the three men from Qitiqliq down, out of the flowing fire, out of the bubbling lake of lava and into hell. It felt, Ez thought, like what sperm must feel, washed in warm salty brine, propelled by the force of life into life yet to be. Infinite goodness consumed him, swaddled him, embraced him. He heard the dim whisper of that woman's voice again, and felt the piercing cold that sought out little cul de sacs of his nervous system. He felt both immensely *loved*, he thought, and yet at the same time repelled.

The steel tongue pulled them through the shaft of blue light and onto a long barge-like thing, four triangles of silver cables rising on either side of them, two towers at each end of the barge. The shaft of light closed behind them, and the barge carried them down into hell.

Innumerable tunnels branched off from the passage the barge took them down. As they rushed down their own way, Ez saw other tunnels — like lava tubes he had seen once near Ercolano — intersecting and leading off from their path. Occasionally a flash of something human whisked by; occasionally a flash of something inhuman followed it. Once they passed through and above a great, glassed plain, two armies on either side hurling stones at each other, the troops of each army covered with a glowing gray dust. Another time they passed by a walled city on an endless sea, two armies clashing, clashing, outside the gates, soldiers in brass chest armor with swords fighting against soldiers in camouflage with automatic rifles.

The barge pulled the four men through hell, through the spongy fabric of the underworld, beyond circles and pits, through vast bubbles of space, over oceans and seas, above cities and towns and nations. Fast comets we must appear to them, Ez thought: shooting stars in the night. Once, he thought he saw Venice, but the vision pained him and he had to look away.

Soon their progress slowed, and Ez saw that they rose through thick, blue-green lava. A red light beckoned at the end of the tunnel, a light that pulled them *down*. Ez tried to pull his feet around, tried to brace for the fall, but his head — and the heads of the others — remained down. He closed his eyes, ready for the impact that would crack his skull and send him back once again to Reassignments.

His ears popped, the way they do when coming down a mountain road, and for a brief moment Ez felt a searing blast of heat and then the cooling wash of water. He opened his eyes, found Barker and Queequeg and Rabbit floating next to him off the shore of an erupting volcano. Rafts of pumice floated past them, ash and smoke swirled around them, re-pelled by a glowing sphere that whipped the debris into eddies in the direction they faced. The sphere turned the water into froth beneath their feet, and they stood on the bubbling sea, like Venus on the half shell. Another sphere glowed on the shore, twenty yards to their left; two figures embraced each other inside the sphere.

"You okay?" Barker asked.

"Yeah," Ez said. Barker had moved to the edge of the sphere, almost through its boundary.

"What is this?" Queequeg asked. He pressed his hand against the bubble.

"Some remnant of the Gap?" Ez said, but wondered to himself: is it really almighty god's Grace, and have we been pulled from hell? Ez moved away from the three men. The sphere followed him, the edge of it moving toward the men. "I, uh, think it follows me." He looked out at the raging fire-storm. "You had better stick with me, all of you."

"But where are we?" Rabbit asked.

"Damned if I know," he said. Ez shrugged, not daring to say it aloud: *Paradise.*

A dark shape moved below them — the barge. Floating above the barge — submarine? he thought — Ez saw that the triangular shaped sails looked more like cables. The silver tongue of the thing rose out of the water and pushed their sphere up onto the shore.

Ez turned, walked away from the thing in the water and toward the other sphere, the other men following him. One of the figures in the other sphere — fuzzy, indistinct — waved to him. Ez moved his sphere to their sphere. As the edges touched, the spheres merged, poured into each other, and enveloped the six souls.

A man in black turned, pushed the blonde women he had been hugging behind him. He raised a blue steeled gun at Ez, shook his head, and lowered it.

"Son of a bitch," the man in black said, "Ezra fucking Pound."

Ez stared at the man, squinting, wondering where he'd seen his face before, then nodded. "Harold," he said. "Excuse me, 'Hart'. Hart Crane."

"Crane, all right," Hart said. "I'm not surprised to see *you* here, you bloody fascist."

"Well, *your* destination was a foregone conclusion — sodomy *and* suicide — not to mention what you did to poetry." Ez spat. "Merde, anyone can use a dictionary."

Barker pushed between the two poets, nervous in the confined space. "Yeah, yeah, it's old home week for all of us, isn't it?" He glanced at Hart's rifle. "You with Satan's great Plasma Pop Gun militia, too?" Barker tapped his M-666. "Big deal. You mind fighting your little battles later? I hate to break up this idle chatter, fellas, but where the fuck are we, and what's going on?"

Hart grinned, nodded. "A blue-hair, huh? And *you*" — he pointed at Queequeg — "you could play Melville's..."

"Enough with this Melville," Queequeg said. "I do not know this Melville, understand?" He pointed the bomb gun at Hart's belly. "I am Queequeg, if that's what you were going to say, yes, but do not say this Melville's name."

"Right." Hart gulped, gently pushed the fat barrel of the bomb gun away. "My good sirs," he smiled, "you are in Pompeii, or what remains of it, in the middle of the latest of Vesuvius's periodic eruptions." Ez felt a chill pass through him: not Paradise? he thought. Not at all. Hart waved a hand at the glowing avalanche coursing around them. "We, fortunately, seem to be safe."

"Her?" Barker pointed at the blonde.

"Em." She shook her head, pushed her still static hair down. "I'm... I'm a little confused."

"Em," Hart said. "She came out of the rocks" — he pointed at the pile by the road — "just in time. This field... I think my plasma rifle generates it."

Ez cocked an ear, listened. "She's gone... the voice. I heard a voice earlier. Harold — Hart, I think this field is part of Paradise, part of... well, god's grace. The rifle? I don't know."

Barker raised his M-666, waved it at Ez. "This ain't Paradise, Pound. You said the Grace would pull us into Paradise. That sure didn't look like Paradise we passed through. Looked like hell."

"Hell, yes," Hart said. "We're still in hell."

"What's going on," Barker turned, followed Ez's gaze, "Pound? *Ah* —"

The rectangular thing with the sails — the barge — rose from the water on three legs, each leg armored with red scales, the legs joining a horizontal structure at the top from the sides of which long arms like cables snaked out. A long tongue waved from the middle leg, two more arms holding the end of the tongue up. Mud and scum and eviscerated bodies fell off of the thing as it moved toward the shore. Lights lit the edges of arms, and swirling lights of red and white rose up and down the tongue. The arms and the tongue writhed toward them, the tongue shooting out, seeking.

"*Shit*," Barker said. He squeezed the trigger of his M-666, pouring round after round at the thing. Queequeg braced the stock of the Pierce & Anger bomb gun against his hip, fired the bomb. Rabbit shot: cool, even shots; click-clack, click-clack; pulling the bolt up, back, forward, and down in quick, firm strokes; shells flying out.

"No..." said Hart, "it's —"

Ez slung the Teller out, snapped the charging button on, waiting the short second for it to power up, then fired five quick bursts through the haze of the plasma sphere. Em raised her Swedish Mouser, lined up the sites and methodically blasted away the lights along the tongue of the thing, ping-*crack*, ping-*crack*, one after another. She slid the bolt faster than Rabbit, the four steps one smooth motion, the jerk of the muzzle controlled and steady — easy to do with the 6.5 mm rifle.

Barker's shots pushed through the sphere, followed by Rabbit's precise rounds and Queequeg's bomb. The bullets pinged off the cables of the thing, a few striking the brick armor of its legs. The bomb burst dead center in the middle leg and made a small crater in the surface, but the thing kept coming.

Ez's plasma rounds hit the arms, and its blue light crackled up the twisting metal. As the rounds tore through their shield, the shield separated, peeling back and behind them, and forming a high wall against the continuing blast of the glowing avalanche.

The towering legs of the thing clomped forward, one step, two, stopping a hundred yards out from shore, and settling into the water. Rising up like an elephant's trunk, the tongue slithered above them, fell down, and rested horizontal at their feet, its supporting arms rising in a gentle incline up to the flat head of the thing. The other arms settled parallel to the tongue, and the lights along the edge of the arms flickered on and off in a running succession up and down its length. Blue light from the dying rounds crackled once more, then coalesced into two shapes walking down the thing's tongue.

"— Only the Bridge," Hart said.

"— ily," the woman said, letting the Mouser hang by its strap from her shoulder. She tugged at her short blonde locks. "I *am* Em-i-ly."

Chapter 14

Job walked with Roebling down the pedestrian span of the Brooklyn Bridge and into Pompeii. The five men and a woman stared up at them, the shield wall holding back the nu'ee ardente of the volcano. The planks beneath his feet rattled slightly, and he felt the Bridge sigh, sending pleasing thoughts up at him. *It is so nice to be wanted*, the Bridge said. *Let my strong cables support you.* Job rubbed his hand down the top of the rail along the walkway, stroked it.

"Is that her?" Roebling asked, pointing at the blonde woman waiting for them. "Is that my Emily?"

Job shook his head, smiled at Roebling. "Not yet," he said. "I'm not sure. I think it is that poetess — *an* Emily, yes — but another Emily, not your first wife. Perhaps she could become your Emily... Anything is possible in hell."

"True," said Roebling.

The Ombudsman touched Roebling's shoulder, patted his back briefly. He's tired, Job thought. It is difficult to be good, completely good, in hell.

Roebling stopped and leaned forward on his cane. He sucked air in through his teeth, stepped back. *"He's* here."

"Who?" asked Job.

"Him - my... W.A.R., the shadow. Him." Roebling pointed at the six people.

"There? Which one?"

He shook his head. "I don't know. He's in one of them, hidden deep inside, but there."

Lady MacBeth, Job thought. Yes, her maneuvers. W.A.R. works for her. He put his hand back on Roebling's shoulder. "Of course he is here, Washington. He will always be here, always with you, as long as you are in hell." Job turned Roebling to face him. "But he is not part of you now. Remember that. He acts on his own. He does not rule you, understand. You are pure and good, and he is pure and evil; but your goodness is greater than his evil, and you will rise above him. You have nothing to fear from him. Is that clear?"

Roebling turned to Job, smiled. "Yes. I will not fear him."

"Good. Let us then face these souls - and him, whomever he resides in."

They walked the remaining span of the Bridge, and stopped ten feet from the five men and the woman. All six pointed weapons at them; two held plasma guns, Job noted. He reached in front of him, undid the sling of his own Samopal submachine gun, held the gun out in front of him by one end of its leather strap. "I do not need this," Job said. He let go of the sling, and the gun floated to the Bridge. The Bridge shimmered over the gun, and the Samopal glowed a bright blue before it flickered away into dust motes. Job nodded, reached under his robe, and pulled out the remaining magazines, which he also let fall to the Bridge. They flared briefly and popped away like little pockets of exploding hydrogen. *Tasty*, the Bridge said to Job. *Tasty bits.*

"I am the Ombudsman Job, come to deliver you from this hell," he said. Or, he thought, at least try to do it.

"What *is* this thing?" the blue haired man said, gesturing at the Bridge with his rifle.

"The Bridge," one of the men with a plasma gun said.

Job reached into a pocket of his robe and pulled out the three leather bound books. He opened one up, glanced at the picture on the frontispiece, then nodded. "You must be Hart Crane. You know this Bridge?" He turned to a page in Crane's book, read, "'O harp and altar...'"

Bless him, the Bridge said to Job.

"'...of thy fury fused,'" Hart finished. "Yes, *The* Bridge. I know it well." He smiled. "I only just destroyed it."

"Not *this* Bridge, Hart," Job said. "This Bridge is a... is a damned being like you. It delivered you to me, as I asked it to."

The tall man with the strange markings on his face smiled. "It is like a ship?"

"You?" Job squinted. "Only three souls were given to me to deliver. But you look familiar."

"Do not speak of Melville!" he warned.

"I do not know of Melville," Job said. "Who is he?"

"Good," said the tall man. "I am Queequeg. We came with *him.*" He pointed at the other man with the plasma gun.

"Ah," Job said, nodding. He thumbed through another of the leather books. "Mister Pound?"

"*Ezra* Pound. I'm sure you have heard of me."

"Of course. Um..." He leafed through Pound's book and read, "'The apparitions of these faces...?'"

"Right, right," said Ezra Pound. He glanced at his companions. "An appropriate passage, though. This place *does* seem to be another station at the metro."

Job chose the third book. Opening it up, he studied the sepia-tinted photo of the brown haired woman on an inside leaf, then looked at the blonde woman. "Miss Dickinson?" he asked. "Surely you cannot be *Emily* Dickinson?"

"I... Em!" she said. "I - am - Em!" Her body jerked, her mouth moved in a rictus of gasped syllables. She clutched her Mouser rifle, lowered it, raised it over her head, then threw it at the Bridge. The Bridge absorbed her rifle. She ran her hands through her chin-length hair, yanked at it, a puzzled look on her face, then shook her head. "I... am Emily Dickinson, yes."

"He is in *her*," Roebling whispered to Job. "*W.A.R. — in her.*"

"*The Belle of Amherst*?" Hart asked.

Emily relaxed, smiling. "Quite the belle, Mister Crane. What did you expect?" She palmed her coiffure, still looking confused, then tapped the upswept ends of her hair as it smoothed itself into shape.

"I... *shit*," Hart said, blushing.

"Forgetting your sexual orientation, Harold?" Ez asked. He turned to Job. "You seem to be expecting us, Mister Ombudsman."

"You, yes — three poets. But Mister Queequeg and these other gentlemen...?"

"Barker," said the blue haired man with the orange skin and violet eyes. "We came along for the ride. Ez, here, brought us on this chase for something he called 'God's Gaps' — some kind of manifestation of *His* Grace here in good ol' hell - or so Ez said. I'd as soon go back to Qitiqliq and slaughter seals, if you want to know the truth." He glared at Ez. "This mission looks like it's heading into major screwup time." Barker jerked his head at his companion. "He's 'Rabbit,' Mister Ombudsman. Rabbit, Queeq, and I kind of come together. Ol' Ez there enlisted our services, per Satan's request." Barker pointed his M-666 assault rifle at Job. "You working for Satan? In case I have to kill you, it's kind of nice to know in advance which faction I'll have pissed off."

Job spread his hands, chuckling. "No need for that, Mister Barker. I am an employee of the Department of In-justice, appointed by His Infernal Majesty himself."

Barker grunted. "Cool. Cool. As long as we know who's who and what's what. So lay it out: I'm getting real itchy for some straight talk here. Been enough bullshit and enough mystery for my liking." He waved his rifle at Pound, then trained it again on Job's stomach.

The wall of glowing ash bulged against the plasma shield behind the six souls. Job watched it nervously, mindful of the volcano still spitting in the distance. "Perhaps you all should step onto the Bridge. Vesuvius grows angrier."

The poets looked behind them, moved forward. Barker held back. "Wait," he said. Rabbit and Queequeg stayed with him. "Where's this Bridge go?"

"Paradise," Job said. "Perhaps — if you can walk across it." He waved toward the span stretching out beyond the first tower.

"I — fuck." Barker stared back at the glowing ashes tum-bling over the top of the shield wall, building up on the sides. "Okay — out of the fire and into the frying pan. Don't matter to me; either way you get burned."

Barker, Queequeg and Rabbit followed the poets onto the Bridge.

The Bridge pulled back from Pompeii, back from the wall of glowing embers, pulling the shimmering plasma shield with it. Like a ferry across rough seas, the Bridge shot across the boiling waters, away from Vesuvius, until it sat safely off the volcanic island. Glowing clouds rolled down the flanks of the volcano, dark ash obscuring the location of Pompeii and its sister city, Herculaneum. The water around the Bridge shim-mered crystal blue, and from its depths mermaids sang softly.

At the other end of the span, where Brooklyn should have been, Paradise beckoned, a great orange ball that the Bridge seemed to reach toward.

"Shit," Barker said again as his M-666 rifle was yanked from his hands. Queequeg and Rabbit whipped around as their weapons, too, flew from their grasps. The guns fell to the deck of the Bridge, flickered briefly as they were absorbed, and vanished. Ammunition popped from their clothes and belts, exploding in small bursts when the Bridge ate the gunpowder. Even the plasma guns of Hart and Ez were gobbled up, their energy feeding the Bridge.

"No weapons on this journey," Job said needlessly. "What obstacles you encounter you must face with only your wits. Come." The Ombudsman took Roebling's arm, then led the souls along the approach to the first tower.

This walkway wound around the center column of the first tower. Two arches like empty cathedral windows opened between the three columns of the tower. Job and his entourage stopped before a brass tablet set into the Pompeii side of the central column. At the top of the table a bronze relief of the Brooklyn Bridge had been sculpted. Job read aloud the words underneath: *"Dedicated To The Memory Of Emily Warren Roebling, 1843-1903, Whose Faith and Courage Helped Her Stricken Husband, Col. Washington A. Roebling, C.E., Complete the Construction of this Bridge, from the Plans of his Father, John A. Roebling, C.E., 1806-1869, Who Gave his Life to the Bridge."*

"'Behind every great work we can find the self-sacrificing...'" Roebling paused as he read, wiping his eyes. "'...the self-sacrificing devotion of a woman.'" He closed his eyes, breathing out slowly. "Ah, Emily..." Roebling ran his fingers over the raised letters of her name. "She is here, Job. Here."

"If the Bridge stretches into Paradise," Job said, "perhaps she waits for you at the other end, and you feel her presence."

Roebling glared up at Job with his steel blue eyes. "She is *here*, in these words."

Job nodded. "Okay, if you wish. She is here." He waved to the left side of the column, at two oak benches resting against the railing. "Sit, all of you. I'll try to explain why the Bridge has brought you together."

*

"*Brought* us together?" Hart asked. "I went to Brooklyn — a new Brooklyn — on Satan's orders, to kill Marilyn, Satan's secretary. Emily here" — he glared at Ez — "looks a lot like Marilyn, which is why I was taken aback at her appearance, *Pound*."

"*You* went to Brooklyn to kill Marilyn?" Emily asked. "I went to Brooklyn because..." She glanced at Hart and Job, mindful that they had declared themselves in Satan's employ. "Because Ché told me to. I was with a trading caravan running drugs to the coast. Yes!" She swung a loose hair back from her face. "I am with the Revolution! And when Satan's minions destroyed the caravan, only I survived, and Mister Cienfuegos told me with his dying breath to go to Brooklyn and follow Marilyn. And I did! *She* told me to cut my hair like this. See, Mister Crane, not the 'Belle of Amherst' you expected. I fooled you, didn't I? You never suspected that I was Emily Dickinson, did you? Marilyn's ruse almost worked." She glared at Hart. "Bastard! You killed her — killed them all, and would have killed me." She stood up, spat in his face.

Hart dabbed at his face with a handkerchief, folded the handkerchief neatly, and stuck it back in his pocket. "I had no real trouble picking Marilyn out." He smiled. "True, seeing five blonde bombshells on the Bridge threw me for a moment. I didn't see six — I never saw you, Emily, *never*. Marilyn... she was easy. Her walk. Her presence. And that cameo ring. I knew she'd have a cameo ring."

"I... I gave her that ring," she whispered, looking down. "From Cienfuegos. He *told* me to."

"Ah: I'd wondered," Hart said. He turned to Job. "But I don't understand: I destroyed that Bridge. I saw it sink into the Sea of Sighs."

"And it rose up from the Sea of Sighs and deposited us in Pompeii," Ez said. "The same bridge?" He shook his head. "But it delivered us from Qitiqliq. *Why?*"

"I asked it to," Job said. He patted the railing. "As I said, it's a remarkable bridge."

"But why?" Emily asked. "Why has the Bridge brought us together?"

Job nodded, thinking of what they said. Marilyn — he hadn't known about that. And Cienfuegos, and the Revolution, and the cameo ring that had set Marilyn up? He didn't see how that fit in with his mission. Other forces were at work here. Lady MacBeth? Mithridates's faction? The shadow? So many players... so much time. He held up the three books, knocked on them with his knuckles. "You are souls," he said, "souls I had assigned to me to help get *him*" — he motioned at Roebling — "out of hell."

"Who?" Hart asked.

"Colonel Washington A. Roebling, Mister Crane," Roebling said. "I enjoyed your poem, by the way. Very stirring."

"*Roebling!*" Hart leaped up, squinted at him. "Of course, you've shaved... All your photographs show you with a beard." He shook his head. "But I killed you, too."

Roebling chuckled. "Not me, I suspect, Mister Crane. Perhaps my shadow."

"Your shadow?"

Job held up a hand. "His shadow." He explained about the evil aspect of Roebling, about Roy's assignment, about Lady MacBeth's machinations, and about the Bridge.

"So we're to help Roebling — this Roebling — get out?" Ez asked. Job nodded. "And we may get out in the process?"

Job nodded again. "Maybe. I can't promise anything. I can't even promise Colonel Roebling will get out. But I do know that you must help him."

"How?" Ez asked.

"Yeah, how?" Hart added.

The Ombudsman got up, waved at the two openings between the central column and the two outer columns, each opening arched at the top, each span of the bridge passing through the openings. The walkway went around both sides of the central column, and joined on the other side. "You poets will walk through on the left, and Roebling will walk through on the right. You will meet on the other side, not all of you together, and not necessarily with Roebling. Some who you will be with will only be projections, not real souls. The Bridge will take you places... I don't know exactly. I will come to you and guide you, give you your task; I don't know what, because Satan hasn't told me. But how you conduct yourselves will determine if you get out, and if Roebling gets out."

"What about us?" Barker asked. "I came to help Ez. These other guys — nothing personal — well, orders are orders."

"You will walk through with Roebling, and aid who you will aid."

"Right," Barker said. "We get our weapons back?"

Job shook his head. "You, maybe, but not the poets. Think with your head, not your piece." He smiled. "That *is* possible, isn't it?"

"Fuck off," Barker said. He slammed a fist into the palm of his hand. "Guns don't solve *everything*."

"What about you?" Emily asked. "Where will be *your* final destination?"

Job looked through the gates, off to where the central span met the other tower. "As I said, I will come to you in the Bridge's hell, and after that I will meet you just before the gate into Paradise," Job said. "Beyond? Those who may continue on I will say good-bye to. But I cannot follow. My place" — he looked down at the Bridge, down at the sea frothing below — "is here, far from my Maker." Job handed the leather bound books to the poets. "Go now. Go before... before the volcano erupts again."

The poets took the books, and walked one by one through the left gate. Roebling went through the right, followed shortly by Barker, Rabbit, and Queequeg. When Job saw their forms shimmer and disappear as they walked across the central span, he followed.

Chapter 15

As he walked through the archway of the first tower, the Bridge took Hart Crane deep under the surface of hell, and deposited him on the beach of a tropical land. Hart walked down the central walkway of the Bridge onto the sand; air rushed in behind him as he stepped off the oak decking. He turned, saw the Bridge recede away out to sea, and when he turned back toward the lush jungle growing on the beach's edge, found himself in the midst of a small cavalry. Men in pointed beards, gleaming helmets and breastplates, and striped shirts with puffy sleeves rode the horses, red banners flapping in the breeze. Ragged men in torn pants pulled longboats up on the sand, and in the milling confusion — horses neighing in their new freedom, soldiers shouting orders in Spanish, foot soldiers unloading cargo — Hart was overlooked.

The soldiers and sailors carried their loads to a clearing at the head of a bay, where a broad river flowed down from low hills. In the clearing the Spaniards had erected a small settlement, a rock fort surrounded by low huts and a small chapel. Trees and brush lay in piles at the edge of the clearing, checking the advance of the voracious vegetation. Hart thought he saw cabbage palms shudder as a brown figure darted back into the jungle.

"You!" yelled a soldier on a small white stallion. The horse stepped over to Hart, and the man in its saddle pointed a short sword down at him. "You, scribe!" the man shouted again, the words clearly Spanish, but Hart understanding them in English.

Hart looked up at him but said nothing.

The man glared down at him with deep brown eyes, grave eyes set under thin eyebrows arching at his brow. A long nose ran down to full, pouting lips and a narrow chin covered by a sparse, pointed beard. The beard barely concealed a thick scar marring the man's lower lip and chin. He waved at another soldier, leading a saddled gray stallion to Hart. "Well, scribe? Aren't you going to mount your horse? On with it!"

Hart took the reins from the foot soldier, tossed them over the horse's smooth neck, placed a foot in the stirrup, swung his leg over, and settled into the saddle. He patted the panniers slung over the horse's rump, smiled at the fine tooling of the leather, the gold initials *H.C.* etched into the hide, but he frowned at the empty rifle scabbard. The soldier stroked the horse's neck and Hart stared back down at him.

"Gracias," Hart said. The soldier nodded. Hart jerked his head at the handsome officer gathering up his troops. "Who is that?"

The soldier smirked and shook his head, humoring Hart. "You do not know, Senor?"

Hart squinted at the Spaniard, shrugged. "No."

"Cortés," said the soldier. "Hernando Cortés — the Conquistador."

Hart nodded. Of course, he thought. He looked down at the soldier, at the gleaming breastplate, the peaked helmet, the plumes, and the pike he held with its banner fluttering in the humid breeze. "Of course," he said as the foot soldier turned sharply and went to help unload a boat. Hart looked up, over the line of trees on the beach's edge, and off toward the plateau rising from the beach, the stepped pyramids hovering on the horizon. Of course, he thought.

Moctezuma. Tenochtitlan.

The last of the longboats unloaded its cargo on the beach. Cortés rode down among the sailors, shouted something in Spanish, and waved his sword at the sea. The sailors looked out to the green ocean, at the eleven Spanish galleons and one rusty steamship, then got in the boat and rowed out to the anchored ships. One by one the longboat went to each galleon — stopping long enough for a sailor to board, do something on deck, and then get back in the longboat — and then the sailors rowed back to shore. Smoke and flames soared up from the first galleon, then the second and third, until all eleven wooden ships blazed against the horizon. When they saw this, several sailors ran to a longboat, but Cortés urged his horse into the surf to cut them off.

"My orders!" he shouted. "We have come to conquer! There will be no hasty retreat. Those of you who triumph" — he waved his sword over the sailors, the marines, the cavalry — "will return to Spain in glory on the *Orizaba.* Those who don't..." He sliced his sword down at the beach.

Hart did a quick calculation, as he imagined all the men doing. No more than a fifth of them could fit on the remaining ship. Cortés either expected a lot of casualties, or he anticipated a lot of involuntary settlers. Hart smiled at the craftiness of the conquistador. Only a few would return on the *Orizaba.*

The *Orizaba...* The ship's name came back to him, a name not out of hell, but out of his life. Hart stared back at the rusty boat, squinted at its lines, its superstructure. The

Orizaba: the last ship he'd been on in the world, sailed on out of Havana in 1932 on his way home to New York from Mexico. The *Orizaba*: the steamship he had gone crazy on, mad with booze, the anguish of his life burning him up until that morning of April 27 when, two minutes before noon, he had thrown off his jacket and leapt over the rails into the sea. The *Orizaba*.

"Hart?" a woman asked.

He turned at the voice and saw that blonde woman, Emily, riding up on a gray mare, still dressed in her tight black jumpsuit, *her* Mouser rifle stuck in a case on the saddle. She pulled back on the reins, stopped her horse next to his. "Emily," he said.

"*Emily?*" she asked. She leaned forward, cocked an eyebrow at him. "Hart, have you been drinking?"

Hart stared at her, and for a brief moment her image shimmered, became that of a woman Emily's height, but thinner, with an angular jaw, a large nose, and straight brown hair pushed back from her face. He sucked in his breath at the sight of her, shook his head, then managed a grin. "Peggy!" His *fiancé* — Peggy — appeared as Emily. "I... no, I'm sorry. I was thinking of Emily Dickinson — that poem I wrote about her? — and for a moment, in the light, you looked like her."

"Hart, Hart..." She shook her head, and the image of Peggy settled back into Emily. "Silly man. It's the air, the tropical air. Exhilarating, isn't it?"

"Yes."

"Are we going to ride horses all day? Or will Senor Cortés provide us lodging at Vera Cruz?" She waved at the settlement at the river's mouth.

"I... " Hart fell silent as Cortés rode up to them. "Ask him." He jerked a thumb at the Conquistador.

"Senor Crane, Senorita." Cortés bowed at Emily. "A thousand pardons. My men" — he turned back at the men on foot — "will be a while unloading provisions. I regret that it may be some time before they will be able to build you a hut. In the meantime, if you follow me I will offer you the hospitality of my pavilion until your quarters are ready. Senorita?" He waved at a line of troops moving along the sand.

"Gracias," Emily said, kicking her horse into a gallop. Hart followed.

*

Cortés' hut had been built in the center of the fort, opposite a roaring bonfire. Logs had been set around the fire, over which a kettle of stew bubbled constantly. An awning stretched out from the commander's quarters, across which Cortés' officers came and went, conferring with him or one of his aides, stopping by the pot to grab a bowl of meat. Sitting around the bonfire, Hart watched the soldiers enter and leave. Not all were Spaniards; the ranks included a mix of Caribbean blacks, Dutch, English, and French as well, though they all wore the heavy cloth armor and swords of the Spaniards. Only the cavalry wore the gleaming steel armor, the breastplates and helmets. Sixteen Spanish horses were corralled at the far end of the fort, near the armory, where the arquebuses and powder kegs were stored under a tent.

Cortés came out of his hut and sat on a log opposite Hart. An Indian woman — who seemed to be Cortés' mistress but also acted as his adviser and interpreter — sat next to Cortés, combing her long brown hair with her fingers; Doña Marina, Hart had heard her called. She talked softly in an unknown tongue to a short Spaniard, Aquilar, sitting next to her. Aquilar mumbled something in Spanish to Cortés; Hart caught the words "gold" and "jade" and a few other words. Gold: Cortés raised an eyebrow at that word. *Gold.*

Cortés looked over at Hart, caught his eye, held up his hand as if he were holding a pen, and waved it at Hart. Hart nodded, looked down at his notebook laid flat on his knees, the miraculous little pen that flowed like water over the page and never seemed to clog. Write, Hart thought.

He stared down at the blank page, sipped from his pewter cup that held only weak tea. *Tea.* How he wished for something stronger in his drink — say, tequila. The humid air reminded him of the fondness he had once developed for tequila. He gripped the pen, and wished for something stronger in his hands, too, more powerful — even a .45 automatic would do, but especially that plasma rifle Satan had given him on the Marilyn project. But. But: tea and a pen. He'd have to settle for tea and a pen. Hart eyed the weapon that Emily — no, had to remember to call her Peggy — laid casually against her leg, eyed the glass of rum she barely tasted. His lips still stung, though, from when he'd tried to drink from her glass, and his hand still burned from just touching — *touching* — her rifle.

Write, Cortés said, and Hart knew what he meant. "Scribe," Cortés had called him. The empty scabbard on his saddle, the fact that no one offered him even a dagger or a pike: Hart could guess what that meant. In this campaign, he'd be a noncombatant. Write. That's what Cortés had commanded: write him a brief account, no more than a few stanzas, of their securing a beachhead. Hart sighed, began to scrawl on the page.

Golden sands on hell's new shore
In azure deep jungle, brown flashes shudder

Moctezuma —

No, he thought, cannot write that yet. Cortés doesn't know of Moctezuma.

In azure deep jungle, brown flashes shudder
Brown King waits to receive the god

Yes, thought Hart: better.

Brown King waits to receive the god
In Undine's flashing sands he is dressed.
Scythe of gleaming steel! Pikes of iron!
The white god bears sticks that thunder,
He waits to ride on the Brown King on
Hooves that thunder, Cortés come to
Civilize hell's new shores.

Yes, thought Hart, *yes*, that would do: not too thick in metaphor, it pays proper obeisance, and yet gives the lines an epic quality. He laid his pen down, let the strange ink dry, and fondled the ripcord at his neck, rubbing the smooth plastic between his fingers. A brief shock came through him as the twine of the ripcord yanked on his flesh. Job's image flickered in the smoke of the flames, but Hart saw by the nonplussed looks of the others that no one but he saw the vision.

"That is not a way out," Job said to Hart. "You keep pulling on that thing, and why is that?"

"The pain," Hart mumbled. "I cannot stand the pain."

"*Stand it,*" Job said. "Endure. If Roebling fails because of your cowardice, I will use whatever powers Satan leaves me with to make your continued existence here *more* miserable."

Hart nodded, let go of the ripcord. Job's image rose on the smoke and disappeared. Cortés looked his way, scowled at Hart.

"Surely you cannot be done already, Senor Crane?"

Hart held up the book, passed it around the circle to Cortés. "It comes in spurts," he said. "When I am so inspired."

Cortés took the book from a lieutenant next to him. "If that is what it takes, Crane, you should hope for much inspiration." He looked down at the page, read, smiled. "Gracias, Senor," Cortés said. "Gracias." He stood up, clapped his hand against the back of the notebook. "Listen: Senor Crane has written some stanzas about our arrival.

"'Golden sands on hell's new shore
In azure deep jungle, brown flashes shudder
A Brown King waits to receive the god who
In Undine's flashing sands is dressed —'

A nice image, Senor: 'In Undine's flashing sands.' Good, good. Um, let's see —

"'Scythe of gleaming steel! Pikes of iron!
A white god bears sticks that thunder,
He waits to ride on the Brown King on
Hooves that thunder, Cortés come to
Civilize hell's new shores.'

Yes, quite good." Cortés smiled at Hart. "You see the slight changes I made? I'm not sure I would keep that 'thunder/thunder'; it seems a little contrived, actually. But not bad, not bad, Senor Crane. We shall yank that epic out of you yet."

'That epic,' Hart thought. He knew which one Cortés meant: the great poem — his second *Bridge* — he had intended to write about the conquistadors, the one he had gotten the Guggenheim grant for back in the world and then squandered in Mexico drinking tequila and screwing Indian boys. Oh yes: *that* poem. He didn't have to guess what thing he would have to do to help Roebling. He'd have to write that poem he owed the world. He'd have to do what suicide had saved him from doing: wrestle with his muse and pin her screaming to the canvas.

Damn it, Hart thought, he'd have to *write*.

Cortés snapped his fingers, and the lieutenant on his right stood up. "Tequila for Senor Crane," he said. "A little glass." The Conquistador held forefinger to thumb in a pinch.

The lieutenant nodded, went into a tent, and came out with a black clay bottle. As he stepped up to Hart, closer by the fire, he saw that the man had blue hair and violet eyes. Barker — that man who had come with Ezra. Barker. Hart almost said his name, but stopped. He was no more Barker than Peggy was Emily. Barker took Hart's glass, turned it upside down, then poured one finger's worth of tequila for him. Hart smiled, took the glass, and downed it in a quick gulp. The liquor barely stung his throat as it went down, and he felt a cool shudder as the tequila scattered into his body.

"Gracias, Lieutenant...?" Hart asked.

"Puertocarrero," he said.

"Puertocarrero." He grinned, held up the glass again. "More, *por favor?*" Barker — *Puertocarrero* — glanced at Cortés, who shook his head. He shrugged, corked the bottle, and put it back in the tent.

"You see how it is, Senor Crane?" Cortés asked. "A little poetry, a little tequila. When you finish your epic, perhaps you may have the entire bottle and get *steenking* drunk, eh?" He passed the notebook back to Hart.

Steenking drunk, Hart thought. He tore the poem out of the notebook, wadded it up, and tossed it in the fire.

*

In the morning, Cortés sat around the embers of the fire, interviewing a Totonec Indian boy from a village just west of Vera Cruz who had been captured in a battle and taken inland to be sacrificed, but who had escaped. The process proved cumbersome: Cortés asked a question, which Aquilar translated into the Tabasco language; Doña Marina, who spoke Tabasco but little Spanish, then asked the question in Nahuatl to the Totonec. Back and forth, a ripple of three languages: Cortés' lilting Spanish, Aquilar's harsh Tabasco, and Doña Marina's melodic Nahuatl.

The Totonec told wild stories of a kingdom to the west containing great riches, of a fierce ruler who demanded tribute from even the tiniest village. He spoke of horrid sacrifices, of victims whose hearts were ripped still beating from their chests, of savage warriors who wore the flayed skins of their captives.

Barker — Puertocarrero, Hart had to keep reminding himself — sat by Cortés' side, Hart and Emily on the edges. Emily cleaned her Mouser rifle, oiling the barrel with gentle caresses. Hart sat with his notebook open in his lap, pen hovering over the pages. He'd found that if he had the notebook open Cortés didn't bother him, even though Hart had scrawled only one word:

Moctezuma.

"At the center of this kingdom is a great city a fair distance from here," the Totonec told Cortés. Aquilar listened to Doña Marina, then translated the distance. "Fifty leagues, perhaps seven days ride."

The scout looked like an Indian boy Hart had once sodomized in Taxco, just as one of the marines looked like a sailor he'd known in Brooklyn. Everyone he saw seemed to look like someone Hart had known in the world. He would stare at the soldiers, the marines, the sailors, watch their images shift back and forth, from who they were to who Hart saw them as, with only Cortés staying Cortés, his image strong and pure and distinct. Barker mostly stayed Barker, slipping into Puertocarrero in strange light, and Emily always stayed Emily, though Hart knew she was Peggy. He rubbed his eyes, looked back at the scout.

"The people there call the city Tenochtitlan," the Totonec boy said, the name flowing from his tongue with ease. "It floats on a great lake, the swamp pushed back by dikes, and in the center of the city rises a wondrous pyramid." The boy waved his hands, his words coming quicker, so that Doña Marina and Aquilar had to speak fast to keep translating. His eyes darted back and forth as he described the city. "The people there have darker skin, bronze almost, not like the black men" — he nodded at one of the Caribbean blacks sitting in the circle — "but with more red. A handsome people. They seem to be getting ready for some kind of festival. Everywhere are flowers, decorations. The streets and buildings are painted incredible colors, as if they grew flowers themselves. The people dress in bird feathers, and some wear golden jewelry that bends their backs with the weight."

Cortés smiled. "Perhaps someone should relieve them of their burden?"

"Oh, yes," the boy said. "That is what they do. They tear off the gold and deposit it at the pyramid in the center of the city, before the people's king."

"Moctezuma," Hart said.

The boy looked up at the name, said something to Doña Marina. "Yes, that is the king's name, the boy says," said Aquilar. "He wants to know where you heard it."

Hart wanted to say, *I read it in a history book. Cortés marched on the city and took Moctezuma hostage and butchered the Aztecs*, but of course he could not. He was catching on to the rules of this little hell. Instead, he shrugged, and mumbled, "I heard the boy speak the name earlier."

The boy, went on: "Anyway, it is a great feast for one of their gods, I think." He frowned, stared out over the river and into the jungle on the other side of the clearing as he waited for the translation. He shook his head. "I get the feeling... I get the feeling that they are expecting this god, that they think he will arrive after many years of waiting."

"What does their god look like?" Cortés asked. Aquilar and Doña Marina translated.

"They had no figures of this god, not in his human incarnation, but they say he will wear a suit of stone, that he will be bearded, and that his skin will be paler." The boy pointed at Cortés, and Aquilar translated. "Like you."

Cortés smiled. "Ah." He looked away, his eyes flashing, then nodded at the boy. "What of their defenses? How many soldiers? What kind of arms?" Aquilar and Doña Marina continued the translation.

"Swamps surround the city, and there are only a few causeways in to the island city, each causeway well defended," the Totonec said. "I could not count their soldiers, but there seemed to be thousands, perhaps tens of thousands, most of them armed with short swords and spears, some with throwing sticks and darts." The boy rolled his sleeve up, showing them a thick scar still not completely healed. "The swords cut deep and clean — they are like clubs, with three pairs of black, sharp stones set on either side. I saw one warrior cut in two with but one stroke of that sword."

"What of guns?" Cortés asked. "Do they have guns?"

The boy smiled as Doña Marina translated. "They did not have the *tepuztli*, the screaming sticks, like you. Just swords, spears, and darts."

Cortés nodded his head. "How much gold did you see?"

"On the people? I counted at least a hundred men and women with much jewelry. And the tribute?" He raised his arm over his head. "This high a pile, and it spread over this large an area." He held his arms out. "Most of the people wore some gold — a medallion, a bracelet, rings."

"How many people?"

"Thousands," the boy said. "Tens of thousands?" He held out his hands, palms up. "The market place teemed with people, the streets were clogged with crowds. Many, many, people, and gold glinting in the sun everywhere I looked."

Cortés rose, turned, gazed off at the mountains rising above the jungle. "Senors, comrades... this city — Tenochtitlan — waits for us. If we can, we will march into the city of this Moctezuma and conquer it."

Cortés' soldiers murmured their assent, looked at each other, a gleam Hart had seen often in their eyes. March into the city, he thought. Seize their king. Hold him hostage. Demand a ransom, and when the ransom had been paid, murder Moctezuma, butcher the Aztecs. Murder and conquest, conquest and murder. Yes, he knew that gleam.

"Commander," Barker said. "Your plan, of course, is brilliant, but there are thousands of these savages. Even with our superior arms, in sheer numbers they could easily overwhelm us. How... why won't they just cut us down as we march in?" He bit his lip, glared at Cortés.

Cortés turned, frowned, and nodded slightly at Barker. "A good point, Lieutenant Puertocarrero. A good point." He glanced at the other men, as if to say: Why didn't you think of that? "True. They *could* massacre us, even with our guns and cannons." Doña Marina whispered something to Cortés, and Aquilar looked surprised to see that she spoke more Spanish than she had let on. Cortés nodded his head, smiled. "But I do not think they will," he continued. "When our Savior rode into Jerusalem, did the Jews throw stones at him? No, they laid palms at His feet. When we ride into Tenochtitlan, they will not harm us." Cortés turned again, into the wind, and took off his helmet. The breeze fluttered in his hair. "No, they will not harm us — they will not harm their savior, and I will be that to them."

Chapter 16

"What do you think?" Cortés asked Hart, handing him the Zeiss binoculars. Cortés wore black, all black, velvet tights and tunic and shirt under gleaming silver breastplate. "A brief stanza would be appropriate."

Cortés handed the binoculars to Emily - "Peggy" - who passed them on to Hart. He took the binoculars, smiling at the seeming anachronism of them, and focused the lenses on the city hanging in a cirque amphitheater from the opposite valley wall. Along the lower slope of the city, a wall completed the enclosure formed by the mountains behind it. Against the mountains, along the edge of the cirque, a great stepped pyramid towered over the city. A pipeline came out of the mountain and down into the pyramid.. At the base of the pyramid, a central boulevard ended in a circular drive lined with a series of monoliths from which dangled long hoses. Gleaming huts lined smaller streets radiating out in neat arcs from the pyramid.

Focusing on a nearer hut, Hart saw it was a long, rectangular shaped box, squares of glass - glass! - along the front and sides, four sets of rubber wheels - wheels! - under the box. Smoke puffed up from the far end of the box as it backed up, its front end turning out, and then moved from a side street and onto the main boulevard. The moving house stopped at one of the monoliths in front of the pyramid. A fat man got out of the house, took the hose, and inserted it into an opening on the house's side.

Hart handed the binoculars back to Cortés, rubbed his eyes. "You want a stanza?" he asked. "How about... ahem:

"Brief wealth tempted the conqueror
Yet the first city hung from mountains,
Not an island floating in azure, but
A city of boxes, wheeled on their bellies."

He shrugged. "I can't explain what they're doing - ask the boy."

Cortés shouted an order and Barker rode back to the column, coming back shortly with the Totonec boy in front of his saddle, Doña Marina behind him. They dismounted. Cortés showed the boy how to use the binoculars. His face lit up, he murmured something to himself, then he handed back the binoculars and spoke to Doña Marina.

"It's Tlaxcala," she said directly to Cortés. Hart chuckled at her rapid learning of Spanish. Aguilar had been relegated to the back of the column, he noticed.

"Tlaxcala?" Cortés asked.

Doña Marina nodded, spoke to the boy again. "'The city of Winnebagos,' he calls them. These people worship Moctezuma's god, but not willingly. They live their entire lives in boxes on wheels, and when they wish to attend to some matter, move the box rather than walk. Moctezuma has subjugated them. The boxes run on something call 'gasoline,' and he controls the supply." The boy said something else to Doña Marina. "He says that they worship an evil god who appears to men in the form of the sloth. The sloth god's piss comes out of the mountain, and they catch it in their temple."

Cortés studied Tlaxcala again with the binoculars. "I see no weapons."

Doña talked to the boy replied for him. "He says the boxes are the weapons. They move around on those black wheels as agile as horses. The boxes protect them like turtles, and should anyone attack the city, the men inside the boxes would drive into the armies."

"Drive into them?" Cortés asked.

Doña Marina nodded. "That is what the boy says."

"Conquistador, may I?" Emily asked, motioning at the binoculars. He gave them to her, and she looked through them at the pyramid. "Hart," she said. "Look at the pyramid, where the pipe flows down. Do you think...?"

Hart took the binocs, focused on the pipe flowing down into the pyramid. The pipe narrowed at a funnel-like opening at the pyramid's apex. Vapor rose up from the funnel. Hart grinned, understand what Emily hinted at.

"This gasoline the boy speaks of," he said. "It is an interesting substance, like... like liquid gunpowder, you see. I understand what the boy means about sloth piss. The temple, I think, contains their supply. Those black wheels - they are like botas empty of wine, all air."

Okay, he thought. Emily wants to make me look good, so I'll have to feed Cortés the facts, the knowledge, and let him come up with the idea. Hart had a feeling Cortés liked to come up with his own ideas, did not like subordinates to think for him.

Hart gave the binocs back to Cortés, and he looked through them again. He nodded, stroked his chin, looked once more at the temple, the pipe coming down from just below a mountain ridge. "This gas is like gunpowder?" Cortés asked. He snapped his fingers. "It explodes like gunpowder?"

"Better. One match, Conquistador, one burning ember touched to it and... fwoof."

"And the wheels? They contain only air?"

"Sí."

Cortés grinned, motioned to Barker. "Puertocarrero, I have an idea ..."

*

The conquistadors crept back into the mountains above Tlaxcala after Paradise - or whatever sun shined at this little hell, Hart thought - had slipped behind the next valley. Cortés, of course, had insisted Hart come along, "for inspiration, no?" When Hart asked if he could have a weapon - "for protection, sí?" - Cortés stared through him as if he were a talking plate of glass. No weapon: all eyes and ears was he to be, and only eyes and ears.

A rock skittered out from under Hart's foot, and he felt the butt of Barker's rifle slam against his hip.

"Idiot," Barker whispered. "Watch your footing or I will kick your cajones up your throat."

Hart grimaced and tried to find a better path.

The raiding party - Cortés, Barker, the Indian boy, Emily with her Mouser rifle, a few others - worked their way up the ridge wall at the top of the cirque. Two men grunted and groaned under the weight of a large cask each carried. Barker had taken out two Tlaxacalan sentries at the ridge flank, and Hart had expected more sentries behind the city. But when they got to the top of the ridge he saw why none were needed. The ridge ended in a thousand-foot high cliff dropping to the next valley below. Cortés hadn't bothered roping the team together. If anyone fell, they fell, and *he* wasn't going to fall, so what did it matter?

The tin boxes of Tlaxcala had shut down for the night. White drapes had been drawn across the windows, and all but a dozen of the Winnebagos had parked on their spots, the occupants asleep inside. Tall poles cast a green light down the main avenue of the city, along the front walls, and over the temple. One lone guard house idled in front of the temple, its headlights dimmed, amber parking lights glowing. A cylinder on wheels pulled in next to the guard house. A fat man got out of the cylinder, pulled a hose from one of the monoliths, and snaked it into an opening on top of the cylinder. The faint smell of gasoline wafted up to them on the ridge.

Cortés stopped, motioned Hart forward. "That round box," he said, pointing at the cylinder, "it is not like the other boxes."

"A tanker," Hart said. "It probably carries the sloth piss to the other houses."

"I see." Cortés turned to Barker, who had joined them. "Puertocarrero, get your grenadiers in position, but wait for my signal." He jerked his head at the refueling truck, the fat man standing to the side as the gas filled. "Wait until that tanker pulls away."

Barker nodded, moved off into the shadows.

The men with the casks scuttled below, to where the cirque wall sloped gently down to the temple and the main boulevard. Unstrapping the casks, the grenadiers set them down, ends out. The fat man fueling the truck stepped up to the hose, pulled it loose from his truck, a little gasoline spilling onto the ground, replaced the hose on the pump, and drove off. The guard Winnebago blinked its lights at the departing tanker.

When the tanker had stopped at the far end of the city, away from the temple, Cortés turned to Emily. She loaded the

Mouser rifle with incendiary rounds, bullets that would blaze light and heat. Emily calmly settled into a prone shooting position, the sling of her weapon wrapped around her forearm.

"Senorita?" Cortés asked. "On my signal you will shoot the casks with your wondrous weapon. Ready?"

"Ready," Emily said.

"Good. Lieutenant Puertocarrero, your grenadiers may release their bombs."

Barker motioned to the two men with the casks, and the grenadiers kicked them down the slope. One cask rolled out onto the main boulevard and the other fell down into the large funnel that received the pipe."

"Now, senorita," Cortés said.

Emily aimed, squeezed the trigger, moved the barrel slightly with the Mouserkick, chambered another round, and fired again. The first bullet hit the cask in the boulevard, igniting the powder and sending forth a shower of shrapnel. The staves shattered into splinters and the shrapnel littered the length of the street. Barker had shown Hart the shrapnel Cortés' blacksmiths had made the day before: caltrops, two nails bent around each other, the tips sharpened further - an old Roman trick to maim cavalry.

The second bullet hit the other cask a few seconds later. When the cask exploded, it blew the end of the pipe off, rupturing the roof of the temple. A glowing cloud of gasoline rose up toward the conquistadors on the ridge. They ducked down, and Hart smelled his hair scorching. The puddle of fuel that the tanker had spilled burst into yellow flames, the flames licking along the asphalt roadway and up the tires of the guard Winnebago. Where the end of the broken pipe had ruptured flames shot out from the mountainside.

"Hoo-hah!" yelled Cortés. "Look! The sloth's prick burns in agony!"

Emily sat up, smiled over at Cortés, and ejected the second shell.

"Good enough, Conquistador?"

"Fine shooting, senorita."

As the casks exploded, the sleeping Winnebagos woke up, a thousand engines kicking to life, drapes flicking back and the soldiers inside springing to action. The Winnebagos nearest the main avenue swung out first into defensive position, rushing toward what they were sure was an assault on the front wall. Their tires shredding on the caltrops, the first Winnebagos made it as far as the front gate, while the following mobile houses stalled in the middle of the avenue.

Winnebagos behind them either suffered the same fate, or rammed into the backs of the other stalled mobile houses. Those that went around got jammed between the dead Winnebagos and the road edge. Some tipped over on the soft shoulders of the boulevard. A tongue of flame licked down the boulevard from the blazing temple, catching some of the Winnebagos on fire. Within minutes the orderly city of Tlaxcala had been reduced to a jumbled mass of stalled, crunched, burning metal boxes.

Cortés smiled and pointed at the city. "Have you ever cooked a turtle, Senor Crane? It is simple. You roll it on its back and toss it on the fire."

Cortés glared at Hart, and Hart knew what he meant. He got out his notebook and wrote:

The prick of the sloth god roared flames,
Scorching his subjects with his scorned blessing.
Like turtles the wheeled houses
roasted in the flames of Cortés' ingenuity.

*

In the morning, the conquistadors rode into the city through the shattered gates. A jumbled mass of scorched metal hulks blocked the way down the boulevard. Cortés led his army around them, between overturned and stalled Winnebagos, down a side street. Hart wrapped a scarf around his mouth and nose, trying not to choke on the stench of burned rubber, burned flesh. Emily rode beside him, the image of her blonde hair rippling in the breeze flickering with the vision of Peggy, her brown hair hanging lank on her shoulders.

Cortés led the army by some Tlaxacalans wandering dazed through the streets, small clusters of them converging on the ruined temple. The Tlaxacalan men waddled with their immense weight, the fat rippling on them, heaving for breath. Supporting them were the Tlaxacalan women, lean and strong, their firm muscles obvious even under their tunics. As the horses clopped by, the men looked down, avoiding the gaze of the conquistadors, but the women glared up, defiant.

At the foot of the temple the fat men milled around, yelling at priests in black robes huddled at the top of the ruined pyramid. The priests were a horrid sight, their hair in long matted locks, their garments stinking of dried blood and grease. Cortés rode through the Tlaxacalans, up to the priests, Doña Marina at his side.

"Tell them their god has been destroyed," he said to Doña Marina. "Tell them they have a new god."

She translated, and the priests kneeled before Cortés. Cortés dismounted, yelled back to his army.

"Padre! Padre, forward!"

A white-robed priest pushed through Cortés' men, a golden cross gripped in his hands. He handed the cross to Cortés. Cortés held it up, so that its shadow fell on the black robed priests, the tortured gaze of the Christ figure glaring down at them. As Hart looked at the cross, he saw it changed into a pentagram, Satan's horned image peering out from the center.

"Tell them," Cortés said. "Tell them that they worship my lord, not Moctezuma's!" He shoved the black robed priests aside, and strode up to the pyramid, to a cairn of rubble. He stuck the pentagram in it, and came back down to the white robed priest. "Padre, get these bastards cleaned up and instruct them in the way of the lord."

A Tlaxacalan woman pushed through the fat men, stood before Cortés, and said something to him.

"What?" Cortés asked, turning to Doña Marina. "What does she say?"

"She asks how their men will move around, now that their houses have been destroyed," Doña Marina said.

"How?" Cortés stepped up to the woman, glared at her. "How?" He reached down, slapped the sole of his right boot. "On their own two feet! Let them walk!" He turned away from her.

The woman grabbed Cortés' shoulder, pulled him back to her. Cortés spun around, his fist raised to strike her, but stopped.

"She asks," said Doña Marina. "She asks the god Quetzalcoatl how her men will defend their city now that they have lost the sloth's piss."

The woman looked at Cortés, and slowly fell to her knees.

Cortés smiled. "Tell her ... tell her they will walk and defend their city with their fat bodies. But tell her the women will ride, will ride horses. No man of this generation will ever ride again, but the women, the women may ride horses."

Cortés took the woman's hands, raised her up, and led her through the crowd, to a soldier holding the reins of a mare and a stallion.

"The god Quetzalcoatl gives her his finest horses" - he handed her the reins - "if she will give the god a tin house and the tanker with the sloth piss." He squinted at her, looking up and down her strong body. Cortés reached out, stroked her long black hair. "If she will give the god a hundred Tlaxacalan women."

Doña Marina translated. The woman led Cortés away from the pyramid, toward a gleaming Winnebago, the gray tanker parked beside it. The woman reached into a pouch on her belt, handed Cortés a set of keys.

"This house is the god's, and our finest maidens are his to take on his conquests," Doña Marina translated for her.

A whoop rose up from the conquistadors. Cortés took the keys from the woman, took her hand, and led her inside the Winnebago. As Cortés shut the door, Hart noticed a sticker on the motor house's bumper: *'If this van's a rockin',* it said, *don't bother knockin'.'*

Chapter 17

The Conquistadors rode west from Tlaxcala, the cavalry taking the point, foot soldiers holding the middle, and the Winnebago and tanker at the rear. Hart stayed on his horse at the front, Emily at his side, Barker and Cortés on the flanks, the Tlaxacalan woman — whom the priest had baptized Linda — riding by Cortés' side.

Linda's sisters had also been given Christian names, so that they would no longer be savages Cortés had made it clear to his men that they would not copulate with heathens, and his men had obliged cheerfully by imploring the priest to baptize every heathen woman they found. The Lord's blessing, however, had not necessarily made the Tlaxacalan women more willing to bed with the Conquistadors, and after several of his men had their throats slit by the Tlaxacalans, Cortés realized that Linda had given him the women for war, not love. The one-hundred Tlaxacalan women marched in the middle of the column, the conquistadors eyeing them carefully.

Two days march later, the army came through a mountain pass and up to a broad terrace covered by a lake that stretched to the slopes of surrounding mountains. Cortés stopped the column, gazed off at the plateau with the binoculars. He handed them to Hart, motioned for Doña Marina to move up next to him.

Though the mountains seemed to have the shape of the Mexican hills he'd remembered, the vegetation seemed strange, Hart thought: not cactus and scrub palm, but purple and red plants, with the highest trees but shrubs lining the valley creeks. High grasses blazed a florescent green on the lake shore. The lake curved around several points of land, two bays cutting into the land in opposite directions. A series of causeways and dikes cut off the westernmost bay, and in the middle of the bay a great city rose up, stepped pyramids arranged in neat rows in the center of the city. Hart handed the binoculars to Linda, showing her how to use them.

She looked through them, pushed them away from her face, then looked again, twirling the focus as Hart had demonstrated. She smiled, then frowned quickly, glancing back at her troops, looking up at the hills, into the vegetation.

"Tenochtitlan," she said. "Moctezuma." She whirled her horse around, and Cortés grabbed the reins, holding her.

"Tenochtitlan?" he asked. "Moctezuma? The city?"

"Si," she said, one of the words Cortés had taught her. "Moctezuma." She glared at Cortés, said something to Doña Marina.

"We are too near, she says," Doña Marina translated. "Moctezuma guards the passes, the causeway, every entry into Tenochtitlan. We must go back, she says — or fight."

Cortés stared at Linda, a cold, hard stare. "Tell her to bring her troops forward. We ride." He took out a handkerchief, polished a dusty spot on his gleaming armor. "Tell Linda that she need not fear Moctezuma. Tell her that she *should* fear" — he put the handkerchief away, thumped his chest — "Quetzalcoatl."

Hart watched Cortés shout orders to Barker, to the other conquistadors, and as Cortés rode up and down his flanks, urging the musketeers forward, placing the Tlaxacalan amazons shoulder to shoulder behind a wedge of cavalry and his foot soldiers, even Cortés' image changed. He sprouted wings, wings of leather like a bat, wings of feathers like a bird, then insect wings, furred wings, scaled wings. His hands became talons and claws, his legs massive thighs like a lion, his armor that of a cockroach, or a beetle. Cortés stopped, for a brief moment gazing at Hart, and as their eyes met, and Cortés' forked tongue flicked out tasting the air, Hart realized who Cortés was.

Lord Satan, Hart thought, fingering the ripcord around his neck. A searing pain shot down Hart's spine, quickly easing, and as the tongue flicked back into his mouth, Cortés nodded.

The tableau changed into the reality of the moment, and Hart urged his horse over to join the cavalry at the back of the wedge, Emily — no, Peggy now — at his side, Barker — no, Puertocarrero — on the opposite flank, Doña Marina next to him. Hart turned back, saw Linda leading her warriors, spears clutched in their hands, leather shields held across their chests.

As he watched, the Tlaxacalan women leaned forward, long braids dangling down their backs. With their shield hand each woman reached for the braid of the woman in front of her, took the points of their spears, and held it against the roots of the braid high on the woman's head. On her horse, Linda drew a long knife, held it up to her own braid, and with a jerk drew the edge through the dark hair. Spears flashed as the Tlaxacalans followed Linda's action. The heads of the women rose up, the shorn hair falling around their faces, like a field of wheat that has just seen a scythe pass over it. In the rear of the army the last row of women turned around, and their sisters behind them repeated the procedure. The women whirled the braids over their heads, a low moaning rising higher and higher as the knots came unfurled and they held whirling fans of dark hair. They threw the fans high in the air, their cries rising to a whoop, and fell silent as the black strands dropped over them.

The conquistadors looked back at this spectacle, at the hundred women screeching a dread battle call, at the points of their spears gleaming, the leather gleaming, the shorn hair gleaming. Their screeching pulled at the harp strings of Hart's spine, and he shuddered, thinking, they are ready to die, they have cut themselves loose from their bodies and are ready to die.

Cut loose as his body already was, this soul of his damned in hell, he thought.

Cortés raised his sword, turned to his army, and pointed at the city on the lake. "Tenochtitlan," he screamed, "is ours!"

They moved down a peninsula jutting into the southern bay of the great lake, a short causeway connecting the southern edge of the bay to the peninsula. The gravel track of the mountain trail widened and turned into paving, hard stones set side by side with paper thin gaps between them. A chill wind flowed down from the mountains, and as the cold settled on the lake, the lake groaned, creaked. On the surface of the lake the water became flat, a dull sheen to its tension, frost spines spreading out in random waves. Hart buttoned the top of his jacket, pulled the collar high over his neck.

As they advanced up the causeway and into the island city, gates at each intersection of the causeways branching off east and west opened up for them. No soldiers manned the watchtowers, no troops manned the gates. Hart listened for the sound of engines moving the gates, but heard nothing. Cortés continued his advance, riding at the head of the col-

umn, flagpole held firmly in his hand, banners flapping.
Barker whispered orders to the foot soldiers to check out each
gate, but they all reported what Hart had suspected: nobody.

Nobody lined the streets, nobody waved at them from
the buildings lining the main boulevard into Tenochtitlan.
Heaps of clothes lay in neat piles along the road, obsidian axes
lying on top of the tunics and shields. Gold lay everywhere,
gold bricks in the road, gold sheathing on the roofs, gold wire
wrapping the shields, gold threads gleaming in clothes. Hart
began a running count of the gold he saw, figuring an ounce
per article of clothing, a pound per brick, but gave up when his
calculations hit a million pounds. Barker still eyed the alleys
and side streets warily, poking the piles of clothing with a pike,
falling back from the column to check out another opening
gate.

Cortés rode proudly, undaunted by the absence of the
Tenochtitlans. When Barker raised the question of their absence, Cortés looked at him and smiled, a reassuring grin.
"They await us at their temple, in the center of the city — Moctezuma, his soldiers stripped naked, his loyal subjects. They
are all there."

Later, Hart would recall those lines, and recognize the
truth in them, and record them thus:

Moctezuma awaited the god,
His armies massed with him,
Their wealth shed, the pure anger,
The pure anger of their might
Revealed.

When the Conquistadors entered the market place of
Tenochtitlan, by the palaces of Moctezuma and his brother
Axayacatl, Cortés' prophecy proved to be right — more or less.

*

Cortés and his Conquistadors came to the final gate on the causeway boulevard leading into the central market place. Like the other gates, this gate slowly swung inward, the shingles of gold rattling on the two doors as unseen forces turned them open. A crack appeared between the pine planking, widening, widening, and a thousand eyes blinked at the splendor revealed. "Sol's skin burning, burning," Hart would later write, hot on gerunds, "a million rainbow'd feathers shimmering, shimmering."

"There," Cortés shouted at his doubting troops, "there are the Tenochtitlans, come to welcome us."

Ten ten-thousand Mexicans stood inside the square, their simple clothes abandoned, now arrayed in robes of jaguar furs, peacock stoles, tunics of toucan pelts, manes of macaw feathers: a sea of iridescent garb, wave upon wave of majestic dress. Women, men, children stood in a semi-circle around the square, their backs to the two palaces, their fronts to a heap of gold and jewels piled before them. Incredible headdresses crowned their heads, their very hair woven into fantastic coiffures glistening with filigreed wires holding thumb sized emeralds and jewels. Their exposed flesh gleamed with fragrant oils, and even their dogs and cats and birds had been dusted with fine powders of silver, gold, and copper. As Cortés rode into the square, a low murmuring rose from the crowd.

"Quetzalcoatl, Quetzalcoatl, Quetzalcoatl..."

Stepping forth from the masses came the most extravagantly attired of them all, a priest attired in a thousand hummingbird skins, the robe rippling down his back from a headdress into a penumbra six feet wide, so that he seemed to rise on cobalt feathered wings. The priest raised his arms, and the blue coat spread from him, its underside golden and hung with rubies and emeralds shimmering in the harsh light of Paradise.

"Quetzalcoatl," the priest said, "I, Moctezuma, living incarnation of Blue Hummingbird, bow before you."

Moctezuma fell to his knees, as did the Tenochtitlans, every man, women, and child falling behind him in rippling waves spreading to the ends of the market place and up to the tops of the buildings. The bowed Mexicans formed the image of a great fan, like the wings of a peacock spread on the ground. A chill wind blew over the market place from beyond the buildings, from beyond the palaces, a strange fog rolling across the backs of the submissive, flipping the robes over and revealing a drab green underside. Ten ten-thousand faces rose from the sea of green, the green like a great dead leaf, the faces aphids on the leaf, until Moctezuma turned his face up to Cortés and beamed.

"But we bow only once, Cortés, and now" — he raised his right arm high, in a clenched fist — "we rise!"

The splendor of their clothing fell away, ground underfoot into the square, and the Mexicans stood, monochrome, monotonous, menacing, ten ten-thousand soldiers in olive drab. Moctezuma raised his hands to his head, pulled the fabulous headdress down, and as it shimmered, adjusted a black beret over his head and smoothed his curly, full beard.

Hart glanced over at Peggy, saw her image dissolve into the woman he had known her as all along, watched the lank brown hair curl up into the flipped blonde bob, saw the brown trousers and loose peasant shirt turn into the tight black jumpsuit, saw the Mouser rifle rise up.

"Ché," Emily whispered. "He has risen."

Booming across the square came a sound Hart hoped never to hear again, a sound that burned the ozone rancid smell of fear in his nostrils, a sound that lesser armies would have died of on the spot, a sound that sent his hand groping for the ripcord at his neck and almost yanking it. In unison, in one quick move, making one single noise, the ten ten-thousand rebels of Ché Guevara's army slid back the bolts on their Hellishnikovs, and locked and loaded their automatic rifles. Cortés glared at the bearded man before him, glanced back at the gates closing shut behind him, looked down at the mound of gold that had turned into a pile of steaming shit as high as Moctezuma and smiled. He smiled. Hart would always remember that smile, remembered the cleft in Cortés' chin rising up, remembered the scars below his lip tightening, remembered the horrid sound of Cortés' sword as he drew it and raised it high.

"Guevara," he said, "we are brothers." And he brought the sword down.

Barker, intensely Barker, not Puertocarrero, kicked his horse forward, taking the right flank. Emily raised her rifle, and in the flash of the battle, Hart could not tell if she aimed at Cortés or Ché. Linda's soldiers roared behind him, a volley of spears flying overhead. The cavalry spread out in a wide vee, Cortés at point, and the foot soldiers moved forward, protected for the moment by the horses. A shuddering rose in the rear, and Hart looked back to see the Winnebago and the tanker reversing, moving forward, and reversing again, battering the closed gates.

The rebels' rifles flashed: 7.62 mm bullets shredding the horses into hamburger, Cortés' cavalry stumbling down. A wave of soldiers around Ché emptied their magazines, ducked down, and a second wave fired. Hart turned in his saddle, looking left and right, watching the Conquistadors fall, watching the Tlaxacalan women string their bows and let loose another volley, bowstrings humming across their breasts. The arrows rained down on the rebels, reducing their ranks by dozens. The tepuztli, the arquebuses of the Conquistadors, answered the rebels' assault. But still the assault rifles barked, still the Mexicans fired on. Bullet, blood, steel, swords... Hart whirled in the center of it, rubbing his ripcord like an amulet, no death seeking him or his horse.

Emily sat stern in her saddle, thighs gripping the flanks of her horse. She became Peggy, Peggy holding her rifle in steel hands, her shots accurate and firm, the bolt clicking in even strokes as she loaded, locked, fired, ejected: *clickety-clack-click, clickety-clack-click.* The barrel of the Mouser glowed a dull blue, a blue that seemed to envelop the rifle, envelop Peggy as she went to Emily and to Peggy and back to Emily again.

Cortés rode forward into the maelstrom, Barker at his side, and with his free arm, reached down, kicking Ché's rifle away, and grabbed for the rebel. Guevara wriggled, rolled free. Barker urged his horse next to him, pinning Che between the two stallions. Ten rebels circled around the two horses, Hellishnikov rifles raised. Cortés reared his horse back, sword raised. The ring of rebels shoved their rifles forward, the points of their bayonets jabbing Cortés' legs. The circle opened up behind Cortés and Barker, the two horses cutting Ché off from his men. Cortés and Barker backed up, toward Hart and Emily.

Emily raised her rifle, sighted down it. Hart glanced over at her, saw it aimed at Cortés, opened his mouth in a yell. The image of her became Peggy again, and the muzzle dropped, kicked as Peggy pulled the trigger. Ché turned at the sound, turned to take the bullet in his neck, smiled at Peggy as she turned back into Emily, and laughed, blood spurting out of his neck as his head rolled off his torso.

"Emily, Emily, Emily," the head of Guevara said, Cortés and Barker moving back from the corpse, exposing the body to the rebels. "Emily, Emily, Emily," Ché said again, a mantra he repeated and repeated until the rebels at the front quit, stunned at the death of their leader, while the shooting was dying down in waves of silence rippling toward the back of the soldiery. "Emily," he whispered, and a few Hellishnikovs answered from the roofs of the palace, and then fell silent.

"Retreat," said Cortés, "retreat to the coast. Retreat!"

The conquistadors moved back, Emily in their midst, the Tlaxacalans covering the rear. Decimated to three dozen men and women and six horses, they slipped around the tanker and the Winnebago as the trucks burst through the gates. Hart urged his horse forward, galloping toward the retreating army. The rebels moved forward, cutting him off from the Conquistadores' flank, shoving him against the city walls. He dug his boots into the horse's side, yanked the bridle, but the rebels squeezed him further from his compatriots. Hart waved at Peggy, at Emily. She shook her head, turned, followed Cortés as they slipped out of the gates. Hart looked down, looked at two dozen rebels raising their rifles at him.

The headless body of Ché Guevara rose, walked over to its head, and reached down. It set the head on its shoulders, gripped the ears, and turned around. Then the cut at its neck healed, the rebel flapped his wings and wriggled his claws, flicked a forked tongue at Hart and ran a hand through his beard. Hart touched his ripcord. The demon flapped his wings again, wagged a claw at him. Hart let his hand drop to his side. Ché folded his wings in and nodded.

One of the rebels reached up, pulled Hart off the saddle.

He grabbed at his saddlebag, yanked it off the horse. The horse reared up, cutting Hart off from the rebels. Digging down into the saddlebag, he took out his notebook and pen, turned to an open page, and wrote.

'Awed at Moctezuma's power,
Subdued by his rage, Quetzalcoatl
Walked backward, his soldiers at his side,
The wheeled box parting a path through
Bleeding bodies. Momentarily, the
Scribe was lost, surrounded by bodies.'

Hart looked up, saw the rebels moving in, Ché picking up a Hellishnikov lying on the ground. He continued writing.

'Bodies bleeding, bodies advancing,
The scribe's horse frothed venom.'

His horse whirled, kicked, fighting its way back to Hart. The rebels moved aside, and the horse came to him.

'Venom, venom, foam on its back,
The horse came, pushing rebels aside.
Reaching, reaching, words flashing,
Action matching, the scribe reached up'

Hart dropped the pen and notebook, grabbed for the reins of the horse as it came by, grabbed the saddle's pommel, ran alongside the galloping stallion, began shouting the poem aloud:

"Taking the reins, foot groping for stirrup,"

... swung a foot into the stirrup, and leapt onto the saddle.

"Settled into saddle, and laughing, leering,"

Hart sat in the saddle, took the reins, and turned back at Ché.

"At the Brown God Moctezuma,
Turned, and followed Cortés away."

Ché grinned, shook his head. Hart smiled, turned and galloped toward the conquistadors. As he passed through the wrecked gate, Hart stopped the horse, waited. His pen and notebook flew after him, and he caught them. He looked at the gates, wrote in his notebook:

> 'As the scribe passed out of the city,
> The gates crumbled behind.'

Hart nodded, put his notebook back in his saddlebags, and smiled. The gates collapsed behind him.

*

Two dozen conquistadors made it to Vera Cruz. The Tlaxacalan women left Cortés' crusade at their city, and he drove away in the Winnebago, his men hanging onto the sides of the tanker or riding the top of the RV. Hart's right hand ached from the words, ached from the painstaking detail he recorded of their journey back east. He refused Barker's cups of tequila, refused Peggy's caresses, refused everything but the power of the pen and the way the words appeared on the paper as quick as he thought them.

Three and twenty men and one woman rode out of the jungle and onto the golden beaches, the god defeated, no gold in his baggage. The *Orizaba* lay at anchor off the coast, her crew shouting at the arrival of the Conquistadors. Boats rowed out to meet them.

Hart sat on a log, his horse tied to a tree next to him, Peggy cleaning her Mouser. His fingers flashed over the page as he wrote the last lines of his epic. Cortés strode up to him, still dressed in black tunic and leggings, still in gleaming armor.

"Are you done, scribe?" he asked. The Spaniard held out a black clay bottle.

Hart looked up. "It's not over yet." He pointed at the rowboat coming toward them.

"Do you treat me kindly?" Cortés asked.

"I tell the truth," said Hart.

"You might as well have this now." Cortés held out the bottle of tequila. Hart looked back at his notebook. Cortés set the bottle down on the log beside him.

And god Quetzalcoatl came back to golden sands
Still dressed in Undine's flashing sands,
Head erect, beard pointed, new scars on his chin.
No gold in his pocket, no lands for his king.
Cortés returned vanquished, defeated, his only reward,
Humility.

Hart reached down, grabbed the tequila, and put it with his notebook in his saddlebags. He led the horse gently toward the rowboat. Rubbing the horse's muzzle, he looked at its blue eyes, its silver mane.

"I've never named you," he said to the stallion. Hart stroked the horse's neck. "Okay: Colonel. I name you: 'Colonel.'"

He led Colonel down the beach and away from hell's new shore.

*

As the *Orizaba* steamed away from Vera Cruz, Hart thought he saw a city of brick buildings rise from the jungle. He shook his head, looked down at the froth being churned up by the ship's propellers, watched seagulls dive in the wake. Hart uncorked the bottle of tequila, raised it to his lips, began to drink it in. The sweet smell of the mescal floated up his nostrils, sending sharp shivers into his scrotum. Upending the bottle, he held it out over the bow of the boat, and, emptied, tossed it into the sea. Peggy moved up next to him at the rail. Glancing over at her, Hart reached out, put his arm around her.

"Why, Mister Crane," Emily Dickinson said.

Hart turned, shook his head at the blonde. The breeze of the sea tugged at loose tendrils of her hair. She smiled at him, pushed her bangs back with a gentle hand, the other hand holding the rail of the ship.

"Uh, Miss Dickinson," he said. "I..." How could he explain? Hart shook his head. "I'm sorry... I thought you were someone else."

She moved toward him. "That's Okay."

He shrugged, put his arm around her, pulled her tight to him. Together they leaned against the ship's rail, passing into the Sea of Sighs, under the Brooklyn Bridge. Hart looked up at the bridge cables that seemed to pull them upward — harp strings, he thought; "dreams filed" the metaphor he'd once used. The towers of the Bridge rose above them and, as Hart Crane leaned toward Emily Dickinson, Paradise began to set behind the windows of the eastern tower.

Above on the Bridge, a horse neighed.

Chapter 18

Ah, this Harold Hart Crane. Here he has dragged me halfway across Mexico, marching on his silly poetic quest, thinking his lost love, his Peggy — his one major tangle with heterosexuality — is the Emily but it is, of course, me! Silly boy. You cannot fool ol' W.A.R., not the Evil Side of Roebling's lost soul. I wander with him across the swamps, ride next to him, projecting that vision he thinks he sees. And for what? For what?

Hah! To mess him up, to make him stray from his task. And the bastard — the *bastard* — goes ahead and writes his damn poetry. He writes it — I cannot believe it — he writes a silly, disgusting, horrible free verse logic-filled metaphor of a poem. And it saves him! Saves him from Ché, saves him from the awful wrath of a million savage *campesinos.* Poetry! Pfah! Can nothing go right in these little hells the Bridge makes? Harold, Harold, you cannot even jump off the *Orizaba.* What good are you? So put your arm around me, go ahead, try to get Miss Dickinson. See what I care. *I've* got big plans, buddy.

This little W.A.R., he's going to hustle Ezra Pound.

Chapter 19

The silver and white Hellcules cargo plane came down hard on the frozen lake, its skis leaving long gutters of slop in the overflow of the heavy snow. The tail gouged a deep crevasse in Lake de Born, a scree of ice pinging on the side of the prop plane. Ezra Pound crouched in a jump seat by the aft door, the hood of his white anorak cinched tight around his chin, the ankles of his snow pants crammed into the tops of his bunny boots.

"All right, girls," Barker, their blue-haired lieutenant, shouted opposite from Ez, "let's move it." He undogged the hatch, swung it open. "Go, go, go." He kicked soldiers in the butt as he pushed them out the door.

Pound's platoon leapt from the plane, rolled in the snow, and scattered across the lake. Ezra fell, zig-zagged away from the Hellcules, sunk his ankle in the icy ditch one of the skis had dug, pulled his foot loose from the water, and ran. *Ran.* Small arms fire popped from across the lake, on the other side of the plane, and bullets thunked into the side of the aircraft, putting fresh dings in the words BRIDGE AIRWAYS painted above the windows. A soldier to his left stumbled, fell down, and came up, clutching his arm, the expanding red spot like spilled wine on a tablecloth, pure and distinct on the white camo, against the gray sky, the gray snow, the gray plane....

And the broad fields beneath them turn crimson, he thought, thinking of his most infamous poem, the "bloody sestina," "Sestina: Altaforte." *Altaforte.* He saw it across the lake, the high fortress rising from an isle, causeways running from it north and south. Altaforte: "high castle." Ez ran toward it, toward its gates, toward the guns barking back in reply, covering their approach, covering the plane.

The door thudded on the plane, and its engine roared as it pulled loose from the sticky snow, the wet snow. Its tail whipped around, the backwash of the propellers sending up a covering cloud of snow and steam, the bow of the plane presenting a narrow target to the enemy across the lake. The plane's pilot gunned the engines and it screamed away into the wind, into the enemy, up and over and away. A relative silence fell on Lake de Born, pops of rifles firing, booms of mortars flying. Ezra glanced up at the plane, a dot disappearing over the mountains that seemed to arc like a bridge to Paradise. He felt his stomach fall as it had fallen ten dozen times before: the last link sundered, abandoned again, cut off, alone.

Barker came up behind him, slapped him on the shoulder. "What're you looking at, Sergeant? She'll be back, don't you worry." He shoved Ezra forward. "Only thing you got to worry about is whether when the Hellky Bird picks you up, you're on your feet" — he glanced down at the water freezing on Ezra's boot, and grinned — "or in a bag."

The platoon stumbled through the back gates of the castle. A soldier on a snow-machine roared out past them, dragging a sled, out to pick up the load of gear dumped by the Hellcules. From the parapets above them a crew of soldiers worked a water cannon, spraying the sides of the fort, building up the thick coating of ice that ran down the walls and around its edge in a jumble of lumpy crystals. Some sections of the walls had been breached, and only the ice filled the gaps.

"Like nanuq, the polar bear," Barker said, pointing at the icicles. "The bear rolls in the water, coats his fur with ice, and no arrow or spear can pierce him. Yukon cement — hah, you can piss such stuff if you have to." The blue-hair herded his troops into the fort, into its warm chambers.

Their platoon assembled in a great hall, doors and hallways running away into other rooms from each wall, a stone staircase spiraling down from a balcony above. A man moved across the balcony, an ermine cape wrapped around his shoulders, two .45 automatic pistols strapped to his hips. A vague shape, like a floating gown, followed him. The taps on his white leather boots clicked on the staircase as he turned the corner, momentarily out of sight. Ez stared straight ahead, listening to the clicks, then quickly glanced to his right as the man moved along the wall and toward them.

His cape whirled behind him, and his left hand clutched a thing... A thing like a lamp? Ez wondered. The man walked in front of the lines of troops, paused, lifted the thing to his neck, and set it in a basket-like contraption strapped to his shoulders. *His head*, Ez thought. The men behind him rustled as the platoon took in the sight. Hardened combat veterans, they'd seen some strange battles in hell, acephalic corpses by the dozen, but not one moving, alive....

Ez stared at the neck, at the gap between axis and atlas, at the way the blood flowed between torso and head, leaping the gap so the cut remained clear. The man swiveled, turned the head with his hand, moving his gaze back and forth along the lines of soldiers. Then he jerked the head out of its basket, gripping it by his hair, and thrust it at the troops.

"Get used to it!" he yelled. "It's not pretty but it's my curse and you'll endure it as I have!"

The man in the white cape swung his arm in a quick arc before the platoon, his head glaring at them, challenging them, staring them down. Ez didn't have to glance over at Barker to see *his* glare, didn't dare move his eyes anywhere but front, knowing that he had to accept the swinging head's visage.

"The swinging head..." the words came back to him, burned like brands into the folds of his brain since that Satan-cursed day Dante himself had recited the entire *Commedia* in a poetic challenge: Ez with *his* Cantos, and Homer trouncing them all hands down with his *Iliad*. Dante, Canto XXVIII:

It held the severed head by its own hair,
swinging it like a lantern in its hand;
and the head looked at us and wept in its despair.

Bertrans, Ez thought. Bertrans de Born.

"Good," the man said, "good, my troops. You will do well. Get used to *this* ghastliness" — he shook his head at them — "and you can get used to far more."

He set the head back in the basket. The diaphanous thing floated next to him, its gown clinging around a woman's torso, nearly invisible hints of arms and legs and head suggesting an intact body. The head shimmered, became solid, then opaque again. In its flickering Ez thought he saw the blonde bob of that saccharine poetess, Emily. One ghostly arm pulled a sheet of paper from under the gown and handed it to the man.

"At ease, gentlemen. I am your commander" — the head swiveled on its own accord, looking straight at Ez — "*En* Bertrans. Since some of you may speak a barbaric tongue as your native language, you may call me 'Lord Bert' if you cannot say the name correctly." Bertrans waved at the floating gown.

"This is the Lady Audiart: Audiart, my help mate, my aide-de-camp, my wife." He reached up, turned his head forward, held up the paper to it. "You are...?" he asked Barker, moving the paper back.

"Alpha Platoon, Task Force Eight Eighty, Special Demolition Unit, Sir!" Barker shouted. He stepped forward, saluted. "Lieutenant Barker, sir, reporting!"

"Lieutenant," Bertrans said. "As you were." He moved along the lines, glancing at their weapons — Hellishnikovs and M-666 automatic rifles, Samopal and Ezekiel submachine guns, even a bolt-action Mouser. — and stopped at Ezra. Bertrans put a hand on his head, pushed his gaze down and up. "You have no weapon, Sergeant... "He squinted at Ez's name tag. "Pound? Why is this?"

Ez stepped forward, saluted. "The Sergeant is a non-combatant, sir."

"Non-combatant?" Bertrans looked at Pound's shoulders. "You are not a medic? A priest? What are you?"

"Your... *jongleur*, sir," he said, thinking: Papiols; Papiols, to the music.

"My jongleur? But my minstrel is..."

"*C'est mort*," Ez said.

"Dead?" Bertrans jerked his head around at his aide-de-camp. "Dead? This is news to me."

Lady Audiart whispered. "Dead, love. This morning. On patrol. We had already requested a back-up."

"So," said Bertrans, his voice breaking slightly. "So... You have experience in war correspondence, Sergeant?"

"I... "How could he explain? Pound pondered. "Six campaigns in hell, sir. I was the *Claw and Talon* reporter at the front for two years, sir."

The Lady handed him a scroll of paper. Bertrans glanced over Ez's vita, smiled. "Well, Sergeant, you have a sestina, I see. A difficult form, difficult. 'Altaforte,' it's called. A charming coincidence, charming."

No coincidence, Ez thought. No coincidence. Planned. Planned, he knew — the Bridge, Job. "Sir," he said.

"Then you shall write another sestina, Sergeant." Bertrans shoved his head down on his neck, and it sealed, spun around, and the face turned to stare at him again, not Bertrans' face, but Job's, Job glaring at him with his intense eyes.

"You will write another sestina, Ezra," he said. "Not a bloody sestina, nothing glorifying war. Call it... 'Sestina: Paradise,' yes? A bloodless sestina, six stanzas, a concluding tercet, using the same end rhyme as the 'Altaforte'— but get the fourth stanza right, Okay? Understand?"

"Yes." He shielded his eyes from Job's glare. "Yes, Ombudsman. Yes."

"Good." Job's head spun around, separated from its neck, and became Bertrans's face again. "Yes, another sestina, something to rival poor Papiols's work." Bertrans shifted his head left and right, reviewing the troops again. "Lieutenant Barker, settle your men in. Get a good night's rest. Tomorrow" — he smiled — "tomorrow, we test you in battle." Bertrans whirled around, his head continuing to look at the troops. "In battle against Le Coeur de Lion's troops." Bertrans reached up, turned his head, and strode off with Lady Audiart.

*

Ez moved with his squad out of the castle under cover of darkness, across the north side of Lake de Born. Three causeways connected Altaforte to the mainland, one north, south, and east. Bertrans had blown the causeways long ago, but the squad scuttled along the east side of the northern causeway, opposite the near shore, using it for cover. The squad sergeant, a tall man whose tiger mask tattoos flamed only for Ez, and who everyone called Sarge Q, motioned to Ez to file out with the other nine men in his squad. A gray-haired private glanced back at Ez, smiled, and took the point.

"Squad A moving into position," Sarge Q said. The sound crackled in the headset of Ez's helmet, the narrow-band radio the whole platoon wore.

"Squad B moving into position," a voice answered back.

That would be Sarge Rabbit moving south, to the other shore of Lake de Born. Barker's plan was to move the two squads up from the south and down from the north, take out the artillery batteries harassing Altaforte — Ez stared at the ADAM backpack nuke strapped on top of the gray-haired private's ruck — and retreat.

"Turn your headset down, Pound," Barker said from behind. "You want to let Richard hear our whole plan?"

Ez reached up, dialed the volume lower. The squad's footsteps made soft crunching sounds in the hoar frost of the lake ice, the sound of insects being crushed underfoot. Lake de Born creaked, then thundered, jagged cracks zigging along the surface. The gray-haired private stopped. What was his name? Right: Washy, Ez thought, recalling the mnemonic he'd devised. Washy, because his clean shaven face always looked pink and scrubbed.

"All right, all right, move it carefully," Barker said. "The ice is thick enough — it held the Hellky Bird, didn't it?"

"Getting warmer, Lieutenant," Washy said.

"Yeah, might even climb to twenty below tonight," Barker replied. "Cool it, Roebling." The squad moved forward, fifty yards from the shore.

"What the hell we fighting for this time, Lieutenant?" another private said — that faggot Hart, Ez thought. "This Coeur de Lion — he Ché-Com, too?"

Ez knew what Hart implied: the factions in hell seemed to either line up for Satan — DEVO Pact, someone called it — or the Dissidents led by Guevara: Ché-Com. But Ez knew that it never was that simple — the Romans, for instance, seemed to have their own agenda.

"Yeah," added another voice. "What's the pay-off?"

"You want to know?" Bertrans shouted in their headsets. Ten hands shot up to cut the squelch. "You want to know why you fight? I'll tell you:

"Henry the Young King, elder of
Geoffrey, Richard, and John,
Son of the Second, desired his share,"

Bertrans boomed.

"What's he doing?" Sarge Q asked. "The asshole's broadcasting live."

"No, no," Barker said. "Loudspeakers. This is for Richard."

Ez turned his headset off for a moment, heard Bertrans's voice echoing across the lake. Satan himself could probably hear him in New Hell, he thought.

"His right," Bertrans screamed. *"His mother, Eleanor —*

"His mother, Pound, got that?" Bertrans said through the headset. "I know what that whoreson Dante called me.

"She, stirrer of strife,"

he continued over the loudspeakers,

Incited brother against brother.

The father, the Second, restored order —
Eleanor in her dungeon of ladies.
Years passed, Sir Yes-and-No, Senher de Niort,
Waged battle against the Aquitane Lords,
Who had risen in rebellion against
His cruel rule; Coeur de Lion roared,
Fought, and Won."

"You got that right!" a voice screamed from across the lake. Ez looked back at Barker, and he smiled. Sure, tell us their position.

"And the Young King, lament, lament,
Fell ill, not to steel's lusting, but
Dread Fever; hah! cursed syphilis."

"Liar!" the enemy voice shouted again.

"Lord of Bordeaux, the Bordello, of the Nuns de Niort,
He made peace with his lords — the peace of steel,
Of destriers frothing, and turned them on
Altaforte.
On he who honored his sister, he who sang praises
Of his brother, he who threw out the tyrant
Constantine de Born, pretender to
Altaforte. Altaforte. Altaforte."

The loudspeaker clicked off, quickly came back on. "Richard, die you dog!"

"You see, my men?" Bertrans said over the radio. "That's why you fight: to preserve justice, to right a wrong, to prevent Richard Lionheart from deposing me from my castle, my home." The channel clicked off, came back on. "And, of course, to crush yet another attempt by Ché and his Dissidents to subvert the Order of Satan's dominion."

Someone spat behind Ez. "What's the payoff, Lieutenant?" Ez couldn't place the voice.

"Yeah, what's our bonus?" someone added on the Squad B channel.

Ez moved forward slowly, keeping in Washy's footsteps, conscious of Bertrans's guns at Altaforte, not doubting for a moment that he'd blow them off the lake if he got pissed enough.

"Bonus?" asked Bertrans. "I thought you were loyal troops, a highly disciplined unit. You want a bonus, my mercs?" Bertrans chuckled. "If that's what it takes, you shall have your plunder. Your plunder, my men, is Richard himself. A king's ransom: that is your reward. Capture him alive — *alive* — and you can name your price. You understand?" No one replied. "You understand!"

Barker answered for them: "We understand."

Yeah, thought Ez. Capture him alive — with an ADAM? Ez knew what the rest of the platoon thought: there wasn't going to *be* a payoff. Barker didn't have to say it.

"Good," said Bertrans. "Ignore the fires flickering to the east; that shore is too far away to be of concern, and the lake too open for Richard to attack across it. Head for the hills. Go into them, search out Richard's batteries, and destroy them before their shelling destroys us. Our walls are already breached, and only the ice mortar shields us now. When the ice melts, as it surely will — Satan damn Paradise's rising! — the wall will break. Destroy those batteries. Destroy them!"

The squad moved onto the shore.

*

Washy led the column up into the thick spruce forest back from the lake's edge. They fanned out into the woods. A branch cracked to Ez's left. The soldiers whirled around, Ez's hands mimicking the action of the other nine bringing their rifles forward, and he felt again the dread absence of his weapon. He squinted, stared at the thing moving toward them.

It rose nearly six feet high, a tiny head poking through the brush, and a rack of antlers spreading ten feet across, with at least a dozen points jutting out from the rack. It stared at them, pulled its head sideways, and fell back into the dark.

"Irish elk," Barker said. "*Megaceros*. Q an' I used to hunt them. Real dumb animals: corner 'em in a forest and inevitably their heads get stuck in the trees."

The squad relaxed, moved to the northwest, up into the hills. Ez felt the blood rush in his veins that he always felt before a battle. He felt his senses go sharper, as if his brain had dialed up sight and sound and smell one notch higher. The night, the forest; the scrape of rifles against camo, the low breathing of Washy ahead pushing through the trees: everything embraced him and flowed around him, pulling him into combat. He felt again the clammy sweat in the small of his back, smelled again the cold of fear tightening his scrotum. Ez's hands longed for an assault rifle, a Hellishnikov, even an M-666, something to hold in his hands, something to send death screaming into bellies, something with which to *kill*. Words formed on his tongue, rolling out his lips, down from the flickering synapses of his mind. He switched his throat mike to record on the private channel to Bertrans, and recited the first stanza of the sestina:

"*Bah! Yes-and-No's wavering is no peace*
His siege but cowardice, dithering music
Come, colonels, gather your troops to clash
Bodies to bodies, sword to sword, soldiers opposing

Don't you lust for battle — the bath crimson?
Blood on mail and shield, your heart rejoicing?"

"Can it, Pound," Barker said.

Ez grinned, walked forward. On the private channel back from Bertrans came one word: *"Bene."*

A game trail wound around the lake's edge, skirting the contours of the hillside, and then down a gully into a creek. Barker stopped them at the gully, pulled out a pair of night-vision goggles, and scanned the draw.

"Looks clear," he said. "But I don't like the brush. Sarge, move your men across one at a time — you first, Pound."

Shit, thought Ez, but he had to agree with Barker's logic: He was expendable. He nodded at Sarge Q, and moved out of the forest and into the brush along the creek's edge.

The bank dropped abruptly away and fell down to a pan of ice. Mounds of frozen water rose up out of the pan where water had seeped and then frozen. Ez moved carefully around the ice, watching the opposite bank, watching the ice. He probed the ice ahead with his right foot; it held. Quickly step-ping across, he ran to the edge and slipped on a sheet of black ice.

Ez danced on the slick sheet, regaining his footing, but his left foot came down hard on a stretch of ice that cracked under him. His bunny boot sank into a stream of water bur-rowing under the ice near the shore. Jerking his foot up quick-ly, Ez grabbed a branch hanging over the bank and pulled himself onto dry land. He looked down at the water freezing his shoelaces, stomped his foot on an exposed rock, listened to the shards of ice tinkle off the white rubber. Luckily, no water had seeped into his boots. He waved across at Barker, pointed down at the open water.

"Can't keep your feet dry, can you Pound?" Barker asked, shaking his head, and waving the rest of the squad over.

The squad worked its way up the draw, inside the forest's edge. Altaforte lay in darkness several miles below, her lights dimmed and only a few lights from quarters in the inner sanctum glowing. Winter covered Lake de Born cast a phosphorescent glow around the castle. Ez had heard that the snow itself held the souls of damned thoughts, crude epithets shouted to the winds. Others had said that snow was the feathers of the fallen angels as they descended to hell and had their wings scorched into bat-like membranes. One damned priest had even said the snow and the rain and the fog were God's tears shed for his wayward children, but Ez had his own theory: the snow radiating like green embers was the frozen piss of dragons and demons.

Several hundred feet above them loomed a ridge separating the creek they had just crossed from another creek south of the ridge. Barker moved ahead, pulled out a map, and motioned to a point marked on it — Richard's north battery. An "X" marked to the south indicated the south battery — B Squad's objective. The lieutenant pointed up at the ridge, and looked at it with his night-vision goggles. He handed them over to Sarge Q, and Ez glanced through the binocular-like device as Q handed it back.

Two smooth, branchless trees poked out of the forest above. The spruce and birch surrounding the two trunks glowed a dull orange; the two trunks were dark blue. A figure walked in front of the trunks. Ez dialed the goggles down to real vision, and the image of a sentry with rifle jutting out from his hip came into focus. Ez passed the goggles back to Barker.

"That's it," Barker said. "You" — he tapped three men, — "head around to the north with the sergeant, and lay down covering fire on my command. You two" — he pointed — "come with me to the south. Pound, you help Roebling and Hart set the ADAM." He handed Washy the night-vision goggles. "Monitor the squad channel, but I don't want any chatter except the ADAM team telling me they've positioned the nuke. Got it?" The squad nodded. "Okay, ladies, let's go."

Sarge Q's group scuttled off into the forest above, and Barker took his men down and around. Washy nodded to Ez and that sorry excuse for a poet, Hart. They headed up the middle, working their way to a spot just below the artillery emplacement.

"Why don't we just set the sucker down right here?" he asked Washy.

Roebling shook his head. "Can't. Lieutenant wants that knob" — he pointed down to a saddle rising up between them and the lake — "between the battery and the lake. The rock will block the worst of the nuke's effects — for us. Besides, the bomb's dialed in for only a quarter kiloton."

Ez looked up at the battery, down at the lake. Two-hundred fifty pounds worth of TNT ought to do it, he thought. Hell, he didn't see why the ADAM - the ADvanced Atomic Demolition Munition -wouldn't just blow Altaforte down, too; they were only about three miles inland. "Right," he said.

Washy looked through the goggles at the battery, nodded when the sentry had moved on. "I only count two guys," he said. "Let's move now."

They scrambled up the slope, coming to a rock outcropping about a hundred feet below the battery. Washy looked at the rock through the goggles. "Okay, here — this rock's still got heat from the day; it'll mask our own heat." He handed the goggles to Hart, who watched the battery. Washy reached behind him, pulled off his ruck, and undid the ADAM from his pack. The mini tactical nuke looked more like a fat thermos than a fission bomb. It had a rounded top, bulky projections on the side, and a flat box on the front. Washy peeled off his mittens, opened the flat box, and began punching keys on a panel inside it. Ez never could understand any of the modern electronics, but the combat engineer worked on the nuke like it was a sonnet: cool, calm, and measured with just a little mystery. Setting the ADAM in a crack below the rock outcropping, Washy glanced at his watch, then tapped a button. A row of LEDs lit up above the key pad.

"Barker going to get Richard Coeur de Lion?" Hart asked.

"Fuck Richard," Washy said, shutting the panel door on the nuke and then putting on his mittens. He clicked on his throat mike. "She's armed," he said over the squad channel.

Hart dropped the goggles, let them dangle against his chest, and pulled his M-666 rifle forward. "We got trouble," he said. "I think the sentry —" A volley of shots cracked through the air, plinking against rocks to their south.

"Give us covering fire!" Washy radioed.

The shots moved toward them. Ez and Hart ducked, rolled, and fell down slope in a rumble of snow. Ez slid down on his belly, rolled around, looking up. Washy stood by the ADAM, shoveling snow onto it — hiding its heat signature, Ez thought. A bullet hit the rock outcropping, and the rock shattered, shards flying towards Roebling. He grabbed his arm, whirled, scrambling down to them.

"You okay?" Hart asked.

Washy clutched his arm, held up his mittens, a blotch of blood across the fingers. "A little cut — the bullet missed me." He winced. "I think."

Automatic fire rattled to their right and left. Washy glanced over at Ez, smiled. The three men moved down slope.

Hart pointed to the creek and the gully below them; Washy shook his head, pointed to the saddle rising above them.

"Get on the other side," he said, "work our way down to the lake, then make a dash across the east-west causeway. But get into the castle *before* the ADAMs blow." Hart, Washy, and Ez split up, moved down.

"Squad B, Squad B, are you in?" Barker shouted in the radio.

"Squad B in and loaded," Sergeant Rabbit replied.

"Okay, move' em down," Barker said. "All squads, let's hit it. I want everyone inside the castle before the candy shop blows."

Ez smiled; Barker didn't have to tell them to retreat. The cannons from the two batteries starting kicking up fire, hitting the west wall of Altaforte. That'd be a problem, Ez thought. They'd have to work their way around the east wall or get blown to bits. He heard his squad scrambling through the woods, saw the whine of tracers flashing. Down on the lake came the sound of rifles firing *up* at them. He rolled to a stop, saw Hart ten yards across from him, hugging a tree.

"See that?" Ez shouted up at him. "Those good guys?"

Hart lifted the night-vision goggles to his eyes, shook his head. "Bad guys."

"Shit." In the faint light of the glowing snow, Ez tried to get a count — a platoon, maybe two platoons of Richard's troops. They'd come down from the north, up from the south; the bastards had worked their way from the east — the far shore — of Lake de Born. A column of four tanks rolled up the east-west causeway.

"Lord Bert, Lord Bert," someone shouted on the platoon channel, "cover our front, damn it. We're getting pinched off." That would be someone from Squad A, Ez thought. If Squad B got lucky, they could move around the south causeway and come in the rear. Then he noticed another column of tanks — ground effects, *physeters,* he'd heard the Greeks call them — moving up the south causeway.

"Hold your positions," Barker said. "Get your asses down and stay off the lake. Repeat: stay off the lake."

"Shit, shit, *shit,*" Hart yelled. "We're cut off."

"Get behind the saddle," Ez yelled. "Get the rock between you and the battery." A bullet pinged against a tree to his right, and Ez ducked, then scrambled through the woods.

Ez dashed through the woods, a mad run, back and forth to clumps of trees. The firing from behind grew fainter, but that didn't help; the booming of the tanks below got louder. Figures flashed through the trees, two, four, eight, he lost count. The head set became an irritating chatter, a jumble of orders and commands from running soldiers. Once he heard a piercing scream, and for a long time someone kept murmuring, low, moaning, over and over, "Jesusmother, jesusmother, jesusmother," which Ez thought absurd considering where they were. And every time the murmur sounded, thunder rumbled, far off: or something very big growled.

He came around the saddle, around the knob of rock between the lake and the ADAM and the battery. If Squad B had done their job right, they'd put their nuke on the southeast side of the south battery. Ez tried to calculate blast rings and fallout rate, but the best figure he came up with was that if he stayed put, the two ADAMs wouldn't fry him instantly, and if he got inside Altaforte within two hours, he'd be safe from the fallout. A figure came around, raised its rifle at him.

"Pound," the soldier said.

"Washy. Hart?"

"Right here." He dashed up next to them.

Ez looked over at Washy, at the splotch of red spreading across his shoulder and into his armpit. "You're hit bad."

Washy shook his head. "It's just a little bleeder. No big deal." He lifted his good arm, looked at his wrist. "ADAM should blow in a few minutes."

"Shit," Hart said. He handed the night goggles to Ez. "Look at that."

Richard's troops had advanced behind the tanks on an assault on the west wall of Altaforte. Machine guns and light artillery fired from the corner turrets, and they picked off stray troops who couldn't get cover behind the tanks. One of the tanks — not a ground effect — had taken a hit in the treads, and it circled around like a drunk with his foot nailed to the floor, chasing soldiers, crushing the ones who couldn't get out of their way. A wave of soldiers — suicidal, suicidal, Ez thought — had assaulted one icy wall, trying to climb up it, and Bertrans' gunners had cut them down. One water cannon sprayed froth on the troops and the tanks, and the hardening water glowed red in the fire spitting from the turrets.

"In Altaforte's gaze stinks much rejoicing,"

Ez muttered into Bertrans' private channel, the lines of the second stanza coming to him,

"Her icy slopes littered with human peace
Paradise gleaming on glass walls in crimson
Funeral dirges sound their sweet music
Such clamor's the noise of swords opposing
When Hell's damned armies set forward to clash."

"Yes?" asked Bertrans. "And?"

Ez sighed, continued:

"Satan swear the heavens' thunder will clash!
Loud screech dread demons in battle rejoicing
Horn to horn, claw to claw, swords opposing!
Rebels, tyrants, and kings — none shall have peace

With mortars and rifles, powders' music
Their souls will sear spilt blood into crimson!"

Something crashed through the woods, ran into the clearing next to them. Hart raised his rifle, dropped it, laughed. "The damn moose again."

"You call that bloodless, Pound?" the Irish elk asked, and its face flickered into Job's image.

"Satan," Washy yelled.

The elk raised its head — not Job's head, Ez saw now — and held out its arms, arms like a centaur, body like a centaur, only *megaceros*, not horse. The elk-centaur held a Hellish-nikov in its hands, pointed it at them.

Hart fired a burst at the thing, cutting its great rack loose from its head, blasting its chest into chopped liver. "A fucking hunter's nightmare," he said as the centaur crashed to the snow.

"Okay, Job," Ez whispered. "No more blood:
"And oh, sweet tastes horrid war's wine crimson
Do pride and duty mixed with death so clash?
Does the sound of tank crushed corpses sing music?
Can you hear the screams of souls rejoicing,
Lost demons moaning at their next new peace?
More happens than two brothers opposing."

Ezra Pound gasped silent, out of breath, drained.

"Thirty seconds," Washy said.

He buried his head in the snow, hugging the rock. Then the nukes went.

Chapter 20

Ez forgot about the snow.

The two ADAMs ignited within seconds of each other, the Squad A nuke exploding first. A shock wave of intense heat obliterated the gravel and topsoil of the ridge underneath the artillery battery; the shock wave thrust the minced mountain upward and out, shredding the forest into sawdust, and crumpling the cannons into exotically flexed pipe cleaners. The soldiers manning the guns disappeared into small clumps of molecules mixed with the ice and rock and snow.

Hugging the snow behind the knob of rock, Hart and Ez and Washy saw the explosions first: the burst of two suns flashing on the mountain. The sound came next, a low rumbling that built to the noise of a titan's fist pounding the earth. It reminded Ez of an earthquake he'd felt once near Pisan, a growling shaking in the ground, and suddenly — *thwack!* — someone playing crack-the-whip with the world.

Ez's parka got warm for a moment as the thermal flash washed over them, the deep cold of Lake de Born quickly rolling back. Up in the hills, the sound of an ocean surf roared. Ez raised his head.

Two clouds flashing with lightning rose to the south and west, flat thunderheads capping them. A faint smell of ozone, the smell of storm clouds rushing across the sea, oozed down the hills. In the gullies and draws and creek beds the snow frothed.

"Shit!" Ez yelled. He jabbed Hart and Washy, pointed at the creek they had crossed earlier. "What the heck is that?"

Hart raised the night-vision goggles to his eyes, then let them dangle. "Lord Satan... It's a flood. A *flood*."

"Yes," said Washy, grinning. "Figuring about four feet of snow cover, and a thermal radius of a thousand feet, it should generate a small tsunami on the lake of..." he shrugged "oh, six feet high." Washy turned to Ez, smiled. "Altaforte's twenty feet above Lake de Born."

"Unholy shit," Ez said.

The creeks swelled, the melted ice and snow pouring down the mountain slopes, collecting in the valleys, and running down to the lake in a sudden spring. Ripping trees from the banks, tearing up clumps of small boulders, the rising rapids shot down to the lake. Standing on the knob rising between two gullies, Ez felt like a sailor astride the stern of a boat, the two creeks propellers churning up water behind a ship.

Six creeks emptied their load of rock and ice and water on the lake, six torrents washing across the smooth calm of de Born, joining in a wave that swelled into one surge, rising to the tops of the tanks. Ez grabbed the night-vision goggles from Hart, stared at the lake.

Richard Coeur de Lion's troops turned, looked at the wave rushing toward them. Men fell before the onslaught, bodies tumbling, arms rising to their faces. The ground effect tanks screamed as their fans fought to climb the water, and then one tank, and another, slumped under as the wave rushed under the tanks' skirts. A turret on a Patton tank turned, snout pointed at the tsunami, and fired just as the front of the wave caught the tank broadsides, and flipped it over.

"Those miserable fools," Ez muttered, handing the goggles to Hart.

The nuclear surge spread out in an arc, the flanks rushing in, and it hit the walls of Altaforte. Altaforte. A boulder in a stream, it stood, the boiling waters of men and machines and rubble sweeping around it, spray rising on the castle's side. She held. Swirling around the island, flattening the causeways, the tsunami swept out across the lake, its force waning slightly as it rolled across in a smooth line to the opposite shore, to Richard's camps.

"There's a broad terrace on the opposite shore," Washy said to Ez. "Richard's built his camp there. It's about, oh, three feet above the lake's surface."

"You sure know your hydrology, don't you?" Ez asked.

"Built a bridge once or twice," Washy said.

The tsunami hit Richard Coeur de Lion's camp, a brief spray of water as it rolled over the lake shore. Hart stared through the night-vision goggles, handed them to Ez. He shook his head, imagined the water sweeping the tents down, imagined it knocking Richard's warriors off their feet. They might be able to stand above it, might be able to hang onto a tree and save themselves, but he doubted it. He'd seen a hurricane once, seen what a storm surge could do to a man. Maybe a soldier could climb a tree, maybe he could lash himself to its upper branches, maybe he could stand the onslaught of water. And maybe he could climb down, find enough wood, and dry himself before his skin froze.

Maybe, Ez thought. Maybe.

The tsunami fell back down from the opposite slopes of Lake de Born, one surge canceling the other, and spreading out north, toward the main body of the lake, the waters dissipating, dying, settling. A dull sheen of rippling water drifted over Lake de Born, trees and rocks and twisted bodies poking up from the quickly freezing ice.

"Poor, miserable bastards," Ez said.

Washy looked at Ez, nodded.

"'War is Hell, Vic,'" Hart said. They glared at him. "*A Boy and His Dog*." He shrugged. "Saw it at the New Hell Bijou once."

*

They came down to the lake where a road from the south ended in a ramp sliding down to the ice to what had been the beginning of the east-west causeway. A group of soldiers straggled up the trail; Ez ducked back into the woods, whispered into his mike. "B Squad, you coming up the south road?"

"Rabbit here — yo," he said. "Who's that?"

"Sergeant Pound, with Roebling and Crane." They stepped out into the road, waved at the men.

Rabbit, some guy named Frost, and a limping soldier Ez remembered was Tully, came up to them. Rabbit jerked his gun at the lake. "You see that?"

They nodded. "Tsunami," Washy said. "It was calculated. That's why Barker gave the order to hold our position — he knew we had to be off the lake — or in Altaforte — before the nukes hit."

"Shit," said Rabbit. "Half our squad was covering for us from the top of a draw south of our battery."

Rabbit dialed his radio frequency to the platoon channel. "Guess we ought to do an all-hail." Ez turned to the frequency, listened to the white hiss as Rabbit said, "Alpha Platoon, Alpha Platoon, this is B Squad leader. Report your position. Repeat: Alpha Platoon, report your position." The six men stood, ears cocked. Rabbit whacked the side of his helmet, repeated the message; then: "Nothing."

"Maybe the EMP zapped their radios," Tully said.

"No electromagnetic pulse at ground zero, Tully," Washy said. "Especially with an ADAM."

"Shit," said Rabbit.

"Maybe they're in the castle," Hart said.

"We'd better be," Washy said. "ADAMs don't kick up a lot of fallout, but you don't want to be in the hard rain anyway."

They poked their way down the ramp to the lake.

*

What was left of the platoon fanned across the ice. A sheen of water that hadn't quite frozen sloshed under their bunny boots. Ez scanned ahead with the night-vision goggles; the others followed, rifles raised.

"There's a *physeter* to the left," Ez said. They'd kept their helmet radios tuned to the platoon frequency; Ez thought of dialing in his private band to Bertrans, but he didn't want to find out about Barker and Q and the rest — yet. He wondered, though, if anyone in the fort was monitoring their frequency, and if they were, why they hadn't answered the all-hail.

Rabbit and Washy scrambled up to the ground effect tank, its back frozen into the ice, the barrel of its gun pointing up at a forty-five degree angle. One of the tank crew had blown the hatch, and a man dangled headfirst from the open cover, body covered in hoar frost. Rabbit scrambled up the tank, looked down in the hatch, shook his head and came back down.

Parts of the causeway still stuck above the ice, a jumble of rocks in a straight line toward Altaforte. Ez ran up to the cover of one rock, stepping around a head sticking up out of the ice like a carrot to be picked. He stopped, glancing at the helmet. Ice obscured the man's features, but the helmet didn't have any insignia.

"I found one of ours," he said. To his left, Rabbit signaled, came to him. He stooped down, cut the helmet loose.

"Marc," he said, reading the name inside the helmet. "B Squad." Rabbit shook his head, turned away.

Ez scanned the high walls of Altaforte, now looming before them. The ice skirting her borders reached high, in some places almost up to the parapets, but the castle had held. Her searchlights still were dimmed — no, shattered, Ez saw through the night vision goggles: a blast wave from the tsunami.

Alpha platoon assembled in front of Altaforte's portcullis. A wall of ice rose before them, sloping up to the roof of the portcullis. Rabbit stood to one side, muttering into his throat mike. The plea came clearly over the platoon channel, then the general channel: "Altaforte, Altaforte, this is Alpha Platoon. Let us in, please." Rabbit kept repeating the message, his voice getting higher.

"Shit, isn't anyone home?" he said. He yanked his helmet off his head, threw it down.

"They might be in the dungeons," Washy said.

"Might," Rabbit said. He looked up at the sky, a glowing cloud creeping toward them. "So how do we get in?"

Washy shrugged off his rucksack, pulled out two steel contraptions that looked like roller skates with claws instead of wheels. He strapped them to his boots, pulled an ice ax out of the ruck, then put it back on. "Climb," Washy said. "That's why the Evil Lord gave us crampons."

The six took out axes and crampons, hacked away at the tongue of ice leading up to Altaforte, and crawled up its walls. As they came up to the top, to the edge of the outer ramparts, they saw Bertrans de Born's head hanging from its hair on a pike.

"Welcome back," he said. The head turned, smiled at Ezra. "Sergeant Pound, do you have another stanza of your sestina for me? I'm dying" — he coughed — "to find out what you meant by 'More happens than two brothers opposing.'"

Ez shook his head. The rest of the platoon looked at him, leaning on their ice axes. "*Okay,*" he said:

"Deep in the night when armies cease opposing
Long after Heaven's light has quit crimson
Still after Bertrans himself has found peace
Then do senher niort and de Born quit clash
Until Papiols rises from death's rejoicing
Come to this Hell to strum his sweet music."

"What?" asked Bertrans. "What is the sound of Papiols's music?"

Ez sighed. "I don't know; it hasn't happened yet."

Bertrans nodded. "Fair enough. Why don't you jerks get into the dungeons before the fallout gets here." The six men climbed over the low wall of the ramparts. "And Pound" — Ez turned at his name — "bring my damn head inside, okay?"

*

Bertrans walked down the staircase, down to the great hall. Ez stood straight, his white camo cleaned, his rucksack at his feet. Roebling stood next, to his right, Hart to his left. He kept wanting to see Barker's blue hair out of the corner of his eye, wanted to hear him shout his orders, wanted to feel him kick his butt. Lord Bert passed in front of the platoon, now barely more than a squad. They clicked their heels, stood at attention.

"Task Force Eight Eighty, Alpha Platoon, ready for inspection, Sir!" Rabbit shouted.

"Very good, Lieutenant," Bertrans said. "As you were."

Lady Audiart floated behind Bertrans. Staring straight ahead, Ez saw her head flicker into solidity, first a woman with flowing brown hair, then the poetess Dickinson with her cropped blonde hair, then a woman with hair black at the roots, blonde in a top knot. Bertrans stopped before Ez. The Lady took out scroll and quill, held the pen poised over the parchment.

"You've had two weeks in the dungeon to think about the last stanza, Pound," he said. "Two weeks to rest. Two weeks to ponder our losses, our great victory. Two weeks to consider the great significance of this adventure. And what is your conclusion?" Bertrans set his head in its basket, and the head spun, the face changing and becoming the face of Job. "What is your conclusion, Ezra?"

"This," he said:

"This is the sound of the jongleur's music:
No more sword to sword, bullets opposing
No more heroes' battle yells rejoicing
Paradise herself all that drips crimson
And only lightning and thunder do clash
When this comes, then will the poets have peace."

Job nodded, and the head spun around and became Bertrans again. "Very good, Pound," he said. Lady Audiart's fingers flashed as she copied the last line down. "Very good. A fitting tribute to your comrades. 'Then the poets will have peace.' Excellent, excellent. Would that I could keep you as my jongleur."

Ez held up his hands. "Lord Satan has other plans for me."

"Yes, of course." Bertrans lifted his head out of its cage, held it up in the air. "Ah, I hear your plane coming. Gentlemen, thank you for your service. Your courage under fire" — he grinned at his pun — "will not go unnoticed. You have been *bathed* in combat." Bertrans chuckled. "Of such are heroes made. Go, my men. Go to your well-deserved rest."

"Tench-hut!" Rabbit shouted. Bertrans and his Lady climbed back up the staircase. "Fall out!" They picked up their rucks and left the great hall.

Outside, just inside the west portcullis, Ez watched the Hellcules prop plane circle the lake and come in for her approach. Paradise hovered over the hills to the west, where Richard's camp had been. The air pierced through the bottom of his lungs, a hard cold, clean and savage. He pulled the white wolf ruff of his anorak close around his face — the ruff Bertrans had awarded each of them, a small measure of his gratitude. On a sled lay Sarge Q, Barker, others of their platoon, wrapped in black body bags, crackly and stiff in the cold.

The plane powered back her props, came in over the tree tops, skis dangling at her wings and tail. She hit the ice, bounced, then settled down, skis cutting into the hoar frost on top of the lake. Ez could read the pock marked letters on her side: 'Bridge Airways.' He smiled. Good old Bridge. The pilot taxied the plane toward them, turned her tail, gunned the props, and swiveled around so the port side faced them. The aft door opened, and a stairway cranked down. The snow-machine driver pulled away from the castle, toward the plane.

"Okay, let's move it. Burning daylight!" Rabbit shouted.

Ez and his platoon scrambled across the ice, heads down. The aircraft's pilot gunned the props, and out of the corner of his eye, Ez saw Washy stumble and fall. The props quieted down, and a crack-crack-crack came from the woods just north of Altaforte.

"Move it, move it," Rabbit shouted. He swung his Hellishnikov out, laid down covering fire. Frost pulled out his M-666 rifle, supporting Rabbit.

Ez turned, looked at Washy. He lay face down in the snow, one arm clawing the air. A bullet struck north of him, then another south — the sniper was getting his range. A blotch of crimson spread across the back of Washy's white camo. His right leg jerked, and another spot of red sprouted on his body. Ez looked back up at the snowmachine and sled. The driver unloaded the last of the bodies onto the plane.

He ran to the plane, jumped on the snowmachine, turned the throttle hard, and pulled away from the plane. The sled swung around, scraping the plane's side. Ez yanked harder on the throttle, ducked down in the snow-machine. Something made a pock-pock sound on the sled; he jerked the handlebars hard to the left, then to the right, zig-zagging across the ice, and pulled up next to Washy.

Rabbit ran up to the snow-machine, Frost firing quick bursts at the forest. The Hellcules roared, taxied toward them. Ez rolled off the snow-machine, landed on his face next to Washy.

"You still with us?" he asked.

"Yeah," Roebling said. "Yeah. Get me out of here, General."

"Right, Washy." Ez looked up at Rabbit, nodded. They pulled him up to the sled, swung him onto it. Rabbit jerked his head back at the sled.

"Hang onto him, Ez," he said. "You want me to drive this thing — I *know* snowmobiles."

Ez grinned at Rabbit, laid down on the bottom of the sled, holding onto Washy. Rabbit hit the engine, turned around in a broad arc, came up alongside the taxiing aircraft, its starboard side between them and the sniper to the north. The plane slowed, and the snow-machine stopped at the open hatch. The snow-machine's original driver hopped off, helped them load Washy onto the plane, then jumped onto the snow-machine and sped for the safety of Altaforte.

Inside the air transport, Rabbit and Ez dragged Washy onto a litter. The platoon's medic ran down the aisle, canvas bag tucked under his arm. He pushed Ez and Rabbit aside, started ripping Washy's pants and jacket open.

"Okay?" Ez asked.

The medic nodded. "He's not going to snuff it yet."

"Ezra..." Washy said. "Your sestina isn't complete."

"I know," Ez said.

"Three lines. What are the last three lines?"

The co-pilot came down the aisle back to them. "You guys want to get strapped in so we can get the fuck out of here?"

"Right," said Rabbit. "*Ez...*"

"Okay, Washy:

"Rising, opposing, cries to Paradise clash
Seize our sins, purge our peace, redeem our souls
In crimson's music, lead us rejoicing."

Washy smiled as the medic pumped morphine into him. "Rejoicing, rejoicing..." he said, drifting into bliss.

"*Now,* gentlemen."

"Okay, Lieutenant — " Ez said, rising, glancing at the co-pilot's name tag: "*Papiols.*"

The Bridge Airways transport throttled up her engines and took off into the dawn.

Chapter 21

Worthless. Worthless! What good is it to be a vision when that vision cannot speak, cannot be more than a wisp? Lady Audiart. Who writes the rules of these little hells? Is it Job? Is it Satan? Is it the Bridge? One would think — *think* — that dear Ezra Pound would froth at the sight of his Audiart, the lady of his poem incarnate. *No*; such is carnality. Damned to be Bertrans' Lady, I can only move seductively while Pound comes and goes from battle. He barely *notices* me, and do we ever get alone? Never. Given a moment alone with him — it would have been fair — and I would have had him. Pound; that other seduction, Battle, War, *she* takes him, caresses him, and tries her tricks. At least there is justice. At least he rejects War, too.

War! W.A.R.! What irony! Oh, this is silly; I should never have thought I could corrupt Ezra Pound, the vainglorious madman. No worry. The way home dawns for me.

Emily. That mousy little poetess, Emily. I have kept my claws in her all along. We shall see, Job, what I do with her. I shall romp in her head, corrupt her, change her, alter her into the woman she should be. Yes, she will become my Marilyn, this W.A.R., this anima, this shadow will travel into Miss Emily, take her, make her, and we'll go back to New Hell and show Satan what's what.

Let me at Emily. Go ahead, Bridge, give her back to me. I *dare* you.

Chapter 22

The dingy aluminum bus pulled into the station. Emily Dickinson leaned against the greasy window, pushing away from the brown-haired woman sleeping on her shoulder in the seat next to her. She rubbed the grime off the window, peering out at the terminal.

Broken amber bottles and flattened silver cans littered the pavement around the building. A cracked concrete patio underneath a tin awning awaited the arriving bus. Pushing a rusty cart, a fat man in a yellowed planter's suit, his string tie cinched tight around his fat red neck, moved slowly out from the terminal. Bullet holes pocked the back wall, and plywood over the windows splintered into long slivers. Hanging above the windows on two doubtful bolts was a sign that read: 'Och Titlan.'

A reddish-brown stain smeared one piece of plywood. Two men in dark blue business suits waited for the bus. One foot up against the wall, Sturm and Drang assault rifle at his side, a merc sucked in the last toke of a cigarette, then flicked it over at the two men, the butt landing in the pants cuff of the taller of the two and slowly smoldering. The man shook his leg and the butt fell out. He turned and glared at the merc; the merc spat. The bus creaked to a stop, and the driver, a slick-haired man in black-rimmed sunglasses, opened the door and stepped out.

Emily sat up in her seat, waited for the bus to empty out. The woman next to her stirred. Tapping her gently on the shoulder, Emily woke her. The brown-haired woman blinked her eyes, ran a thin hand through her shoulder length hair.

"We're here, Norma," Emily said.

"Huh? Yeah, 'Old Chitlan.'" Norma brushed dandruff off the shoulders of her navy jacket, tightened the scarf around her neck. "You getting off here, Emily?" Emily nodded. "What are you going to do?"

"I don't know. Clerk. Wait tables. Write poetry." Emily shrugged. "Got any ideas?"

The brown haired woman in the blue blazer opened her tan briefcase, handed Emily a card. "Try this place. They always need help."

Emily glanced at the card, put it in a pocket of her black jumpsuit. "Thanks," she said, standing up.

A half-dozen young kids in old blue jeans and sweatshirts moved up the bus aisle. One guy rubbed the back and sides of his head, and a tall girl with pumped-up muscles tugged at the inch-long hairs of her flat top. Their scalps gleamed pale and shiny under the short haircuts. Recruits on their first leave, Emily thought. One soldier glanced at her, smiled. Emily smiled back, reached up into the overhead rack for her leather valise. The soldier suddenly grabbed the bag, helped her take it down. She smiled at him again, turned to Norma.

"See you," she said. What was that phrase the New Dead used? Emily thought. Oh yeah. "Later."

"Later," Norma said. "Good luck."

Emily shuffled up to the front of the bus. The driver straightened when he saw her descend the steps, stuck his cigarette in his lips, and helped her down, shoving an old lady aside.

"Miss," the driver said. "Welcome to Och Titlan."

"Don't listen to him," the mercenary said, waiting to board. "Folks around here call it 'Titland.' And looking at you" - he stared down at her breasts and smiled - "you're gonna fit right in."

The driver turned from Emily, glared at the merc. "Weapons go below, soldier."

Shaking his head, the merc slung his rifle over his shoulder. "Like I said, don't listen to him." He boarded the bus.

Stopping by the door into the terminal, Emily turned, looked back at the bus. On the side of it, below the windows, the palimpsest of a dog's leaping form showed through a thin coat of gray paint. Emily smiled. The dog reminded her of Carlo, Carlo who had died in that attack on the trading caravan weeks ago. Over the image of the dog a crude picture of a two-towered bridge had been painted, and next to it the bus company's name: Bridge Bus Lines.

The driver lowered his shades to stare at her, tipped them back up, smiled, and got on the bus. It backed out of the terminal and down the causeway, away from the island city, into the hills surrounding the lake Titland was in the middle of. Emily went inside the terminal.

Plastic covered seats, the stuffing exploding through rips in the fabric, lined the center of the waiting lounge. A man dressed in six layers of clothes lay curled up on five chairs. Next to him sat a woman in a gray jacket, tightly clutching a tan attaché case. She glanced up at Emily and quickly looked away, her shoulder-length gray hair bobbing with the motion.

Against one wall was a row of lockers, most of them missing doors, a few hanging on bent hinges. A line of white haired ladies, the kind of person who worked behind counters in state bureaucracies, waited for the baggage claim office to open. Something rubbed against Emily's leg and she looked down to see a big black cat slink by, a rat almost as big as it in the cat's jaws.

A wall on her right had a big bulletin board with tattered notices, and on either side of the board were doors marked 'Men,' 'Women,' and 'Whatever.' Emily waited for a woman to come out of the lady's room, then walked in. She stepped over a puddle of puke and up to a sink. The silvering had eroded from around the edges of the mirror, but she could still see her image. Emily frowned, set her valise on the sink, and took out a small toilet kit. She brushed her short blonde hair, combing out the tangles, then sprayed it with that sticky stuff Mister Frank had used on her.

Pulling out a gold lamé dress and a pair of spike heels from under a distressed brown leather jacket in her bag, she started to pull off her boots, looked at the puke again, and thought better of it. She lifted up the jacket and an Ezekiel automatic mini-submachine gun beneath it, and then put heels and dress back in her bag, gun and jacket on top. Emily unbuttoned another button on her black jumpsuit, reached down in the bottom of her toilet kit, and slipped a string of fake pearls over her head. OK, she thought. Classy and cool.

At the curb outside the terminal, Emily took out and read the card Norma had given her. 'Bert's Disco,' the card read, 'Exotic Dancers — Girls - Boys Girls!' A man in a blue suit strolled past her, flicked his eyes quickly in her direction, straightened his shoulders, and hurried on. Another silver bus went by, diesel belching as it shifted gears, a harsh sulfur smell wafting through the air. Emily waved for a cab, and a battered lime-green sedan with fins pulled up at the curb. She got in, handed the card to the driver.

"Take me there," she said.

*

The cab pulled out onto the main causeway running west out of town, turned north, and after a few miles stopped at a driveway hooking around an upside-down pyramid. A broad parking lot covered a swampy area east of the pyramid, and the front of the pyramid faced the swamp and the lake. Emily paid the driver with a dime diablo, walked up to the discotechque. A pink neon sign that said '*Bertrans*' in art-deco cursive lettering buzzed in a little window just to the left of oak double doors. She tried the door, rattling the thumb-switch lock. It didn't open. A bras gryphon's head door knocker stared down at her, and she rapped it against a plate. The gryphon opened its mouth, flicked out a tongue, and licked her palm. Emily jerked her hand back. Ruby eyes fluttered open and tracked her.

"Yessss?" the gryphon head asked.

"I'd - I'd like to see the manager, please," she said.

"Do you have an appoint... ment?"

"No."

"Come back... laa-ter."

Emily glanced up at the eaves of the awning over the door, noticed a video camera panning across the entranceway. "A Miss" - What was the name of that woman on the bus? She thought - "Uh, Norma, yes, Miss Norma Jean told me I should come here."

"Miss Norma Jean? That tight-assed little bitch?" The gryphon curled its lips and spat, the spittle hissing on the concrete walkway and burning a pit in the pavement.

Damn, Emily thought. She looked around, couldn't see any other doors on the front. Maybe around back? No. Ah, of course, she thought. Reaching into her valise, she felt the cold plastic handle of the minigun, then grabbed a velvet pouch and pulled it out.

"Hungry?" she asked the gryphon, holding out a silver quarter-diablo.

"Yesss," it said, opening its jaws and sticking out its tongue as if taking the sacrament. "Pleassse. Yesss." Emily laid the coin on the knocker's tongue, and it clamped its mouth shut. The coin rattled down a chute inside the door. "More? Pleassse?" Emily fed it another quarter. "Gooood. Thank you very much." The latch clicked and the door swung open.

A man with a tiger face glared at her. Emily stepped back, breathed slowly, smiled. The tiger man held the door open, motioning her in, his arms spreading enough for her to see a long-barrel magnum pistol in a shoulder holster. Emily glanced over at him, checking out his face again. Whirls and lines outlined the contours of his high cheekbones, the sharp relief of his chin. He'd greased his hair into a thick topknot, some sort of bone stuck through the knot.

Queequeg, she thought.

"I know you?" he asked.

"I don't think so," she said, stepping inside. "I'm new in Och Titlan. Miss Dickinson - Emily Dickinson."

"Titland," he said, correcting her. "*Miss* Emily?" He snorted. "Call me 'Q.' Do you want to see Bert?"

Emily nodded. "About a job. A friend told me he always needs help."

"Yeah," Q said. "High turnover." He smiled, patted the revolver. "Rough clientele." He turned, waved at a glass elevator to the right. "This way."

They walked past a coat check stand, a chain-link barricaded armory behind it, through a metal detector that Emily hoped was off, and by a staircase opening up into a main ballroom. The elevator doors opened, and Q touched his thumb to a depression in the control panel. The elevator descended, the view of a pit-like dance floor quickly passing by.

"Let me hold your bag," Q said. Emily smiled, handed it to him. He snapped it open, pulled out her gun. "N-Mini Ezekiel. Nice choice." He slid back the action and peered into the chamber. "Nobody home. Good." Q ejected the magazine, slipped it in his pocket, handed her back the submachine gun and the valise.

"If Bert hires you, you can keep the sidearm in your room. No guns upstairs in the disco." Q pulled back his lips, showing two gleaming gold canines. "Well, almost no guns."

The elevator stopped at a long hallway, and the door slid open. Q walked down the hall, stopped at a heavy oak door, cast iron bars set in the wood, and rapped on a brass knocker, a twin to the one upstairs.

"Entrez," a voice said from inside. "Barker, let them in."

A bolt slid back from the inside, and a tall man with blue hair, pale orange skin, and photo-flash red eyes pulled the door open. A Devil Imp .44-magnum automatic pistol hung in a holster on his belt, the strap across it unsnapped. Q nodded at the blue-haired man. The man looked Emily up and down, then nodded and let them back in.

"Lady to see you," Q said. "About a job." He lead Emily up to a massive hemlock desk.

A tall, thin man, hair brushed back with a razor-carved widow's peak, stood up. He had a neatly trimmed goatee under thick, puffy lips. Around his neck he wore a bright purple scarf wrapped tightly.

"Mademoiselle," he said, bowing. "I am Bertrans de Born. En Bertrans. Bert, if you wish." He stepped out from behind the desk.

She held out her hand. "Miss Dickinson. Emily."

Bertrans held her hand to his lips, fluttered his lips over it, spit flecking her skin. Emily stood straight, shifting her weight back and forth. Bert lifted up her pearls, let them fall back on her chest, his fingers flicking across her cleavage.

"Charming, charming," he said. "You seek a position?"

"Yes. I'm willing to work in most any job. In New Hell, I... well, I worked at the library, and in my free time, wrote poetry."

"Ah, a poet?" He touched her hair, pushed her chin up, and nodded. "Excellent, excellent. Well, we have no openings for poets here, not those who use words ..." Bert laughed at his little joke. "But we do have some interesting positions, interesting. Are you - how do I phrase this delicately? Would you be willing to work in our recreational division?"

Q coughed. "Lord Bertrans means..."

"I know what he means," Emily said, blushing and looking down.

"I see," Bert said, smiling at her embarrassment. "Well, we always need waitroid units - barmaids, waiters, bar-things. Do you have any problem with that?"

"Oh, no. That's fine." Emily looked up.

"Good. Pay's six diablos a week, room and board and costumes included." He turned, sat back down behind his desk. "See, Miss Emily, at Bert's we like a consistent theme, so you'll be playing dress-up a lot. Q will take you to Trixie - she's the artistic director - and Trixie and Mister Hart will set you up."

Q and Emily moved toward the door. "Wait," Bert said. "There's one thing you should know, Miss Emily." He reached up, unwrapped the scarf from around his neck. A thin gap, almost like a wire necklace, showed at the base of his neck. "Just so you aren't surprised."

Bert pulled his head away from his neck and tossed it across the room to Barker. Emily jumped back, held a hand up to her mouth. Bert chortled.

His head spoke to her from Q's hands. "A little defect, Miss Emily. 'I bear my brain / divided from its source.' Check your Dante. The Gideons have obligingly put a copy in every-one's room." Bert walked over to Barker, took his head, and put it back on his neck. "Be seeing you."

*

Q led her around twisty passages and to a gymnasium area. A woman with short, tight red curls led four rows of men and women in an aerobic workout. Some sort of music with a thumping bass beat boomed out of loudspeakers in the ceiling. They contorted their bodies in an exercise that involved bend-ing their necks around their ankles.

"Trixie?" Q asked.

"And a fifty-and-one and a fifty-and-two - bend those thighs, Darlene - and a fifty-and-three - that's right, feel the burn," the redhead said.

"Trixie."

The redhead turned, stopped, twisted out of position, and stepped over to Q with lean, cat-like steps. "What, Q?" she asked over the music.

"New meat. Miss Emily. Fix her up." He nodded at Emily, reached into his pocket, and handed her the clip from her pistol. "Good luck," he said, and walked away.

"Well, Miss Emily. Welcome, honey." Trixie gave her the long glare Bert had given her. "You, uh, in recreation?" Trixie glanced over at the group, still gyrating away. "Good, good," she yelled at the dancers. "Robbie, take over." She put an arm to Emily's back, steered her down a corridor off the gym floor. "Well?"

"No, ma'am," Emily said. "Barmaid."

"Barmaid? Fine." They passed by a room with steam oozing out. "Showers. Don't hog the hot water. Mess is up the hall. Meals are three times a day, open snack bar, but don't overdo it - you'll be penalized if you're overweight, a dime a pound." Trixie stopped in front of an open dutch door, banged a bell on the counter. "What size are you?"

"Eight."

"Shoes?"

"Seven."

A dark-haired woman in pink leotards stepped up to the door. "Eight, seven in shoes," Trixie said, looking at Emily again. "Uh, tiger camo, lamé." The dark-haired woman nodded, rummaged through a bin, and handed Trixie a plastic package and a pair of shoes.

They continued down the hall, halted at a red door. "Your quarters. It's a single." Trixie pushed the door open, waved at a narrow bed, a dresser, a chair, and a small closet in the corner. She handed Emily the package. "Go ahead and get settled. Change into this. I'll be by before we open and we'll go see Mister Hart. Punk - circa nineteen seventy-seven, not that twenty-first century stuff - is the look this month." Trixie grinned. "I hope you like purple hair."

*

The walls of Bert's boomed with the beat of a million bass guitars screaming on overdrive. Mister Hart scurried around a room stinking of hairspray and greasepaint, men and women sitting before a bank of mirrors applying make up, barmaids and hookers and dancers running back and forth across the room. Trixie led Emily into costuming.

"Showtime," Trixie said. "You just hustle drinks, hon, so Mister Hart's not going to do too much with you."

Emily looked down at her legs, at the silver leather high-top shoes and the tiger camo pattern of her tights and leotard. Her back felt cool where the leotard plunged, and the v-neck in front didn't offer much more insulation. She scratched at the stubby hairs on her nape.

"Mister Hart," Trixie said. "New one for you."

Mister Hart stood over a woman with waist-length fluorescent orange hair. A cigarette dangled from the corner of his mouth, ashes falling onto the shoulders of his black floppy jacket. He looked up, pushed a lock of hair back from his fore-head. Electric shears buzzed in his hand and, as he glanced at Emily, he pulled up a section of long hair and buzzed it away. He flicked at the shorter hair with a wide comb, held it steady and clipped the top of her mane into an inch-high flat top.

"Let me finish up here," Mister Hart said. He smeared some gel into the orange locks, poking it into little spikes. "Okay, Bambi," he said to the woman. "Get out of here." He patted the seat. "Next."

Emily gulped, sat down. Hart, she thought. Hart Crane, that poet - the one who'd killed Marilyn. She glared at him. Bastard. Hart looked at her, squinted, then grinned.

"First time at Bert's?" he asked, putting a black plastic cape around her.

"Uh, yeah." *This* killed Marilyn? she asked herself. It wasn't him, not really, not that cool assassin she'd met in Pompeii. Emily relaxed, smiled back at Mister Hart. Harmless, she thought. Harmless Hart. "First time."

"Well, you're gonna love it here." He stood before her, sucked on his cigarette, clippers still humming in his hands. The clippers shimmered, changed into a chainsaw, and Hart's image shifted. His head turned around, and his face became that of a gray bearded man, that man on the Bridge.

"Miss Dickinson?" he asked. "Does it seem to fall into place for you? You wanted to break out of your shell? Well, here you are: a hard place, a tough place." He jerked the chainsaw's starter cord, and the sharp little teeth on the chain whirled around and around on the track of the chain bar. "This is where all the people who have broken out of their shells come. This is where they take their rest. This is where they grapple with the beasts inside them. This is it, Miss Dickinson: pure, raw, savage emotion. Do you want this? Write of this, Miss Dickinson. Write of this, not your silly little rhymes about death. Write of savage emotion."

"Mister Ombudsman...," she said. "I —"

"You want transformation? You want change? You want redemption?" Job lowered the chainsaw toward her, touched it to a lock of hair curling away from her neck. The ends of the hair blew away. "You don't know what you want, Miss Dickinson, but I know. Write me about love, Miss Dickinson. Write me... a sonnet." He grinned. "If you can. Yes, write me a classic Shakespearean sonnet. Then you may become the soul you are supposed to be." Job pulled the chainsaw away from her neck, let the motor idle. His head whirled around and became Hart Crane once again.

"Yes, indeed," Hart said. "You'll love it here." He looked at her, combed his fingers through her blonde hair. "Hey, some dark roots here. Nice cut, though. Hate to mess it up." He gunned the chainsaw. "But why not? It's Punk Month!"

"Please," Emily said. "No." And a voice insider her echoed: No, don't destroy me; don't destroy Marilyn.

"What? No? Not even, say, clipped at the sides, little spikes on the top?" The chainsaw became electric shears again, and he hummed them over her neck.

Emily jerked her head away. "No."

"Oh, okay. I'm just kidding. You're a bar maid. We don't need to fuss too much. But let's clean up the back here."

He ran the clippers over her nape, trimming the hairs that had grown long there, and set down the electric shears. Hart squirted some foamy purple stuff on her hair and worked it in: "Ah, mousse. I love the smell of mousse in the morning." Hart molded her into a mess of spikes and random tufts of hair. The coloring in the mousse gave her platinum-blonde hair a purple tinge. He ran a blow dryer over her hair.

"Okay, it's cool," Hart said. "Knock 'em dead. Trixie! Get this girl the rest of her outfit."

Hart swept the cape off Emily. She touched stiff spikes and erratic clumps of hair, looked at herself in a mirror, grimacing at the odd color.

"Showtime," Trixie said, leading Emily to a rack of skimpy skirts.

"That was close," Emily said.

"The color will wash out. You should have seen the month we did the French Revolution." She laughed, looked back at Hart, who ran the clippers over the ears of a woman with a foot-high fan of hair.

"Woo-hah!" Hart said. "It's Mohawk time!"

*

The disco rose up from the dance floor at the center of Bert's: an inverted pyramid, each floor opened up on the floor below it, so that from the domed ceiling the building appeared to be a square pit, each floor a ledge, the stage at the center. A glass elevator in each corner rode down slanted tracks to the bottom. The top two of eight floors had windows overlooking the center atrium of Bert's. Prostitutes lounged in the windows, the boys and girls beckoning to the patrons, who had binoculars on every table for the clientele to examine the local talent better. Open stairways rose up to the next floor in each corner, and the mercenaries and camp followers and battle-weary old men and women circled the great pit of Bertrans', cruising for a cheap thrill, around and around and around.

Emily worked a cluster of tables on the fourth level, her station a bare spot of counter at the bar running around the entire edge. Inside cages hanging from the domed ceiling naked dancers shimmied to the slow number playing from the band below. A small cluster of couples hugged each other on the floor. Above the bar, a smoke-eater crackled, a demon licking its lips as it sucked in the thick, smoky air.

Dangling from her feet, a woman swung back and forth on a trapeze, her silver braid swishing into the faces of a group of grunts as she moved from balcony to balcony. One soldier pulled out a knife, made a half-hearted swipe at the woman.

Barker, working the floor that night, grabbed the grunt's knife hand and slammed it down on the table edge. The knife tumbled over the balcony, where a beam of intense ruby light whisked out at it, vaporizing it before it hit the floor.

Emily stood by the table, biting her lips. Barker motioned to her and she moved forward.

"Don't mess with the talent," he said to the man. "Not while they're performing." He jerked his chin at Emily. "Tell the lady you want a drink."

The soldier looked at Barker, at his hand pinned to the table. "I, uh, want a drink."

"Tell her you want to buy your buddies a round."

"Yeah, sure," the soldier said. He tried to pull his hand out of Barker's grasp.

"What will your buddies have?" Barker looked at them, then up at Emily.

"Scotch."

"Whiskey."

"Uh, bourbon."

"Why don't you get a bottle of Diabhalvulin?" Barker asked. "Say, maybe a nice eighteen-year-old bottle? Emily's new here and she can't remember all those complicated orders."

The soldier nodded. "Sure, sure. That sounds nice."

Barker released the man's hand. "Enjoy yourselves, boys. And don't forget to tip Miss Emily nice, okay?" He moved off, toward two women clawing at each other.

Emily went to get the grunts' order - a whole diablo a bottle, she remembered - and glanced over at a gray-haired man in a quaint blue uniform sitting by himself at a table near the railing, sipping a bottle of pilsner beer. He caught her eye, held up a finger, pointed at the bottle. She smiled, set her tray down at the station.

"Bottle of Diabhalvulin 18, four glasses, and a pilsner," she said to Rabbit, the bartender.

He reached above the bar, pulled down the Scotch, kicked open a fridge behind him, took out the beer, and set everything on her tray. She popped the beer bottle cap, and he handed her four shot glasses, a fresh beer glass.

"Diablo and five," he said.

Emily opened up the coin box on her tray, counted out the change. "That guy over there," she said, pointing at the gray bearded man. "He come here every night?"

"Every night for the past two weeks," Rabbit said.

"He ever *do* anything?" she asked. "I mean, go upstairs, dance — anything?

"Sometimes he orders some potato skins," Rabbit said. "Mostly..." He pointed at him. The gray-bearded man had taken up a pair of binoculars and scanned the windows above. "Mostly he just watches."

"But he doesn't go upstairs?"

Rabbit shook his head.

"So what's he doing, looking for something?"

"You got it," Rabbit said.

Emily took the bottle of Diabhalvulin over to the grunts, set the glasses down, then took the pilsner to the gray-haired man.

"Your beer, sir," she said.

He set down the binoculars, glanced up. A spotlight played its beam across her face. Emily felt the brief glow from the light, was conscious of its hard glare highlighting every blemish on her face. She touched the dark roots of her hair against her scalp. The man squinted at her, his mouth dropping open. Her face passed back into shadow again. He shook his head.

"Something wrong?" Emily asked.

"No," he said. He pushed his empty glass and bottle back at her. She set the chilled glass down, poured beer into it. "It was just that for a moment there you looked like... well, my wife." He waved at an empty chair. "Please, sit down."

"I can't. I..." She looked over at Barker.

The man followed her gaze, smiled. "I see." He pushed a diablo at her. Barker nodded.

"Well, it's about time for my break." Emily sat down. "You seem to come here often, um, Mister...?"

"Roebling. Colonel Washington A. Roebling." He half rose from his chair, bowed. "And you are Miss Emily?"

She touched her name tag. "Yes."

"That's my wife's name - Emily." He took a sip of his beer, wiped a foam mustache from his clean-shaven upper lip.

She shrugged. "It's a common name. Is your wife here in...?"

"Old Titlan? I think so. We were separated because - because of the war. But I'm on leave, and I understood she had taken a job here." Roebling pursed his lips, took out a photo from his wallet. "I think she's a recreation specialist. You wouldn't by chance have met her?" Roebling handed her the photo.

Emily sucked in her breath, seeing the photo. The woman with the dark brown hair piled into a bun, the handsome face, and the deep brown eyes looked just like the woman she'd met on the bus — 'Miss Norma Jean,' she called herself. Emily shook her head.

"I don't know... I haven't seen anyone like that at Bert's, but I don't know the people upstairs well. Sometimes their appearance is a bit altered. I'll ask around." Emily looked over at Barker again. "I'd better get back to work." She stood, picked up the diablo, slid the photo back to him. "Thanks, Colonel."

"May I see you later? After your shift?"

"Sir, I'm not supposed to, uh, fraternize. I'm just a bar-maid. Ask upstairs."

"Oh no," he said. "I didn't mean that. Just to talk. That's all. I wanted to ask some more about my wife, see if maybe you know who she is."

"But if she's in recreation, you should ask *them*."

"I want to ask you. I think you know her." He smiled.

Emily sighed. "Okay. But not here. Meet me out on the pier, after closing."

The colonel pushed another diablo toward her. "Thank you, Miss Emily, for your trouble."

Emily took the second coin and walked over to another table where some women in leather were whistling at her.

*

A chill wind blew off the north end of the island, scream-ing through the channel between the pier and the mainland. Less than a mile away, the steady light of the ferry landing blinked back at Emily, a green spot whirling its beam on the hills, the island, the lake, the hills. Emily pulled her leather jacket tight around her, felt the butt of her little submachine gun digging into her side. "If you have a gun, use one," Q had told her.

Someone walking with a cane tapped his way up the pier toward her. Emily turned to see a man in light blue coming toward her. A spotlight from a corner of Bert's flickered across the pier, briefly lighting the man, then swung around again. Gray hair, shiny buttons, a broad trooper's hat: Roebling. Emily relaxed, stepped toward him.

"Miss Emily?" he asked. "Thank you for coming." He waved at a bench on the pier, near the ferry ramp. Roebling took out a handkerchief, dusted the seat. "Sit down, please."

She sat, unzipping her distressed leather jacket halfway, and put one arm along the back of the seat, leaning forward slightly, her hips away from Roebling, her knees jutting out toward him,.

"Your wife?" she asked, prodding.

Roebling nodded, sitting stiffly, head turned slightly to her. "The last campaign... I'd been away a long time, longer than I expected. The army was supposed to forward my pay to her, but the bureaucracy fouled up. Her letters were erratic, strange, but I understood that she had taken a job there" - he jerked his chin at Bert's - "at *that* place. I wrote her, told her I had some leave coming, that I would come here." Roebling smiled. "It's a favorite place with the DEVO-pact troops, Old Chitlan. All the young privates speak highly of it. I've been here two weeks, every night, and I haven't seen her. But she *must* be here."

"I'm new here myself, Colonel. And I'm not in recreation, as I told you."

"But you must see the prost - the recreation specialists. I understand they have dormitories, a cafeteria, many shared facilities. Surely you see some of the other women - and men - in recreation?"

"Well, yes, in the cafeteria, maybe in costuming... but I've only been here a few days."

"Please," Roebling said. "Look for her, for me. I'll reward you handsomely. You don't have to tell her anything. Just let me know. I think they're hiding her from me - Bert and his people. Maybe they've changed her appearance. I look at every woman, even the men - you never know. Look for..." The searchlight swung around again, shining on Emily's face. "Dark roots." He reached out, touched her bleached hair. "You look so much like her, so much."

Roebling ran his hands across the edge of her scalp, his fingers soft; not rough like other men, delicate. Catching a strand of her hair, Roebling pushed it back behind her ear and slid closer to her. Emily pulled her legs back, shifted her hips next to him, turned her face to his. The little voice inside her whispered, *Take him, take him.*

"So much like my Emily," Roebling said softly, his fingers moving through the hair at the back of her head.

"Colonel, I *am* an Emily. Please..." She felt a curious warmth in her thighs, *that* feeling oozing up her spine. "But not *your* Emily, don't you see?"

"Yes, yes," he said, his hand at her neck, rubbing the muscles there.

Something splashed below the pier. Emily turned at the sound, pulling away from Roebling. "Colonel, someone's below us."

Roebling smiled at her. "Washy. Please, call me 'Washy.' Emily did."

"Yes, yes, Washy. What is it?" She stood up, pulling out her submachine gun.

Roebling got up, grasping his cane, pointing down between the planks of the pier. "No need for that. It's nothing - smugglers, perhaps. Bert has an underground passage that comes out here, I understand." He reached into his coat pocket, took out a square photo.

"I'd better go," Emily said, slipping the gun back into her jacket. "Curfew." That feeling oozed up her spine, into her head, making her scalp and the ends of her hair tingle.

"Yes, of course. Take the picture, please." He held out the photo print, handed it to her. "If you see my Emily, I'm at the Pink Pussy Motor Court."

Emily took the photo, glanced at it. It was the same one he'd shown her in the club, the one that looked like Miss Norma Jean. How could she tell him she'd seen his Emily on the bus? She couldn't; she couldn't. He must have hope, had to believe she wasn't heading to... Emily knew where the men and women in the blue suits went. They went into the bowels of hell, into the bureaucracy, into deep cover. The Devil's Own, they were supposed to be. Lawyers, accountants, loan officers, that's what they were. A grunt like Roebling, even a colonel, didn't have a chance of finding her again, because if she wore the blue suit, she didn't want to be found - couldn't be found except by chance.

"If I see her," Emily lied. "I'll let you know."

She turned and walked away from him, up the pier.

Chapter 23

Mister Hart smeared the silver greasepaint into Emily's cheeks, rubbed it into her neck. She hated the feel of the make-up but liked the incidental massage. Silver greasepaint: the waitroids at Bert's wanted to lynch the idiot who had shown the boss a video of Fritz Lang's *Metropolis*. After seeing the robot woman, he'd gotten it in his head to do girl robots that week at the disco. The stuff itched and it ran when you sweated and if you got it in your eyes they burned. Emily leaned back as Hart brushed her hair and pinned it up.

"Getting some serious dark roots here, Emily," he said.

She knew that. It had been over a month since she'd been at Bert's; she counted the weeks by the schemes Bert came up with to torture the workers: that safari phase, jodhpurs and pith helmets; the mime week, when everyone saw their tips plummet because they couldn't speak; the brief Jackie Kennedy day with the pink pillbox hats. And now this: Metropolis, layers of carbon dioxide fog swirling around the floors, laser light shows, and silver greasepaint.

"Want me to fix 'em?" Hart asked.

"Yes," Emily said, echoing the voice in her head. "Um, no. No telling what Bert will be up to next. With our luck he'll get his claws on that World War Three movie and make us shave our heads." Emily shuddered; Trixie had told her about *that*, how they'd heard *Amazon Platoon* was supposed to be on Titland's cable network, and the rec specialists had seduced the cable programmer into "losing" the video. Hart spun her around, and Emily looked at herself in the mirror, seeing the reflection of Hart standing behind her. The image of him reminded her of the Ombudsman and his demand.

"Okay?" he asked.

"Yeah, fine," she said, shrugging. "Hart... You ever write a sonnet?"

"Why should I have?" He put a close fitting helmet on her head; little knobs stuck out over her ears, and a raised band stretched from ear to ear over the crown.

"Didn't you write poetry? I mean, you know, in —," she jerked her chin upward.

"Nah. Always did heads." Hart pasted little letters on the helmet: *'E-m-i-l-y.'* "But you... I read your stuff. Gloomy shit about death, always the same silly meter and rhyme. Did you know you can sing every one of your poems to the tune of *'The Yellow Rose of Texas'*?" His voice got squeaky as he sang, "'Because I could not stop for death / He kindly stopped for me...' Sheesh, Emily."

She cringed. "I happen to like iambic tetrameter."

"Oh, it's not a bad meter, but you sure ran it into the ground. A sonnet, though... *There's* a poetic form. You know my favorite? Shakespeare's One Thirty. I had to memorize it in ninth grade. It's really an anti-sonnet, though. Has the form but it's not Plutarchan, not all gushy and idealistic."

"Yes, One-hundred-thirty," she smiled. "'My mistresses' eyes...'"

"Shhh," he said. "Not like that. One mistress, okay?" He put the last letter on her helmet, stepped back, leaned against the counter, left arm across his waist, right elbow resting on left hand. He rubbed his chin, pointed. "Like this:

My mistress' eyes are nothing like the sun;
Coral is far more red than her lips red
If snow be white, why then her breasts are dun;
If hairs be wires, black wires grow on her head.

"I love that line, 'black wires grow on her head.' You see the irony, how Shakespeare builds the sensory image? This next quatrain's wonderful." Hart stood up, waved his hands, orating:

I have seen roses damasked, red and white;
But no such roses see I in her cheeks;
And in some perfumes is there more delight
Than in the breath that from my mistress reeks.

"*Reeks*," he said. "Shakespeare's a cruel bastard, isn't he? It gets worse."

I love to hear her speak, yet well I know
That music hath a far more pleasing sound;
I grant I never saw a goddess go;
My mistress, when she walks, treads on the ground.

"*Treads* on the ground?" Emily asked. "I'd forgotten that line."

"*Treads*," he said. "Makes her sound like a tank, eh? Wire hairs, treads. Ahh, but there's the concluding couplet, so beautiful in its honesty:

And yet by heaven, I think my love as rare
As any she belied with false compare.

"Wonderful!" She clapped her hands. "Very good, Mister Hart."

He bowed, a mock bow almost. "Shakespeare's poem, my performance. But a truly amazing little work. Horrid as the speaker makes his mistress sound, it's not affected, but ironic. And it's *his* mistress, dun breasts and all. Now you do one, just a quatrain."

"Now?"

"Sure. On your feet. Iambic pentameter, da-duh, da-duh, five measures to a line, end rhyme of ay-bee ay-bee. Hit it!"

"Uh..." She frowned, greasepaint crackling, thinking whom she could write about. Washy; okay, that odd man. "Okay — how's this?"

His eyes blaze not at all like Paradise
Deep thunder booms like his voice when it roars.

"Good, good. Get the rhyme right now: -ise, -oars."

Emily grinned, felt the words bubble up in her like they did when it hit right, when she'd found the spot at the back of her mind where the words came from, the ideas, the symbols, the metaphors. It came, better than sex, a crisping crinkling roaring orgasm of the head.

"Hands, toes, chin and cheek have the feel of... ice."

"Great! Great! Go on..."

"None will touch or bed him, not even..."

She laughed, leaned forward, pursed her lips together and blew the word at Hart. *"Not even... whores."*

"Fantastic!" Hart yelled. "Miss Emily, you are a marvel. I love it, I love it." He whirled the apron off her, waved her out of the chair. "Get out of here, sweetheart. I got heads and faces to do." She stood, and he pushed her toward Trixie, and the rack of robot suits, the silver clamshell forms with their airplane-fuselage bras.

*

Rabbit plunked six bottles of hell's most common beer and a pilsner on Emily's tray. "Busy night, yes?" he said.

She counted out the change to him. "No kidding. Seem to be a lot of grunts here."

Rabbit handed Emily her change. "I hear Bert made a deal with one of the generals. They like their soldiers to have a good time, but they don't like them getting too messed up. Bert guarantees their safety, doesn't let 'em get too trashed — or sick." He pointed upstairs. "Sam's Oasis down the way doesn't like it, though."

She waved at one of the barmaids serving a clump of tables opposite the section. The woman nodded, went on. Emily squinted at her. "That's Bambi, isn't it?" she asked Rabbit.

"Her station," he said. "Hard to tell with all that grease-paint but, yeah, that's the name on her helmet." He tapped the top of Emily's helmet. "It doesn't figure, though. She hasn't said much, and you know Bambi." Rabbit held up a hand, flickered his fingers like a chattering mouth.

"Huh. Maybe she has a cold." Emily took clean glasses from Rabbit, set them on her tray. "Lot of new help, isn't there? I don't recognize a lot of the waitroid units."

"Hard to keep track. You know, high turnover. You're an old timer now, Miss Emily."

"Yeah," she said. "Six weeks." She glanced over at a table where a woman with a pink flat-top was waving at her. "Got to go."

She served the beers to Pinky's table, took another order, then walked over to Washy, gave him his pilsner.

"Thank you, Miss Emily."

"Emily, Washy; just call me 'Emily,' okay?"

"Emily, then. Sit for a moment." He pulled an empty chair away from the table.

She looked across the room, across the balcony, beyond two trapeze artists in robot costume dangling from the ceiling, ruby smog rising around them, over to Barker leaning against the rail. "Can't," she said. "Too busy."

"Okay." She poured his beer into a stein; he raised it, took a sip. "You haven't seen —"

"*No*," she said, thinking, I can't tell you I've seen her. Emily looked at him, at his short gray hair, baby-smooth face, the ice-blue eyes; at the faint smile on his lips, the hope, the longing; at the nose twitching slightly at the smell of her, at the smell of the disco. He knows, she thought, the words of her sonnet's quatrain coming at her the way the poems sometimes came, not a gentle washing of words, but a thrust, a bolt out of the blue.

Through Hell's last quarter, Emily he seeks, she thought.
A couple, separated: lost or gone
What ill wind blowing from Bertrans' so reeks?
She's been there, he smells it, the missing one.

"No," she said again. "I haven't seen her — seen your Emily." Damn, she thought, It's getting harder to lie.

Washy nodded. "I just thought — well, with these robot costumes, she might slip in, you know."

Like Bambi, Emily thought. Washy might be right. She shook her head. "No, I don't think so. I would have noticed someone new in costuming, or in the cafeteria."

"Of course," Washy said.

She glanced over at Barker; he glared at her, jerked his head toward Rabbit. "Look, I can't talk now."

"See you later? At the pier?" He smiled.

"I —" She smiled back. "All right. But it looks like it will be a long night, and I have to wash this stuff off." She rubbed her face.

"I'll be waiting."

*

Washy and Emily met on the pier and strolled down a boardwalk running east. Paradise hovered on the north horizon, sliding over the edge of hell, bouncing back up, wobbling around, then bouncing up again, a chaotic perturbation. Two soldiers, man and woman, weaved toward them. The man held up a bottle, toasted them as he went by. Washy put an arm around Emily, pulled her close.

"Assholes," he said.

She shivered in the cold, moved toward his warmth. Yes, move toward his warmth, the little voice said. "They're just having a good time."

"They don't have to be so loud about it." He turned, glared back at them.

Emily and Washy passed under a bridge heading north, across the swamps and the lake to the opposite shore. The boardwalk wound around, in front of another disco. Loud music still boomed from the club, and patrons milled around on the lawn, shooting off firecrackers, whooping, couples necking and screwing in the grass.

"Sam's," Emily said. "They're supposed to be closed for the night; he's asking to get his license pulled."

Washy stopped, looked at a cluster of marines sitting on the lawn. "It's off limits to the military. Those kids ought to leave — the military police should be sweeping up soon."

"They're not technically *in* the club."

Washy smiled at her. "You talk like a lawyer; ever think of being one? My Emily wanted to be a lawyer once."

"Do we always have to talk about Emily?" she asked, putting an arm on his shoulder. Her scalp crackled with some odd electricity and her thighs grew moist.

"No, no, of course not." He leaned back from her, turned his head, looked at her funny. "It's just that — I thought... Well, I mean, aren't you supposed to be helping me find her?"

"Washy..." I should tell him, she thought. Tell him about Miss Norma. "Washy, I think you should know —"

"Emily!"

He whirled her around, moved in front of her. Something climbed up and onto the boardwalk: A thing, all scales and not much skin, plopped onto the decking. It dragged a tail longer than its body, swished it against the railing, knocking the posts down. Its teeth gleamed yellow, and red blood dripped from its claws as it slid silver dagger-claws in and out of its sheaths. Eyes flickered back and forth, focusing, stopping on Washy and Emily. The pupils dilated, and the thing hissed and scuttled toward them. Another like it crawled through the wrecked opening of the rail, and Emily heard thumpings beneath the boardwalk.

"What *are* they?" she screamed. She dug underneath her leather jacket for her submachine gun, cocking the Ezekiel as she yanked it out.

"Swamp demons? Shit, I don't know." Washy held his cane out at them, flicked a button on the cane's head. "We get them up in the swamps at the front, but I thought Titland had wiped them out."

The first demon advanced toward them. Emily and Washy walked slowly backwards, toward Sam's. Something pushed up on the decking next to them, and the plank creaked as it pulled loose from its nails.

"Can we make Sam's?" Emily asked.

Washy shook his head. "Inside? Not near enough. My motel's over there." He waved at a pink building, neon letters humming on a sign that said *'The Pink Pussy Motor Court.'*

"I've got — I've got a Hellishnikov assault rifle in there, if we need it. We'll have to run. Take out the first one. On three. One..."

"What's that cane *do*?"

"Shut up. Two, three!"

Emily held the submachine gun out, a shooting stance, fingers wrapped around fingers, and fired. Washy squeezed something on the head of the cane and a shot flamed out, hitting the lead demon's chest. A glob of jelly spread out over the chest and ignited. The thing clawed at itself, turned, rolled onto its stomach. Emily's three shots bit into it, the bullets digging into its left eye, its crotch, and into one shoulder. Washy had pulled back the head of the cane and was cramming another round into the gun's chamber.

Emily whirled, aimed her weapon at a claw bursting through the deck, and fired from three feet away. The claw whipped back, fingers shredding off, and slid back down the hole. The first demon rolled over again, chest up, on its back, and then its chest exploded. The thing twitched, paws flailing around, ripping the boardwalk up in its throes.

"Explosive bullets with a napalm tip," Washy said. "Banned by about eighteen military treaties in the world." He aimed his cane again at a third demon, Emily following his sight. "Take that one out and then let's get out of here." They let go with another volley. Washy's shot caught the demon in the head, and its face started flaming. Emily went for a heart-lung shot — if they had hearts and lungs — and ran as the demon tumbled backward over the edge.

*

The pink-neon sign flickered through the iron grating across the front window of Washy's room, casting long shadows across his chest. Emily ran a fingernail over his nipple, watching her hand like it was someone else's, numb and distant and aloof. She circled the nipple with her finger, pinched it. He reached up, touched her breast, flicked his tongue up at her, and pulled her down on top of him. Emily raised her eyebrows, rolled over off him, landing on her feet on the floor, and grabbed the Hellishnikov.

"*Again*?" he asked.

Cocking the rifle as she stepped to the door, she turned sideways, poked the barrel through the gun slit, and fired a burst across the parking lot, letting the barrel kick from side to side in the narrow opening. Two demons moaned, fell back. Emily pulled the assault rifle out, ejected the magazine, flipped it over, and slid a fresh magazine in.

"Yes," she said. She set the rifle down next to the bed and rolled on top of him, "*Again*, Washy." And the voice inside her echoed: Again, dear one, again. Though no climax could follow, affection in hell was rare and precious.

*

Paradise wobbled at a point in Titland's sky approximating high noon; yellow-orange light seared through the edges of the venetian blinds in Washy's window. Emily pushed two slats apart, looked out on the parking lot at the demons' bodies melting into the tarmac. A Bridge bus rumbled down the coastal highway. The sight of it jolted her, made her remember. She sighed and thrust her hands in the pockets of her jacket. Got to tell Washy, she thought. Enough lies and deception. He has to know.

"Washy..."

He came out of the bathroom, buttoning his gray pants, tucking a shirt tail in. His wet hair, slicked back from a widow's peak, gleamed in the harsh light. "Emily...?"

"Yes, Emily," she said. "Your loved one, me, *her*." She pulled the photo from her pocket, stared at it, handed it to him as he came across the room. "I've seen her."

Washy rushed to the window, pulled back the blinds. "Where? Out there?"

"No." She grabbed his shoulder, whirled him around, facing her. "On the bus, when I got here six weeks ago. She... Her hair was cropped at her shoulders, and she called herself 'Norma.' But it was her. I'm sure of it."

"My Emily?" He pulled back from her. "Why... why didn't you tell me?" Washy took her shoulders, shook her. "*Why*?"

"Your... your Emily wore a blue suit." He squinted at her, shook his head. "Do you know what the blue suit means, who the men and women in the blazers, the white shirts, the plain bows and ties, with the neat haircuts and the bulging briefcases... Do you know who they are?"

"Lawyers..." Washy said. "She always wanted to be a lawyer. I thought when she wrote that she worked for Bertrans she meant hooking. She was his lawyer!" He laughed, a false laugh, too happy.

Emily shook her head. "No, not his lawyer. The *Devil's* lawyer. The blue suits? They collect the Devil's taxes. They balance his books. They interpret his laws. They are his own, his bureaucrats, his executives. When you put on the blue suit... you disappear, Washy. No way can you be found, unless you want to be found. She told me that on the bus — not as Emily Roebling, but as Norma Jean. That's why I didn't want to tell you. She's *gone*, Washy, gone to you and gone from anyone and gone to hell."

"My Emily... Not Bert's lawyer — the Devil's lawyer?"

She nodded. "A blue suit." She pushed him away, left him standing by the window. No, the voice in her said, No, don't reject him. No... She scratched at her itching scalp.

"My Emily?" he asked. "A lawyer, a lawyer?"

She couldn't stand it. Emily opened the motel room door, stepped over a melting demon, its head ripped away, and walked back to Bert's. On the way back, the last quatrain came to her.

*

The next Friday afternoon, Emily stopped by the supply office to pick up her laundry and that weekend's costume. The supply clerk pushed a clear package across to her, a little clear bag with an electric razor and a bottle on top.

"What's this?" Emily asked, holding up the little bag. "I've already got a shaver for my legs."

The clerk shrugged. "Orders. It's a heavy duty shaver," he said. "Gets real close, ya know?" He rubbed his stubbly chin.

Emily opened the package up, held out the desert camo tee-shirt, the khaki pants, the webbed belt. A little A-shaped insignia had been pinned to the front of the shirt. She rubbed the brass between her fingers, felt the little star in the background of the pin.

Trixie came down the hall, stopped. "You're late, Emily. Get dressed and to Hart in five minutes," she said. "You're the last head he's got to do for tonight."

"Trixie, did —?"

"Go," Trixie said. "And bring the little bag." She walked off.

Partitions had been set up in front of the long row of chairs by the make-up mirrors, and curtains draped between the partitions, so each chair was separated from the other. Privacy? she thought. Emily smoothed her top, pushed something away with her foot. Two- and three-foot lengths of red and blonde and black hair lay on the floor. "Sheesh," she muttered, "Hart's gone crazy." She rapped on the edge of his partition.

Hart poked his head out, and behind him Emily saw the gleaming flash of some Army recruit's clean-shaven head. "Hang on, Emily." He ducked back in, and Emily heard the low hum of an electric razor. It stopped, the recruit gasped, he left the cubicle, and then Hart pushed the curtain back.

"Okay," he said, waving at the empty chair, hanks and hanks of florescent-orange hair — Bambi has orange hair, Emily thought — hanging on the arms of the chair like skeins of yarn. "You bring your shaver?"

"Yeah," she said, handing it to him. He set it on the counter. "Why?"

"Just sit down, okay?"

"*Okay.*" Emily sat in the chair and let Hart put the plastic apron with the poodle pictures around her shoulders. He cinched it tight on her neck, ran his fingers through her hair, pulling it up from the apron. "Uh, time for a trim?" she asked, looking in the mirror at the blonde ends hanging to her shoulders, the dark roots over an inch long.

"Maybe," he said. He spun a colored wheel mounted on a stand like a fan, and as it slowed, ratchets clicked, and an arrow passed over pie-shaped sections, images of various soldiers in uniform pasted on the sections. The arrow clicked over the picture of a woman with general's stars on her cap, seemed to pause on a clean-shaven recruit, then finally stopped on the picture of a blonde woman. "Close," Hart said. "You got the Lieutenant." Hart brushed the orange hairs off the arms of the chair. "Not so Bambi — she got the new recruit."

"Recruit?"

Hart nodded, pointed at the electric shaver on the counter. "Fucking Bertrans, asshole's got me doing chop jobs like when I was a boot camp barber. And he won't let me shave the bad cuts or anything; got to let the 'wheel of fortune' decide. *Jerk*. And now even the ones who don't *have* to get shaved want it. 'Solidarity,' they say. I'm an *artist*, damn it, not a butcher."

"The video? He saw *that* video?"

"*Amazon Platoon*, yeah. Some dickhead mailed it to him, like with *Metropolis*. Messed up some good heads because of it." He smiled, began brushing her hair. "But not yours, toots. You got lucky. You don't have to be like all the others, insisting I shave them even when the wheel says otherwise. Sure, everyone else asked me to shave them, but you don't have to. No, you don't have to do that." He grinned at her, pleading. "But you *do* have to fix those roots, though."

Yes, yes, said the voice in her, make it like Marilyn's. As Hart brushed her hair, she felt that presence ooze out of her head, up toward the strokes of the stiff brush. Emily stared at her reflection, looked at her dark roots, at the style that didn't feel like her, never had — it felt like Marilyn, of course, her idea; she was someone else, not her, not the Belle of Amherst. Got to purge myself, she thought. Like Job said, I seek transformation, redemption, change. This is it: a cleansing. Got to cut loose one last time.

"Shave it, Hart," she said. No! the little voice said. Yes, she replied. "Yes, *shave it*, Hart. If Bambi gets the new recruit then so do I. You said solidarity, okay? Tell Bertrans *that*. We'll stand by each other, all of us."

"Emily, you *don't* have to do this," he said quietly, setting the brush down. He picked up the clippers and flicked them on, gunning them. The way he stared at her, though, Emily knew he wanted her to do it.

No, the tiny voice protested. "Yeah, I do." Emily looked at Hart, the clippers buzzing in his hands, and thought of the first time she'd sat in his chair, when he'd turned into Job. "So why don't you get it over with, okay?" The strange feeling tried to slide back down into her head, but Emily closed her mind to it, closed it to the shadow.

Hart smiled at her. "*Okay.*" He shook his head. "Damn it, you're *all* doing this. But okay."

Emily ran a hand along her scalp, pulling the hair up. She felt the shadow grab her skin, relaxed her fingers, and let the strands fall away. "I finished the last quatrain," she said. "My sonnet."

"Good." He spun her chair around, away from the mirror. "Why don't you recite it while I — while I take care of you?"

"Okay," she said. "Here goes:"

"Here goes," said Hart, moving around behind her.

"*Emily is me and I am like her,*" she said. Hart touched the clippers to the nape of her neck, and they whirred as they bit into her hair, the hair screaming. "*She has touched me, too, a sister to my heart,*" she continued. The warm air of the clipper's motor washed over her bare skin.

"Go on," Hart said, pushing the clippers over her ears.

"But for me his blood beats and his thighs stir," she said. The black-blonde hairs rustled like paper as they fell on the plastic apron. Hart walked around in front of her, pushed the shears up from her forehead. *"I ride him, take him..."* He ran the clippers over the crown of her head, hair fluttering down in front of her eyes, a shrill voice yelling at her as it fell. *"I ride him, take him, feel his piercing dart."*

Hart stepped back, set the clippers down, and with a whisk broom brushed hair off her scalp and shoulders and into her lap. "You have a beard on your head now," he said, taking the little bottle and dashing the fluid on her skin. "You'll have to shave every day. Recite it to me again." The little razor hummed over the brush of her crew cut, a tiny voice screeching one last complaint.

"Emily is me and I am like her," she said.
"She has touched me, too, a sister to my heart,
"But for me his blood beats and his thighs stir,
"I ride him, take him, feel his piercing dart."

"Excellent, Emily, excellent — it's a new kind of poetry for you; a new poetess." He set the shaver down. "You wanted to do this; I'm sorry. Hold out your hands." He gathered the apron up, shook the ounce or so of hair into her hands, then opened the little shaver up and dumped the tiny hairs on top. "A souvenir." Hart held open a plastic bag and Emily dumped the long and short and blonde and brown hairs into it. He whirled her chair around.

"Yes, a souvenir.... A souvenir of someone I was not meant to be."

Emily ran a hand over her smooth scalp, felt the smooth bumps of her mastoids, the high flat forehead, the gentle roundness of her crown. Clean, she thought, like a Buddhist. Clean. She looked up at her reflection, amazed at how small her head looked, at how light it felt. The contours of her skull looked like deep valleys in the harsh lights of the mirror. She sighed, smiled. "Hey: you got rid of the dark roots. Thanks."

"Right: no dark roots." He tied up the plastic bag of hair, handed it to her. "Now, go see Trixie."

Emily got up, and walked down in front of the rows of chairs. The electric clippers hummed again, and she glanced back to see Mister Hart shaving another head. He caught her eye, smiled, and continued his shearing. She went to Trixie in costuming. In front of a rack of uniforms, a woman with red fuzz on her scalp turned to her.

"*Trixie?*" Emily asked. "You didn't have to...?"

Trixie shook her head, rubbed her scalp, then Emily's. "I did. Screw Bertrans. I wouldn't ask my crew to do something I wouldn't. Here." She handed her a toy plastic pistol, its lines smooth and futuristic. "A plasma pistol, just the thing for the Amazon Platoon." Emily clipped it to a magnetic clasp at her waist. "Hey," Trixie said. "It'll grow back, nice and thick."

"That's the idea," Emily said. She walked out onto the floor of Bertrans', into a sea of bald pates and camo tee-shirts and tight-fitting khaki fatigues. As she passed by an open fireplace, Emily tossed the plastic bag into the roaring fire.

*

More laser light shows lit up the balconies of Bertrans'. From the ceiling, a helicopter with a fuselage like a Japanese beetle spun around and around, beaming shafts of light down on the dance floor. Every barmaid seemed to be bald, their skulls shining, and Emily could hardly tell one from the other, noses and mouths and bodies inaccurate distinguishing traits. She nodded at Bambi cruising her station next to Emily's, but in the dim light, even Bambi with her thin waist, her deer-like long legs, seemed hard to identify. Among the new recruits in *their* camo uniforms, *their* black boots, the waitroid units — how apt was Bertrans' term, Emily thought — seemed to disappear among the customers. But, she realized, the recruits had a boot camp's six weeks of fuzz on their heads, and no toy guns.

"Two tequilas, a rum 'n' coke, a Manhattan Banzai, a Planter's Punch, and a pilsner," Emily recited, setting her tray down before Rabbit.

"*Emily?*" he asked.

"Yup," she said, scratching her scalp.

"You people look like the *qilalugaq*." His hands flashed as he mixed drinks and set them up for her.

"Kill-a-what?" She counted out change, paid for her drinks.

"Beluga whale — a little white whale with a big head." Rabbit smiled.

"White whales — don't tell Q," she said.

Emily set down all the drinks except the pilsner at a table of boot camp graduates. "Two diablos total, kids," she said.

"Sure." A tall girl, barely a teenager, pushed two coins across at Emily. "You join up, too?" she asked, knocking knuckles on her own brush cut.

Emily smiled, shook her head. "You kids have got no imagination."

"Sure we do — I saw that flick," a guy said. "You're supposed to be one of the grunts in that all chick platoon. They're like real savage. There's that big desert battle where they blow up tanks from the back of pick-up trucks. I remember. *Nasty* chick soldiers." He looked over at the girl who'd paid for the drinks. "Shit, Galla, what century are *you* from?"

"Second Common Era." She winked at Emily. "Ignore these barbarians."

Emily laughed. "Not while they're tipping good."

Someone beckoned from across the room; Emily nodded, worked her way over to another table of grunts — not recruits, they had the hardened look of combat veterans — took their order, and swung by the gray-haired man she knew would have ordered the pilsner. She set the bottle down before him. "Your drink, sir," she said.

"Thank you, Miss," he said, looking up. "How did you — *Emily*."

"Washy."

"You, uh..." He pointed at her head; she nodded. "It's quite... That's not one of those bathing caps, is it?"

"Real skin, Washy."

"It's quite becoming, yes. Highlights your cranial features nicely. This is an odd little show Mister Bertrans is putting on tonight." He pointed down at the stage, where a band of people with hard carapaces on their skulls were beating out some syncopated song. "That man is rather strange at times." Washy sipped his beer.

"Got to run, Washy."

"Yes, of course." He stared at her, then shook his head.

"Something wrong?"

"When my Emily and I were building the Brooklyn Bridge, she once picked up a bad case of head lice from one of the workers. There were things that could be done — kerosene and such — but she was not a vain woman, and so she had me shave her head, because it was so much simpler." He looked away, his eyes focusing on the far wall. "I remember gathering her braid up like a rope, cutting it loose, then lathering her scalp, pulling the straight razor through it...." Washy shivered, sipped his beer again. "You look exactly like her, Emily Dickinson. Exactly."

"I am not your Emily, Washington. I told you where she... I never told you my last name. How did you know my last name?"

He sipped his beer again. "We are contemporaries, Emily. You, me, my wife." Colonel Washington A. Roebling stood, leaning slightly on his cane. "Come with me, Emily. Come away with me."

"You... Your wife. What of your wife?" She glanced over at Barker, watching her, raising her hand to signal him. She did not like this, what was Washy doing, she felt nothing for him, nothing, that night at the Pussycat, that had been something else, someone else.... "Your wife is gone with Satan."

Washy shook his head. "My wife has never been here," he said.

"She —" Emily turned toward Barker, toward the transformed man, looking for his blue hair, his violet skin, *where was he*, she had to stop this. A shiver ran down her spine, she felt herself drawn to Roebling. "I *can't*, Washy, I cannot, I..." Barker. There he was, by the rail of the far balcony, pulling his Devil Imp automatic pistol from his belt. No, she didn't need *that —*

A blue bolt like a small glowing marble screamed across the room. Emily whirled at the sound, tracking the light like a flashbulb continuously popping as it landed in the chest of the Second Century girl she'd just served, Galla; Galla jerking backward, arms/ heart/lungs/diaphragm misting away and her head rolling onto the table. Emily tracked the source of the shot, saw one of the barmaids, a barmaid in Bambi's station, raise the toy gun, the plasma pistol, and fire it at the table of combat vets.

"Em —," Washy said. He turned, raised the cane up, pointed it.

She raised her hand at the glare, felt for the toy pistol at her belt, yanked it up, and squeezed the sticky trigger. The gun felt warm in her grasp, and a glowing thing seemed to shudder from it, pulling the pistol from her hand, yanking it across to one of the swamp demons crashing through a skylight above.

"— I —," Washy said. He raised the cane.

Barker turned toward the barmaid in Bambi's station, hands clasped tight around the automatic pistol, and fired, the big slugs cracking, one-two, *thunk-thunk* into Bambi.... It couldn't be Bambi (no, not Bambi), into the woman's head, into her shooting arm. The bald woman jerked, first up, then around, little pieces of muscle and bone spraying out into the flickering laser light. The plasma pistol fired one last time, a bolt hitting the helicopter mobile, its saucer dome exploding into droplets of dripping plastic.

Emily stood, walked around the room, edging toward the counter, toward Rabbit crouched behind the bar, pumping a shotgun. Around the room bald heads popped up, plasma guns held before them: quick, methodical, firing at tables of crew-cut grunts; at combat vets; at recruits; at whores doing table dances; at couples dancing below. Spherical blasts, dozens of miniature suns, careened across the cavern of the disco, flashes bursting next to her head, flashes splattering bodies and table legs and glasses of beer into so many elemental parts. A plasma bolt cracked behind her and as she turned she saw a blue ball whiz by her, charring her tee-shirt, and slam into the back of Bambi's head.

Energy crackled around her, dancing over her skull, down her neck, over her camo and khaki costume. It shimmered, searing her eyelashes and eyebrows. Bambi's bald head glowed in a nimbus, and the plasma bolt melted her skin and clothes and slid harmlessly off her, burning its way through the floor. A thing with a titanium skeleton, a gleaming skull, rose from Bambi's ashes and raised its pistol at Emily.

Yes, Emily thought, seeing, Ah, yes, terrorists had been infiltrating Bertrans' for weeks, putting their people in the club — waitroid units, literally. Emily looked around her, at the dying and dead bodies, at the suns bursting and bursting around the room; at the dead grunts, the dead barmaids. How clever, she thought, sending that video, tricking Bertrans into costuming the real barmaids so that they looked like the intended victims. Kill 'em all and let the devil sort 'em out? Wasn't that how it worked? And if they were real units, real cyborgs, why, they could shoot at each other and all they'd lose would be their facade.

"— ly!" Washy shouted. He swung his cane up, sighted at the Bambi-thing aiming at her, and pulled the trigger on his cane gun. The thing took the blast in its face, napalm flooding the sockets of its cameras, the flame blinding it.

"Emily, *get down*," Rabbit yelled at her. "It's Sam's — his people, they're taking over the club."

She walked by him, little globs of polyester dripping off her charred shirt. In the distance she heard Barker's gun firing, intellectually sympathizing with him as he looked for a target — friend or foe? — among the dozens of bald people stunned or shooting. She stopped at the balcony, leaned over, clutching the railing with both hands.

Bertrans — *En* Bertrans, Lord Bertrans — stood on the stage, head thrust out in one hand, a machine pistol in the other, head whirling around, pistol following. He thrust the head up at Emily, and the muzzle moved toward her, then quickly shifted.

Something itched from under her scalp.

"Washy!" she screamed. He turned toward her, head of the cane flat against his left palm, his right hand jamming a round into the chamber.

"*Listen*, Washy!:

His eyes blaze not at all like Paradise
Deep thunder booms like his voice when it roars
Hands, toes, chin and cheek have the feel of ice
None will touch or bed him, not even whores.

"What are you saying?" Washy yelled back.

"This is for you." From the balcony below she saw Hart standing next to Trixie. He nodded up at her, and she smiled back. In the corner of a room, some bald woman's plasma pistol exploded in her hand, the negative shadow of her body flashing onto the wall behind her. Another explosion, another shadow: Emily's scalp ran with sweat, and something soft brushed over her head.

"*Through hell's last quarter Emily he seeks*
A couple, separated: lost or gone
What ill wind blowing from Bertrans' so reeks?
She's been there, he smells it, the missing one."

"Do you understand?" she asked Washy. One of Sam's bald commandoes aimed her pistol at Emily; another little sun died in the pistol's chamber, another shadow seared into a wall.

"I think so," he said, moving toward her.

"*Emily is me and I am like her,*" she continued,
"*She has touched me, too, a sister to her heart*
But for me his blood beats and his thighs stir
I ride him, take him, feel his piercing dart."

Bertrans moved to the edge of the stage, reached toward a panel behind a curtain, and pressed something. Gears ground in the floor below and the dance floor began sliding back. Deep dark water loomed from an open pit below the floor. Bertrans pressed another button, and underwater floods lit the pool.

"This place is going to blow," he yelled. "Jump into the pool — it leads out to the lake."

Washy walked up next to her, turned her around. She faced him, long strands of something falling in front of her face. "Go on," he said.

The noise in the disco died down, low moanings, a few more pops of energy seizing space. She brushed the hair away from her eyes, pushed it back from her ears.

"When Paradise rises and the Bridge returns.
With his lover he walks while her soul burns."

"You'll go with me?" he asked, reaching up to touch the soft brown hair falling down over her shoulders.

She nodded. "I think I might love you, Washington A. Roebling. I am your Emily — at least this Emily, at least here."

He put an arm around her, and they looked over the balcony. Hart and Trixie leapt over the edge, following Bertrans into the pool. Rabbit straddled the rail to their right, Barker to the left, emptying their guns, and then together they jumped into the water. Emily looked at Washy; Washy looked at Emily. Together, they climbed over the balcony edge, and together they fell into the maelstrom of the pool.

When they surfaced out in the lake, a ferry boat puttered toward them, the words 'S.S. Bridge' painted on its bow.

Chapter 24

Hart Crane's hands, that damn poet's hands, pull me from her head. Oh, the caress of the boar bristles on her scalp, on Emily's scalp, lures me from where I had hidden, and up-up-up I come, into the long luscious protein strands crackling with static on her head. Screw the science, okay? I went into her hair. Well, can you blame this shadow, can you blame W.A.R.? I thought Mister Hart was going to do a Marilyn. I thought he'd bleach that dowdy essence of Miss Emily Dickinson. Here I had worked hard to make Emily a Marilyn, and Mister Hart, bless the bastard, was going to correct the ravages time had done to her.

Shorn! She told him to cut me loose. The bitch! Lured out from her body, basking in the locks and hanks of her head, she tells Hart to shave her head. What is this? What woman in her right mind would shear every strand from her scalp, remove any essence of femininity from their head? I do not understand this. She does this, he complies with her wishes, and the pain, the horrible pain as the whirring little blades roar through me, through this shadow, and the brown-blonde strands, me inside them, drift away. Liberated! She refuses me.

Ah, but I crawl down to the edge of the shaft, seek entry, am denied. So I stay, my essence spread thin over the stubble left on her scalp. Marilyn is gone, that wonderful blondness is gone, but I hide in what remains. Hart smears some odd lotion on me. The stubble stiffens, my power is held in bondage; and then he makes another pass, a smaller razor, just a humming little shaver, and I am ripped lose one last time from Emily. Farewell, dear poetess! He empties me into her lap, she dumps me in a plastic bag, and I writhe among the wreck of the Marilyn's deception. Oh, I am a genie in a bottle, captured here forever. What cruelty, what torture.

Ah. Ah, deliverance. Miss Emily tosses me into the great roaring fire. There is a brief moment of intensely wonderful agony as the flames sear at me, licking at me, devouring me, and then I rise up into the smoke, up the chimney, adrift in the air. My ashes rain down on this little hell, down to the lake, and I see two bodies swimming through the water. I stick to one of them: the male. Ashes plastered to his flesh, I ease into the cracks and crevices of his face and cling to the shadow of his beard. We join together, this body and me.

Well, what do you know? Surprise, surprise. It is Washington Roebling, this male body, swimming with Miss Emily. And now, me: W.A.R.. The Bridge comes for us now.

Well, well, well.

Chapter 25

"They are delivered," the Bridge said to Job.

Job stood on the central span of the Bridge, facing the Emily Roebling inscription on the east tower — the inscription that had been on the *west* tower, the one they'd walked through before to get to the central span: the Bridge had become a mirror of itself. Job shook his head, glanced back. To the west, the ruins of Pompeii glowed ruby red, reflecting the light of Paradise shining from where Brooklyn had been. The poets passed through the northern arch of the east tower, walking around the central column, while Barker and Rabbit and Queequeg came through the southern arch, from the other side. Hart staggered through, black coat slung over his shoulder, Emily at his side. Touching his throat, he rubbed his skin, a blank gaze in his eyes as he searched for something not there. He glanced over at Emily, raised his arm to hold her around her waist, shook his head, let the arm fall.

Ezra Pound swaggered through, cape flying behind him, a red-blotched bandage across his forehead. He whistled, smiled at Job. "Like the sestina?" he asked. Job frowned.

Sestina?

White skirts swirling behind her, Emily Dickinson followed the other two poets. A hot breeze blew off Pompeii, pushing loose strands of her long dark hair in her eyes. She reached up, patted the bun at her crown, then combed a loose hair down over her shoulder, touching the ends, staring at them.

"Washy," she said, whirling around.

Colonel Washington A. Roebling walked behind them, dress blues clean and pressed, tapping a gold-topped cane. He rubbed the bristle of his short trimmed gray beard, stopped, straightened his collar. Behind him, through the portals of the east tower, three visions flickered by: a great stepped pyramid, a medieval castle, a glass and steel inverted pyramid, and then a steamy lake, a frozen snowscape, a turbid swamp. Pompeii and Vesuvius reappeared from the sea to the west. Roebling walked up to Job, handed him three slim volumes.

"For your records," he said.

Job took the books from him, glanced at the titles: "Conquistador," "Sestina: Paradise," and "Sonnet to My Colonel." Ah, he thought, *that* sestina. "Thank you," he said, slipping the books inside his robe.

"They performed well," Roebling said. "Courage. Duty. Love." He brushed past Job, up to Emily, and took her hand. "Come, my love. Let us go."

"Go?" she asked. "*Go?* Me?"

"*Her*?" asked Pound. "That poetess?"

"Yes, *her*?" asked Hart. "Why not...?"

"Come, my Emily," said Roebling. "Take me home."

"*Your* Emily?" she asked. "I am — yes, I said, I know, but not your Emily — no, not *her*."

"Her," said Roebling. He looked up at the sky, watched a spittle of sun fall away from Paradise. "Emily Roebling." The glowing meteor, its light fierce in its intensity as it came closer and closer to the Bridge, fell down on the brass inscription on the east tower, absorbed the raised words, and shot out like a reflected beam toward Emily Dickinson. The beam wrapped her in its blazing white embrace. Hart and Ez, Rabbit and Q held arms over their eyes, cowered from the holiness enveloping her. Job stared straight ahead at the nimbus.

In hell, the legend went, every soul had its Judge. "My Judge," said Washington A. Roebling, gazing into the light.

*

Job stared at the poet, watched her body shimmer and flicker. The meteor spun around her, paralyzing her, wrapping her in a silver cocoon. Emily Dickinson, dressed in a high-necked white dress, her brown hair parted in the middle, braided and coiled in a neat bun, doubled, grew larger, became two: two women, two glowing clouds. The Emily closest to Roebling's side shrank an inch, her hips growing larger, her face becoming wider, arms and shoulders gaining flesh. Her dress rippled, ripped, regrew itself, tighter at the hips, a low scooped collar with frills rustling across her wide bosom and over her shoulders. She turned to Roebling with only the faintest trace of the thick Dickinson lips and wide set eyes, and then turned back to the other Emily, the poet.

That Emily stayed the same height; her waist became thinner, her bust filled out; her legs stretched and swelled: thin ankles, firm calves and thighs. Her face stayed the same and the neat little bun unraveled, long brown hair sweeping back from her forehead; the ends whisked away at her shoulders and ragged bangs appeared above her brow. As her dress flamed away, a black jumpsuit, bandolier slung over her shoulder, appeared beneath, two buttons loose at the top. She patted her hip, and a handgun in a holster appeared there, hanging from a black canvas utility belt. She held out her hands before her, and a Hellishnikov assault rifle smacked against her open palms. She kicked a boot at the bridge decking, and shoved a black nylon rucksack upright. *That* Emily turned to the other Emily:

"You going to take him?" she asked.

"He is my husband, I his wife," she said.

"Groovy," Emily said. "You sure as shit ain't me."

"*I'm* Emily" — she looked up at Washington A. Roebling — "Emily *Roebling*, dear. I've come to take my husband home."

Emily spat. "Well, *dearie*, I'm Emily *Dickinson*, poet, and you can have the little cocksucker." She ran a hand through her shoulder length hair, looked down at her jumpsuit, at her weapon, seeming to notice it for the first time. "He's no hot stuff, if you ask me." She slung the assault rifle over her shoulder.

Roebling blushed and turned to the poet. "Emily," he said, "we had something... something in Old Titlan."

"Titland," she said. "Look, Washy, I was a little confused. Too many hormones or something." The poet reached out, pinched his cheek. "Yeah, it was fun, but you've got your little wifey now. Now that I think about it, she doesn't look a bit like that Norma Jean on the bus." She shrugged. "Don't know who Norma Jean is — was, will be."

"But you know who you are now?" Job asked. He held his hands up, fingers steepled.

Emily Dickinson looked at him, grunted. "O Ombudsman, cut the existentialist — that's the word, yes? — cut the crap. Does anyone know who they are? We just try on different personas, you know?" She smiled, looked down at her body, ran her hands over the tight jumpsuit. "Miss Marilyn seems to have loaned me parts of herself, but I think this persona's mostly me." She shrugged. "Well, it will do. Yeah. I know who I am — for now."

Emily Roebling took Washington's hand, sniffed at Dickinson, and turned to the last tower of the Bridge. "Come, dear — I *can* take him, can't I?" she asked Job.

Job shrugged. "Walk through the gate. The way I understand it, if these poets have done their job — and I think they have —you can take Washington into Paradise." Don't you know? he thought. Don't you know that you're his Judge?

The couple turned from the poets, turned from Job, turned from Barker and Rabbit and Queequeg, and walked toward the final tower, Emily Roebling passing on the left of the central column, Washington Roebling on the right, by a clean, bare spot on the granite where Emily Roebling's memorial had been. Their bodies glowed as they walked through the gate. Emily's clothes fell from her. Her braid came undone. She blazed a bright platinum silver — her skin, her hair, her body. She rose up from the Bridge, its roadway rising to meet her steps, and turned to Washington.

A maelstrom whirled around him, a black mist spinning from his body. Roebling dropped his cane, slapped at his clothes, ripping them off, whirling to look back at the poets. Emily Roebling turned to him, grabbed his hand, and pulled. Roebling remained, his feet stuck in his boots, the boots seemingly glued to the Bridge. Emily yanked at him, he pulled at her, but he could not rise up.

"Come, dear husband," she said. "Leave your sin behind. Come to Paradise. Though you never appreciated my efforts, never could be the husband you should have been, I love you nonetheless." She glanced back at the clean square of masonry where her bronze tablet had been. "Though I went through — yes, hell — to help you build your damned Bridge, you never thanked me, never truly showed your appreciation. *I* built your Bridge, Washington A. Roebling. It is my Bridge as much as yours, as much as your father's." She pulled on his arms again, the skin and muscles taut. "But never mind, Washy, never mind. All is forgiven. You are worthy. Come with me."

Job walked toward them, through the gate, a membrane-like spider web parting before him. A scream echoed in his head. *I will not go, I will not go,* the voice roared. *I will not go to the Place of Good, leave me here in the Place of No Return. I will not go!*

"The shadow!" Job yelled. "The shadow keeps you in hell."

"My... W.A.R.? The dark side?" He pulled a hand loose from Emily's grasp, touched his chin.

Job nodded, pushed Roebling's hand aside, reached for his beard. It wriggled in his grasp, felt like putty, like writhing worms. "You must... You must leave it here." The Ombuds-man held out his hand, and a portion of the glowing cloud surrounding Roebling manifested itself as a gleaming silver razor.

No, the tiny voice said. *No, that is not what I want. You cannot, you cannot, not again and again.*

"Yes," Job said. He drew the razor down Roebling's cheeks, up his neck, over his chin, over his lips. The little gray hairs fluttered down to the Bridge, wriggled together, and became an imp, a glowing red thing, a simulacrum of Washington A. Roebling.

"Go, bless you. Go!" Job shouted at Roebling.

"I... I cannot." He looked down at his boots, at his feet stuck in them. Colonel Washington A. Roebling let go of Emily's other hand, reached down, grabbed the imp, the sha-dow, and held him in his hand. "This *thing*, this evil demon, it is me, can you not see that? I must have it."

"Washy!" Emily Roebling screamed. She hovered over him, reaching for his hand. "Washy, you cannot bring that to Paradise. Leave it! Fly up with me! I absolve you of sin!"

"I cannot, dear one."

The Sea of Sighs frothed and boiled, and a thing rose up out of it, its black hide running with blood, enormous teeth clacking in its huge jaw. Leviathan reared back, stood on its flukes, and the head became smaller, the fins grew into arms, the snout into a nose, lower jaw into chin. The black hide stretched back from a forehead, a white spot on the whale's skin settling over the face, and the beast became a woman, shiny skin, hair that turned into hide, clean white teeth in her small mouth. She smiled.

"Give *me* the Shadow," she said. She rose up out of the water, as tall as the Bridge, head towering over them. "Give it to me, Colonel, and you shall be free."

Queequeg, Rabbit, and Barker ran to the side of the walkway, guns and harpoon pointed down at the beast. "It is him," Rabbit yelled.

"No, not him — not our friend Qavvik," Queequeg said.

"Lady MacBeth," Job said. "I had thought you through with the Shadow."

She shrugged. "He is so... so valuable. And charming." She held out a massive hand to Roebling. "Give him to me, Washy, and you can go."

"No, Lady," Roebling said. "No, Emily, dearest. You do not understand: I *cannot* go into Paradise without this Shadow."

Emily Roebling nodded. "Then you cannot go at all."

"I do not believe that," he said. "Even the blessed have some Evil."

"We have cast it out!" Emily Roebling screamed. "We cast it down into hell, like the Dark Angel himself."

"No," said Roebling, glancing over at Job. "That is not what humans do. We take the evil, control it, recognize it, and let it become us."

He knows, Job thought. Like all men, he knows. An antinomy. That is what we are, created in God's image: antinomies.

"We *eat* our evil," Roebling said.

"No!" roared Lady MacBeth. "Give him to me, give me my child!"

No, the shadow said, *let me free, let me free.*

"No," said Emily Roebling, "Cast off your evil."

"Yes," said Washington Roebling, and he raised the squirming shadow to his mouth, opened his lips, and bit down on its head. The imp twitched, arms raging, then relaxed. Roebling stuffed the torso, legs, and arms in his mouth, chewing slowly, pinkish blood streaming down his chin. He swallowed, burped, and gray hairs grew again on his face. "Now. Now, the evil is mine to control." Roebling clenched his right fist, shook it at the sky. "Mine alone, do you understand?" His body began to glow, brighter than Emily Roebling's, and he rose up out of his boots.

A great force, an unseen hand, slammed him back down to the Bridge.

Job stepped forward, his robes flickering with St. Elmo's fire. "Let him go, damn you!" he yelled. "It is only a little evil. You know that. He controls it. It is only a little evil."

"*So little and yet so strong*," a voice boomed from the sky.

"It is part of him, Lord," Job said. "You know that. All souls have some evil. Take him. This soul does not belong here."

"You do not belong here," the voice said. *"Come to me, my child."*

"Lord... Lord, I cannot do that."

"Then Roebling stays. Come to me or he stays."

Job looked back at the poets, back at the Bridge, back at hell. Emily Roebling hovered above her husband, her glowing husband straining against the force pushing him down. The poets looked through the gate, squinting at them. The mercs looked down at Lady MacBeth; she looked up at Job, at the three of them beyond the gate. He looked down at the Sea of Sighs, across to Pompeii, thinking of New Hell, of the millions of souls he'd met, of the few others like Roebling that might be worthy enough of escape. Job felt... He felt an intense love for hell, felt compassion for his people. Y**H did not know. He did not know who he was. And He was wrong. Job did not belong with Him. He belonged in hell. But for Roebling...

"I will go then," the Ombudsman said.

Colonel Washington A. Roebling flew up from the Bridge. He grabbed for his wife's hand, took her (and the builder, the father of the Bridge), ran up its ramp, hand in hand with his love, the mother of the Bridge, running into Paradise, two glowing bodies sucked from Hell.

The raging wind died around Job. His robes ceased glowing, and the electricity ceased crackling around him. He looked up at the ascending comets, motes against the face of Paradise, down at the piles of clothes at his feet.

"He didn't take me," he whispered, thinking — what? — disappointment, and then relief. He let me stay here.

Do My work here, a voice said inside his head. *Do Good, Job. Do Good.*

Lady MacBeth groaned, fell back to the Sea of Sighs, rolled, turned back into the whale, and slapped her flukes against the ocean. She dove, fins slapping the surface, spouted a great breath, and the beast disappeared beneath the black waves.

Job walked back through the gate, toward Pompeii.

"Welcome back," Hart Crane said. Job nodded.

"Well?" asked Ezra Pound.

"That's a deep subject," Job said. He passed by Emily Dickinson, touched her shoulder, moved on toward the ruins of Pompeii, then turned back to Paradise. It fell, setting behind the far tower, casting the Bridge into darkness. The far span stretched into a point, vanishing into an amorphous void. "Where's it go?" he asked.

"To wherever in hell you need to go," the Bridge said.

"To Brooklyn?" Hart asked.

"If you want it," the Bridge said. Hart Crane walked through the far tower.

"To Venice?" asked Pound.

"I think so." Ezra Pound followed Crane.

Job smiled at Emily Dickinson, at the mercs. "Well?"

"I don't know...," said Emily. She looked down at her legs, smoothed her jumpsuit, touched the leather strap of her Hellishnikov. "Something doesn't feel right... something's missing." She twisted the leather strap around her hand, pulled on it, then looked up. "Carlo," she said. Emily whirled, faced the east tower of the Bridge. "Carlo! *Carlo!*"

"What?" Barker asked. "Where's that?"

"Carlo!" she yelled again. "Come here!"

The east tower shimmered, and a big hound — part Rottweiler, part blue tick, spotted on its chest and with big floppy ears, deep brown eyes — came bounding out of the gate. Emily kneeled down, and he ran toward her. As he passed Job he suddenly veered, stopped, and sat. Job scratched his head.

"Good dog," he said. "Go to momma." He touched the rail of the Bridge, thinking that even Satan has some mercy left in him.

"Carlo." The dog turned at his name, stood, nuzzled Job's leg, and sauntered over to Emily. She hugged him, rubbed his stomach. "Carlo. *Good* doggy, good boy." Carlo wagged his tail, looked around at Job and the other men, smiled a dopey grin — I'm a good dog, aren't I? Aren't I? he seemed to be saying.

"Yeah," Emily said. "*Okay.*"

Barker glanced at Emily and the dog, shook his head. "Shit," he muttered. "A girl and her dog." He sighed, looked at Rabbit and Queequeg. "I don't know about you guys," Barker said. "You want to go back to Qittiliq?" He clicked the bolt on his rifle, ejected a live round, then locked the safety on.

"It's been awfully cold there lately," said Queequeg.

"The hunting's been lousy ever since Qavvik got Leviathan," Rabbit said.

"Yeah," said Barker. "I've got some scores to settle, starting with the guy who made my hair turn blue."

Job smiled. "You ever hear of a bar in New Hell called the Oasis? You'd like it there — lots of adventure."

"New Hell?" asked Emily Dickinson, standing. "There's an old brick house there whose windows I'd just love to shoot up." She raised her weapon, slid the bolt back. Carlo jerked at the noise, then wagged his tail again. "Let's — what's that phrase about rocks, Barker?"

He smiled. "Rock and roll."

"Yeah," she said. "Let's rock and roll."

Job nodded at the four mercenaries and the dog, looked up at the second tower of the Bridge, at the black haze stretching beyond. "Brooklyn Bridge," he said. "Take us to New Hell." The Ombudsman turned to the mercs, waved at them, began walking toward the far span.

"Take us home."